Steel Hand, Cold Heart

Rachel Menard

ISBN: 978-1-08-102280-8

To all the girls who were told, "no,"
and did it anyway.

"All the horrors thou wilt not get to know which Hel's inmates suffer. Pleasant sins end in painful penalties; pain ever follows pleasure."

Edda of Saedmund the Wise

CHAPTER 1

✖

They called me Carina the Unstoppable. No, the name did not render men to terror like Merciless Merle, nor did it inspire awe like Dagna the Destroyer, or command attention like Odda Ironfist. But the moniker was mine. I earned it for the many times I had been knocked flat on the training grounds or limped on bleeding limbs to finish a fight. It was how I earned my place as one of Hel's Daughters, the Hand of Death Herself.

I leaned over the rails of our longboat, *Jörmungandr*, aptly named because the figurehead was carved in the image of the giant sea serpent, wriggling its way through the water east toward Frisia. A strong wind held our mainsail, and we bobbed back and forth on gentle waves. These smooth waters were a blessing from the sea giant, Aegir. He approved of our quest, speeding us along our last raid of the season, the last offering to Hel before the long winter.

This was the Daughters' last raid of the season but my first. I could hardly contain my excitement. I wanted to be there already, to see the villagers' faces when we arrived on their shore in droves. When we offered their blood to the Goddess Hel.

I curled my steel fingers into a fist. On the eve of my initiation, Thora warned me attaching my steel hand would hurt. Her exact words were, "It feels like cutting your fingers off one by one and pissing in the wound." Vidar warmed the steel gauntlet in the coals until it glowed sunset red, and I grit my teeth as he slid the molten metal over my fingers. The steel hand burned through flesh and muscle until the metal touched bone. My eyes

1

had watered. A violent scream had gathered in my chest.

I held it back. I didn't have the luxury of showing weakness, and once the hand was seared to my fingers, I belonged to Hel. *She who bears the steel hand has the Goddess's blessing to take life.* That was three months ago. It took that long for my hand to heal, to become useful again.

"Oy, Carina!"

My fist curled tighter at the sound of Dagna's voice. She made the application of the steel hand seem like a hangnail in comparison. Whereas the steel only burned me once, Dagna burned me again and again and again.

Slowly I turned, on my time, not hers.

She stood opposite me on the port side of the longboat, still too close for my liking. Her gold hair glowed under the pale moonlight, tied tight into a perfect braid that resembled a thick coil of rope. She stood tall and lean, bright-eyed and fierce. With her broad axe slung over her shoulder and the cruel smile on her lips, one look from her caused men to fall to their knees and weep for mercy. She painted the perfect picture of one of Hel's servants, and I despised her for that.

"When we arrive at Frisia," she said. "I hope you don't forget who you should be fighting. It will be easy to get confused in the dark. Should you find my axe in your back, forgive me. You blend so well with blackness."

Her cruel smile widened. This was an old joke, a tired one, except a few of our Sisters still laughed. It stuck at me like nails. I was not the perfect picture of Hel's Daughters. I had been claimed by a raid in the Southern Isles years ago, brought back as a spoil of battle at three. I had olive-toned skin and black hair, wood brown eyes, and even though everyone could plainly see it, Dagna felt the need to shine a painful light on my differences.

I should have been glad she at least warned me she might stab me in the back this time.

She had officially tried to kill me three times and maim me more times than I could count. The breeze lifted her tunic, revealing the edge of a long pink scar. I gave her that one on the practice field, self-defense with a touch of vengeance.

"A good, healthy rivalry," Merle called it, seemingly proud that when it came to fighting, neither Dagna nor I held back.

But it was not exactly healthy. If one of us were stabbed, or trampled, or drowned tonight, the other one would open a bottle of mead and drink in celebration.

"Look there," Thora Legbreaker said. "Land approaches."

She thrust her steel finger north to a gray shadow rising up from the waves. The only sign of life on the island was a pair of flickering torches. Merle followed the line of Thora's finger, marching up the length of the boat for the spyglass. She held it to her face and stood, one leg on the bow while her red, fox fur trimmed cloak billowed out behind her.

She was breathtaking in a way she had not been when I'd been in training, learning to sail with the Daughters on trade expeditions to Brezadine. This was different. This was Merciless Merle on her way to show her devotion to the Goddess Hel, dressed in her finest cloak, her steel claws freshly oiled, and her belt heavy with her sword and bow.

Merle was always something to behold. Not a scrap of fat on her bones. Every bit of flesh and muscle was worked to perfection, each sinew and joint made for one thing—dealing death. As children, we had our own stories about the fearsome chieftain: that she walked from her mother's womb exactly as she was now. Her mother died in childbirth and our tale was that it happened because Merle had been born with a sword and cut her own mother in half to escape her body.

Mostly we told that story because none of us could picture Merle as a plump, round baby with gold curls and rosy cheeks. It was hard to imagine her as anything else besides steel and iron and blood. I would never reach the fine-tuned, immortal strength of Merle. That was something that couldn't be found with training or practice. It was born into you. It lived in your blood.

All I could do was prove I deserved my place. I could show her that she had been right to spare my life, to bring me to Helvar, and to raise me as her own.

She tossed the spyglass back to Thora and grinned at the rest of us. Her one, silver tooth glinted in the moonlight.

"Lower the sails," she shouted. "Take to the oars. Before morn, the Goddess Hel will be fat with blood!"

"Hah!" We all called back in unison and raised our steel fists. My blood pumped hard as I sat down at the oars. I locked my steel hand around the oak handle and sank my claws into previously made marks. As the sail came down, I pulled against the water.

Horrible Hild kept one hand on the *styr bord*, and her steel fist banged against the back of the boat to keep rhythm. I plunged the oar into the water when she struck and yanked it back in the beat of silence. Dagna sat across from me, pulling her oar to the same rhythm.

"Be careful," she mouthed silently.

I looked away from her and focused on the ever-growing land mass rising up in front of us. Odda Ironfist warned us that it was easy to get carried away on your first raid, to gain a thirst for blood.

"The blood is not for you," she said.

It was for the Goddess Hel. Each life we took tonight would be a new soul in Niflheim, the land of the dead, and in exchange for that soul, Hel gave us life: food, riches, weapons, bountiful crops, fat livestock, rivers of fish, good health for our children, and plentiful game. The more death we doled; the more She gave, and if we did not satisfy Her with enough souls for the winter, She would take them from our people, in the form of starvation or sickness. If we failed, our people failed.

One life for every life on Helvar. That was what we owed, and we could always give more but no less. There had been two seasons since I'd been on the island when we'd fallen short. The year of the storms, eight years ago, when then Daughters were stuck on the island due to the dangerous waters. That year, the crops soured, and thirty children died of stomach sickness. And four years ago, the year of revolt. Some of the villages we raided in the past came for vengeance. We lost fifty-two lives that year, too busy defending ourselves to make our claims to Hel.

Hild's heavy hand beat faster, harder, and I stretched my arms to meet her demand. We would make our claims tonight. We would end the season with blood. Silently we swept across the water, moving through the waves instead of bouncing over them. We had to come in quickly, quietly, to gain a solid position before the village discovered our arrival.

Our longboat slid up to the sand, along with the twenty-two others that left Helvar with us three days ago. I released the oar and reached for my sword, a gift from Merle after my initiation ceremony.

"What will you name it?" she had asked.

I carefully examined the longsword, carved with runes in the golden hilt. *Death must be satisfied.* "Gut Spiller," I'd said, because that was usually where I aimed my kill strike—along the middle.

Merle nodded with approval. "Gut Spiller," she'd said.

Now I took Gut Spiller and climbed onto the sandy beach with the others, tense and waiting for Merle's command to strike.

She made her way in front of us and stood on a boulder buried in the sand. The breeze off the ocean fluttered her cloak behind her. She looked like a goddess herself.

"This is our last raid of the summer, Sisters," she said, clicking her steel fingers together. "Whatever food and riches we take will have to sustain us for the long winter following. Whatever blood that seeps into the sand will have to satisfy the Goddess Hel until we can draw blood for Her again. While we are out there, we cannot forget who we are."

Her steel blue eyes found me in the crowd, and I fought the urge to shrink away, standing taller instead. I knew who I was, who I was meant to be.

"Remember that Death has no mercy," she continued. "She must be satisfied, and if She is not satisfied here, then She will take her blood from our people. We are the Daughters of Hel, the hands of Death." Merle raised her steel fist over her head. "Tonight, let us show Hel that She need not take what we freely give. That She has no cause to leave the underworld and claim what is Hers, because we shall gladly give it to Her! Join me, Sisters!"

"Oy!"

Our voices were like one, giant fist, striking at the silence. Merle climbed down from her rock and led the charge up the hill toward the flickering torches of the village above. I found a comfortable place in the center of the mob, surrounded by warrior women with swords raised and teeth bared.

A sharp elbow struck my side and a blonde braid whipped me across the cheek. "Try to keep up, Carina." Dagna shoved her way forward.

This was not her first raid. She was a year older than I, always slightly ahead.

As usual, I followed in her wake, fighting to catch her. She reached the village first. Our chant awoke the villagers. That had been the intention. Although Death did not discriminate, She would take sleeping children as readily as virile soldiers, there was no skill or glory in taking the life of someone asleep.

A man in a sodden tunic and a dull sword rushed at Dagna. She swung her axe, cutting clean through his neck. His head rolled into the grass, and his headless corpse fell bleeding. There was no quicker or cleaner way to send someone to Death. It had been a flawless attack.

"Go swiftly to Niflheim," she said and moved onto her next kill.

Steel-handed women flooded the village, spilling blood on the sandy path. I pushed ahead, stepping over fallen bodies and around my Sisters. Screams of terror blended with screams of victory, and the air smelled strongly of sweat, fire, and blood.

A man launched himself into the path in front of me, brandishing an axe.

"Go home, Daughter of Hel," he said, raising his axe high.

I thrust Gut Spiller forward, plunging the blade into his stomach. He let out a final gasp and collapsed. I knelt beside him. He was my first kill, my first offering. It had been easier than I thought. Years of practice, of fighting with trained woman warriors, I acted on instinct. He appeared; I stabbed.

"Go swiftly to Niflheim," I whispered and picked up the axe. I hooked it on my belt. What had been his was now mine and my Sisters', the gifts Hel gave in exchange for life, and I needed more. I could not go back to Helvar with only a rusty axe, not on my first raid, not being who I was and having to face Dagna.

My Sisters mobbed the village, dropping down from the thatched roofs, climbing in through the shuttered windows of the stone houses. I turned further up the hill where a single light burned through the trees, perhaps a small group trying to escape. I grasped Gut Spiller and charged after the light, leaping over fallen bodies and weaving around a herd of loose sheep. You could not escape Death. You could outsmart Her for a while but She would always have you in the end.

When I breeched the trees, I plunged into a deeper darkness and quiet, away from the shrieks of the village. A single light shone ahead of me, unmoving. It came from inside a building, a small, stone building with a tall turret in the center--a church.

The people of Frisia worshiped the one, male god. Instead of blood, they offered their god celibacy and gold—ridiculous. What kind of god needed silver and gold? But my people would have great use for it.

I reached the carved oak doors of the church and paused. They were slightly ajar, and on the other side, I heard a woman.

"No," she whispered. "I cannot. I will not!"

I heard no other voice. Either she was alone, or the person she spoke to wasn't responding. Either way, there could be no more than two, easy enough.

I shouldered open the door, and a single priestess spun to face me. The burning candles on the altar behind her flickered. She kept her hands behind her back and her white hood dropped over her forehead. She was old, possibly as ancient as Thorvald the Drunkard, the oldest man on Helvar. Liver spots marked pale cheeks that hung heavy from sharp cheekbones. She had probably been striking once, before age dragged on her.

Keeping one eye on her, I scanned the rest of the room, around the wooden benches and along the tapestries clinging to the walls. "Where is the other one?" I asked.

"There is no other."

"Then who were you talking to?"

"Him." She raised her eyes to the altar and the carved marble statue of her god, dressed in long robes with arms outstretched. "Have you come to kill me?" she asked.

It was a useless question. Of course I had come to kill her. That was what being the Hand of Death meant, except now that she asked, something under my skin tugged at me to stay my blade.

It was the rot of cowardice given to me by my true father, the one Merle had taken me from. It was a sickness in my blood that I could not cure, not with a thousand hours of practice, or even with a steel hand. It was the foul odor that Dagna smelled on me and what made her sneer when I passed. I didn't just look different from them. I was different from the other Sisters, inside and out. They had been given the strength of the Goddess at birth. I had to earn it.

I raised my sword with both hands. I just had to kill the woman and be done with it. I should have done it by now. My hesitation cost me. I moved to her, and her yellowing eyes followed my every step, unflinching, judging. I could drop my sword and split her in half; she was so fragile. Instead, I lowered my blade to the ground.

Hel's fury, what would the grand Goddess of Death want with a wasted old priestess anyway? She would have her soon enough from age.

"Don't do anything that will force me to kill you." I pushed by her to the altar, snatching a gold chalice encrusted with rubies. I unfurled the sack on my waist and shoved the chalice inside, followed by two silver candlesticks.

In a cabinet below the altar, I found a large jug of mead. Thorvald would enjoy that. Watching the priestess, I ripped down her velvet curtains too. We could turn them into cloaks or trade them in Brezadine for seed or weapons. I stuffed them into the top of my bag, pleased with my take.

Merle would be pleased too.

Unless she discovers you spared the old woman.

"You know, she will not give you what you seek," the priestess said, "your vile goddess."

"How do you know what I seek?" I plucked two gold figurines from the windowsill and shoved them into my pockets.

"Acceptance," the woman said.

I flinched. "That is not what I seek, and your god cannot protect you from Death."

"No, but He can provide everlasting life."

I tied my sack closed. Making my way to the priestess, I prodded the point of one steel claw into the underside of her chin. She eyed me from the end of her nose.

"Everlasting life is an affront to the Goddess," I said. "All have their time to live, and once that time is done, they belong to Her. You will too."

"Perhaps," she said. "But who will you belong to? You don't belong to them. You come from the Southern Isles. You are not one of them."

I ignored her. "What are you hiding behind your back?"

"Nothing, at least not to you." She pulled her arm forward and flattened her palm. On her wrinkled skin sat a simple rock. "It's a prayer stone, but any prayers you say on it will not reach your fiendish Goddess."

I jabbed my claw into her skin. "Keep talking, old woman. You will bleed out faster if your tongue is moving when I cut it out." I snipped my steel fingers together, and her sallow eye finally sparked with fear.

That was enough to satisfy me. She could keep the last few threads of her life and her worthless stone. I had her god's riches, and I would give them to my people instead.

I turned for the door, and a figure appeared there. I heard the click of a crossbow, and the wisp of a dart cut by my ear. It lodged into the old priestess's throat. Blood spurted from her lips, and she fell. The stone clattered across the floor. Crimson ran down her chin to her robes while her eyes remained open in a judgmental glare at the ceiling. I took a breath as Merle marched toward me, slinging her crossbow over her shoulder. Blood streaked her cheeks and stained the blade at her belt.

She did not look at me as she passed. I should have killed the woman myself. Why had I let her go? What sickness had come over me?

"You have a good eye for worth." Merle examined the inside of the church. "Not for detail." She nudged the old woman's leg with her boot.

The rot of my heritage seeped up through my pores. "I'm so—"

Merle held up her hand. "It is our nature, our human nature, to preserve life." She pressed her steel hand to my cheek, warm, not cool. Heated from battle. "But when we become one of Hel's Daughters, we must go beyond nature. Death does not spare the young, or the weak, or the infirm. That is usually who She takes first."

"I understand."

Merle shook her head. "No, Carina, you do not. But you will. When you spare a life, you commit someone of Helvar to die in her place."

"I know."

"Do you?" Merle nudged the dead woman's leg again. "Don't disappoint me again, or I will make sure you're the one we send to Hel. Now, come with me and prove you deserve those claws." She flipped her bloodied cloak over her shoulder and made for the doors. I shook off the yearning to cry. Hel's Daughters did not cry.

As I followed her, I kicked something on the ground--the priestess's rock. I picked it up. The gray stone was simple, something you would pluck from a riverbed, except this one was etched with a circle of two snakes, tied into knots.

I tucked it into my pocket so I would never forget how I shamed myself this day.

CHAPTER 2

✳

Flames burst from the center of the fire pit, tickling the roof of the longhouse. With the crush of bodies and the spray of fire, it felt like we were in the pit of Niflheim with Hel.

The *skalds* fought to have their song heard above the din. They sang the tale of the glorious raid of Frisia—at least that was what I took from it in the few words I could hear. It was nearly impossible for the musicians to compete with Odda Ironfist and Aslaug Bloodmouth slamming swords against each other. Odda jumped onto one of the tables and knocked over a few horns of mead. Aslaug followed her and struck at Odda with her fist. Aslaug caught Odda's hand and pulled her in for a kiss while the others around them cheered.

The end of summer celebration was always a celebration to be remembered. This one I would be happy to forget. The take from Frisia had been bountiful with little assistance from me. Merle let me claim the spoils from the church as mine. She didn't tell everyone else that I had failed in killing the priestess, or she would have to admit she had made a mistake in keeping me and raising me as one of them, and she couldn't do that.

Merle didn't make mistakes. She was infallible. Chosen by the Goddess.

At the front of the room, Merle held the golden chalice from the church. It sat beside her on the armrest of her whalebone throne, filled with blood red mead. To persist with her lie that I succeeded on my raid, she'd had a new cloak made for me, cream-colored linen embroidered with golden

10

thread.

Death does not show mercy, the runes read.

It was less a gift and more a punch in the mouth, another reminder of my failure, and it would be an entire year before I could prove myself again, twelve months to quash any remnants of my weakling blood and show my worth.

"More wine, Carina?" A girl with one arm stood over me, perching the jug of wine on her severed stump.

"Yes." I held up my empty horn, smiling at her with something of a grimace.

She topped the horn and moved onto someone else. I exhaled and drank deeply. At least I would have another chance. I hadn't been Disgraced, yet.

At age seven, all women of Helvar made a choice. We could train to become one of Hel's Daughters or choose to hunt or fish or farm or sew— to provide for the island in another way. I, like the Disgraced, chose to train for nine years, learning the many ways to kill someone with a variety of weapons. At the end of my training, at the beginning of the summer in my sixteenth year, this year, I faced Horrible Hild in my final battle.

She had towered over me like a bear in her cloak made of the same, deep brown fur. She raised her sword over her head with both hands, blocking out the sun, and when she came down on me, it took all the strength I owned to keep her from cutting me in half. The second strike, I missed. It sliced down my side in a long thin arc. The third nicked at my knee, and tears stung behind my eyes. I choked them down and persevered.

If I had failed, they would have taken my hand. If I had failed, I would be washing dishes and serving wine. If I had failed, Dagna would be right.

Hild struck me eight times. I only hit her once, a well-placed blow to the back of her knee. It brought her down, and I earned my claws, my place among the Daughters. That one strike was what put me at this table.

One fight, that was all it took. The line between warrior and washer, and my fight wasn't over yet. If I didn't perform as a true Daughter of Hel, they would claim my steel hand, and I would be one of them. I would have to fill Dagna's horn with wine while she smirked at me with her perfect blue eyes. I would be Disgraced.

I would kill a thousand elderly women to avoid that fate. I would do better.

Another body dropped beside me, hard enough to rattle the bench and spill wine onto my fingers. Von sat facing me, one leg on either side of the bench, the inside of his thigh against my knee. I drank heavily of my wine and pushed back against Gunnar behind me to put space between us.

"Nice cloak," he said and picked up the gold-trimmed hem. He rubbed it between his rough fingers while his taut muscles danced like two cherubs in a tent. He had grown tall and strong with sun-kissed hair braided at the back of his neck. Hands calloused from spearing fish and caribou. A thick beard growing in along his jawline. He was a Son of Hel, worthy of the name. While Merle took the Daughters on raids for Hel, Von and the other Sons hunted the game, planted and tended the crops, and built new homes for growing families. We all had our purpose.

Von was also Dagna's older brother, Merle's nephew, and he and I had been raised together in this longhouse, as part of Merle's family, the *chieftain's* family. He was my closest friend until he decided to kiss me at the first summer celebration. He blamed it on too much wine after I pushed him away, but it was too late. Things were strange between us and couldn't be repaired.

I snatched the cloak from him and tucked it under my legs. "Von Whalehunter, if you drop one speck of wine on this, I will cut you." Even worse than having my shame cloak would be to stain it with wine.

He laughed, deep and rich, causing several heads to turn, including Dagna's. If glares could cut, hers would have sliced me from ear to ear. Von was one more reason for Dagna to hate me. Von always preferred my company to hers, and then she had been witness to the stolen kiss. I touched the scars on my collarbone where she jabbed me with her claws afterward.

"I'm sure there will be many more fine cloaks if the stories are true." Von tipped back his wine.

"What stories?" Did they know that truth? Did they know about the priestess?

"Didn't you hear the *skalds*?" He cleared his throat. "Then young Carina marched up the hill, where she slaughtered the priestess for riches galore and sent the old maid to Death evermore."

I winced, almost as much for his singing as for the content. "It's an exaggeration." Now I wondered what other stories about the raids were lies. Had Odda Ironfirst really punched a man's head off his neck? I seriously doubted it before. More so now.

I pulled the stone from my pocket and rolled it in my fingers.

"What is that?" he asked.

"A rock I picked up on the raid." I did not mention the priestess.

"Let me see it."

He snatched the rock from my hand and held it close to his nose, squinting at it with one eye. "You know, I think this might be Rorik's stone."

"Rorik's stone?" I had never heard of this.

"It's a legend, from old Perdita. Rorik was a soldier in the king's army. He went to battle in Murus and returned to find his two sons dead and his wife on the verge of death. He took the blood from his dead sons' veins and etched it into the stone, in the shape of two snakes, one for each son. Legend says he was able to call the boys from death and return them to their bodies."

"Impossible," I said. "No one escapes Death." The *skalds* sang about a man who tried once and he paid the price.

> *Gustaf the brave had fought and bled,*
> *Then found himself cold and dead.*
> *He pleaded with the Goddess Hel,*
> *That if She would only make him well,*
> *He would kill ten men that night,*
> *And send them to Her without a fight.*
> *She agreed and took him back,*
> *To his body bent and black.*
> *When his spirit stepped inside,*
> *The pain and rot forced his cries.*
> *He begged Her again to set him free,*
> *Which She did most generously.*
> *Death cannot be fooled or bought.*
> *Best be gone than left to rot.*

Von handed the stone back to me. "I'm not saying it's true. I'm only telling you the story. Regardless, the stone is valuable because many people believe it is. You could fetch some good coin for that."

"How good?" I asked.

"If it's the real stone, and you found the right trade," he shrugged. "Two, three hundred pieces of gold."

I held back a gasp. Three hundred coins? For this plain, gray rock? The foul priestess lied to me. She knew its worth and tried to hide it. I wished more than ever I had killed her myself. But nothing else we claimed on the raid was this valuable. This could possibly soothe Merle's disgust of me.

"I need to take this to Merle."

Von grabbed my hand. "Let us dance first. Merle and the stone aren't going anywhere."

"I can't."

"One dance?"

"No, Von. I can't."

I wrenched my hand away from his and made my way through the crowd. My face burned. I hated him at the moment. I had few allies here, and now I felt like I didn't have him either. My acceptance always sat at the tip of a blade, one Merle could easily tip.

I was an exercise in cruelty, not greatness. On a raid in the Sothern Isles, a pathetic man offered his only daughter in tribute to Merle in exchange for his life. Merle took the daughter and killed the man for his cowardice. She never explained why she let me live, why she brought me here as one of their own. My best guess was that I was an experiment, to see if someone else, with enough training and teaching could become a Hand of Death. If I failed that experiment, she would have no need to keep me.

I elbowed my way toward Merle, ensconced in the ribs of her whalebone throne. Large, drunken bodies held me back. The fire in the center of the room spat flames and sparks. The room suffocated in wine and sweat and fish.

Sweeping around another body, one blocked my path, tall and bronzed with flowing gold hair.

"Carina." Dagna always said my name like a curse word, rolling it on her tongue like she could bite it off.

"Dagna." I stepped to the side. "Excuse me. I need to speak to Merle."

"I'm sure you do." She snorted derisively as if she knew something I didn't. I worried she knew the truth about the old priestess. "Come have a drink with me first. I have a proposal to discuss." She held up two horns of wine.

I hesitated. I trusted Dagna about as well as a poisonous snake. But if she knew the truth about the priestess, I could not let her reveal it, for my sake and Merle's.

"Fine. One drink."

"Good. Let's get some air." She handed me a horn of mead and we swept through the longhouse doors. The temperature dropped drastically. The sweat on my skin turned to chill. Cold wind blew off the water and smelled like salt and fish

I loved this island. Even though I had come from another one.

The Daughters of Hel were on a raid to the Southern Isles, Orsalia, to be exact, thirteen years ago. Orsalia was the westernmost island of the Southern Empire. When the Daughters invaded, people often begged and pleaded for their lives, but not once had anyone offered their child freely as sacrifice. They usually clutched their babies close and begged their lives to be spared.

But not the man who had born me. Oh no. Even a dog fought harder for a bone than my father fought for his own child. Merle found it amusing to take his sacrifice and then kill him anyway, and I was glad she had killed him. I was glad she took me.

Dagna drank her wine and stared at the moon, hanging in the black sky.

"You did well on the raid, Carina. Better than I expected."

"I did?" This was unexpected. I thought she brought me out here to shove my folly in my face, not compliment me.

"I think it's time we end our feud." She held out her steel claws. "Whatever has transpired between us before, we are Sisters now in the eyes of the Goddess. I would like to start anew…without trying to kill one another, if possible."

My mouth dropped open. She must have been impossibly drunk. As far back as I could remember, Dagna had wanted me gone. Dead, preferably, but gone would have sufficed. I invaded their island, tread upon their lives. I stole Merle's attention. I wedged myself between her and her brother. I understood why she despised me. I didn't like it, but I understood it.

She only approved of me now because she believed Merle and the *skalds*. She thought I killed the priestess. But I would be a fool to ignore her outstretched hand. I might never have this chance again.

"I would like that." I clapped my steel hand into hers. Our fingers locked together briefly until she took hers back and wiped it on her leggings.

"This doesn't mean I'm going to sit by while you take all the glory," she warned.

"I didn't think you would."

"And your hair is still an unsightly color of squid ink." She swirled the wine in her horn. "But it doesn't matter. You don't need to bear children, which is a good thing. Because no man would want you, or woman, really. You're lucky you're somewhat capable of handling a sword, otherwise you would be useless." She held her cup aloft. "To Sisters."

"To Sisters." I raised my horn and drank deep of my wine.

As it rolled down my throat, I felt strange. Weak. My leg buckled underneath me as if it had turned to water. I fell to the dirt. My arms collapsed beside me. My wine spilled. I could not move. I could not speak.

"Honestly, Carina, you are far too trusting." Dagna picked me up under one arm and carried me down the hill.

My dead legs scraped through the dirt. Something had been in the wine. She poisoned me! That was the coward's way to kill someone, the way people who could not fight or aim a crossbow killed people. I never thought Dagna would sink so low, and perhaps that was why she had. She knew I'd never expect it.

"She had a bit too much to drink," Dagna called to two men outside the longhouse. "I am going to dump her in the cold water to sober her up."

They laughed. I couldn't see who they were. My eyes turned black at the corners, and my tongue sat like a dead fish behind my teeth. My throat tightened. I couldn't make a sound.

"You are a mistake," Dagna said under her breath while she pulled me down the hill. "You do not belong here. Hel does not want you, and neither do I."

When she said this to me before, I had been able to deny it. Now I couldn't, in part because I couldn't speak, in part because she might be right. My back scraped against something hard, and other hands took me, laying me flat. Above me, pinpricks of light broke through the darkness. Stars, possibly, except they moved in swirls.

"Take her," Dagna said. "Take her and drown her or gut her and leave her for the gulls. I don't care as long as I never have to look at her vile face again."

CHAPTER 3

✕

I awoke surprised to feel breath in my chest and warmth in my toes. My cheek pressed to rough wood--oak, coated in a dusting of salt. It coated my tongue too, and the floor beneath me swayed. I was on a boat. Not one of our boats. I was inside the boat. This was one of the fat, slow ships from down south.

Slowly, I pulled my legs underneath me and sat upright. My head throbbed with the remnants of whatever poison Dagna had slipped into the mead coupled by the ache of my own foolishness. What beast stalks it prey for thirteen years only to befriend it and feed it wine? Not Dagna. She had been playing the long game, waiting for the right moment to strike. Her only mistake had been not killing me. When I got out of this cage and back to Helvar, she would learn the true meaning of vengeance.

I moved to stand, and the world turned sideways. My stomach churned, and I sat back down to catch my breath. Thick iron bars held me in a small cage. The rat droppings in the crevices of the wood told me I was not alone. I straightened my leather armor and swept my tangled hair behind my shoulder.

I patted my waist. My sword and belt were gone. I had also been wearing a fish knife, a gift from Von on the fateful night of the unwanted kiss, but it was a nice knife, hand-carved. My steel hand they couldn't take, and they left the rune stone in my pocket. I took it out and lay the stone flat in my palm.

The fool kidnappers didn't take the most valuable thing I owned. What did they want with me? I could be on a slaver ship bound for Kievan. Or

17

meant for something worse. But if Hel had not seen fit yet to take my life, then She still had purpose for me.

This travesty could actually be an opportunity. I could kill the kidnappers, give their lives to Hel, and take the ship back to Merle. A fat cog ship filled with bounty would be a nice gift to the island. Paired with the rune stone, Merle would forgive me for the priestess, and Dagna would be punished for betraying me. I would not have to wait another year to show my value.

But first, I needed to get out of this cage.

Footsteps sounded overhead, creaking across the floorboards. I dropped the stone into my pocket and listened. It sounded like three men, possibly four. The steps were off. There could be more men inside the ship with me. The belly of it seemed to be divided into rooms, like a beehive. I would have to make a quick, quiet escape, sneak up on them and slit their throats with my claws before they could rally. I reached around one of the bars and stuck my clawed finger into the lock, scratching at unseen mechanisms.

Escaping from cages hadn't been part of my training. Hel's Daughters weren't captured. It was impossible, unless one of your Sisters poisoned your wine and handed you to the captors. I wondered how Dagna managed to arrange the kidnappers. Usually any ship approaching our island was shot at with flaming arrows until it turned around or burned.

I would be sure to ask Dagna all of these questions before I cut out her eyes. She would be in too much pain afterward to provide any useful answers.

My finger scraped inside the lock to no avail. Nothing clicked or opened. If I couldn't open it the standard way, I would have to try and saw through it, which would take much longer and leave more time for me to be caught.

A door opened and slammed shut. I drew my hand back and sat poised, every muscle tensed from toe to jaw. An unsteady set of steps came near. Shuffle, clump. Shuffle, clump. When the owner of the steps appeared, I found out why.

A sliver of a boy stood in front of me, a wooden cane hanging from one arm, a plate of bread and dried fish in the other. Though he was probably closer to my age, sixteen years or so, he looked young. His left leg was thin and twisted. Even from behind his leggings, I could see it was nothing more than bone and shriveled skin. The rest of him didn't appear to be much more. He had no muscle, no color. A strong gust of wind would topple him. A hearty sneeze. A boisterous laugh.

He did not look like your standard slave trader. I didn't know what he was.

"You're awake," he said, his voice quaking. He spoke in the Southern tongue, which was not my best language. Merle had done her best to teach me all the languages I would need, but I spent less time practicing the Southern words. I was afraid my mouth would fall too easily into the sounds, as if I had been made for it.

The boy stood, motionless, staring at me with drooping brown eyes. He was terrified of me, quivering from the crown of his black hair, down his sunken cheeks, across his hunched, concave chest, all the way down to his shrunken leg. This was my captor. A weakling who couldn't face a woman behind bars without quaking. When I returned to Helvar I would be sure to make him sound more menacing. Add some girth to his body and perhaps some superior sword skill.

"Let me out of this cage," I said between my teeth, or at least that was what I intended to say. The boy looked confused. I must have mistaken my words.

"Eat," he said and leaned toward me with the plate of food.

His heavy, stunted breath fell hard on my ears. He was right to be afraid of me. I planned to kill him. As he bent lower, his cane dangled closer to the bars, just within reach. I seized my opportunity, and his cane, and the boy toppled, dropping my tray of food. He landed hard to the wooden slats, and I shoved the curved end of his cane into his throat. I drove it hard into the jugular. His heavy breath gained a slight whistle as it struggled to get through a half-closed windpipe.

"Don't move," I said, and while I held him, I snatched the fallen bread with the tip of a claw. I bit off a hunk and chewed slowly.

The boy who had been afraid before was now terrified, dark eyes so wide, white rims circled around them. If I thrust my arm forward, I would close off his air and he would suffocate within a minute. I knew this because Dagna had done the same thing to me once with a broom. The first time she tried to kill me.

We had been charged with sweeping up the longhouse after a celebration, a punishment for breaking a basket of eggs earlier in the day. Dagna and I had each taken a side of the larger room, trying to race one another to clean up faster. I pulled ahead of her, using unknown muscles to push the broom back and forth. I had nearly finished when she caught me, swept my legs out from under me, and jabbed the broom in my jugular.

"You will never beat me," she hissed.

I thought I would meet the Goddess that day, until Von came into the room and wrestled Dagna away from me.

"Open this cage," I said to the boy and bit off another hunk of bread. I couldn't fight on an empty stomach, and I couldn't send him to Niflheim until I was free.

"I can't," he wheezed. "I don't have the keys."

"Then I will shove this cane into your throat, and perhaps Hel will grant me my freedom for your life."

He didn't move. Did not speak. Either my translation had gone wrong or I'd rendered him speechless.

"Mat!" Another voice called. More footsteps. My arm wavered. Dagna's poison still dulled my senses.

"Good God, what are you doing?" another boy said. Two of them stood at the base of the stairs. I gave them a quick glance, long enough to see neither one of them had aged past twenty. The first had oiled black hair turned into curls and wore what looked like rouge on his sharp cheeks. The other had darker skin, longer hair pulled into a tail at his neck. He was Eastern, not Southern like the other two. I was held captive by three boys, barely men.

"Let me out of this cage, or your friend dies," I said.

"Now, now," the rouged one said. "Let's not be hasty."

I pushed the cane deeper into the boy's throat, and the whistling breath stopped. Red veins slashed across the white rims of his eyes. I couldn't show him mercy like I had given the priestess. Perhaps if I hadn't failed then, I wouldn't be here now.

A knife cut through the air and landed square in the center of the cane, hard enough to push it from my grip. The boy collapsed in gasps while the cane clattered across the floor. I slammed my steel fist into the bars, rattling the cage. That never would have happened had I not been weakened from poison. The rouged boy picked up the thin one and dragged him across the room, muttering something I couldn't understand. The other boy, the one from the Eastern lands, walked by my cage like a bear on the hunt. Step by step, never tearing his eyes away from me. He bent down, retrieved the cane, and plucked the knife from it.

It was *my* knife. The fish knife from Von.

"Give me that," I said.

He didn't respond. He only dropped the knife into his low slung belt, where it hung over the tops of his baggy, woolen pants.

"You want to eat?" He kicked the fallen plate away. "You behave yourself."

He went with the other two up the stairs, carrying the skinny boy between them. As soon as they were gone, I finished the dry crust of bread and went back to the lock. It didn't matter if they fed me or not. Before nightfall, I would be out this cage, their bodies would be dropped into the sea, and I would be sailing their ship back to Helvar. We couldn't be more than a day away. If Aegir gave me smooth waters, I could handle the boat myself. I'd been sailing since age four.

Unfortunately, by midday, I hadn't managed to open the lock, and it seemed like the boys were not going to be back for me. My parched tongue ached for water. I switched from trying to pick the lock to attempting to saw it open. I rubbed one of my metal claws along the outer edge and imagined I was sawing through Dagna's rib bones to reach the dry, shriveled organ she called a heart.

When I returned with the ship and the stone and told Merle what Dagna had done, our places would change. She would be the one they questioned, and I would torment her, like she had tormented me for years and years. The thought tasted sweet on my parched tongue. Water would have tasted sweeter.

By nightfall, I gave the lock a rest and went to sleep, trying to forget the hunger and thirst. In my dreams, I imagined a table piled with roast lamb, stewed potatoes and broiled codfish. As I was about to gnaw the meat off of a dripping leg of lamb, someone sat at the table across from me—the dead priestess. "You failed," she said and raised a gnarled finger to me.

I snapped myself awake, mouth still watering from imagined food.

My head pounded from lack of water, and I heard them, walking above me. I stood on the bars and pounded my steel fist into the ceiling. The priestess's voice still haunted me. I'd failed in killing her. I failed in escaping this cage.

"Let me out!" I shouted.

They ignored me and so I kept pounding and shouting until they poured a bucket of cold seawater through the cracks.

Salt water burned my eyes. I felt the foreign ache of budding tears and stuffed them down, rolled them into a tight ball to add them to my mass of hate and shame and things I needed to prove or vanquish. I shook off the water and sat down to work on my lock.

Why imprison me if they only planned to starve me to death? They didn't plan to starve me was the answer. It was a test of wills, one they would lose. I was Carina the Unstoppable. If a large, menacing woman with a sword couldn't stop me, if perfect Dagna couldn't kill me, then three pathetic boys wouldn't either.

I scraped my finger back and forth across the metal while small shavings dropped to my leggings. When I did get out of this cage, I couldn't decide what I would do first: raid the supplies or wrap my steel fingers around the boys' necks in turn, grinning while their last breaths left their bodies.

Death was not for me; it was for Hel. I was not supposed to take it as my own, or delight in it, but I had a feeling in this case, Hel would make an exception.

By the third day, my stomach became a creature of its own, a monster that could only be satisfied by a cup of clean water and a roasted piece of fish. I raised my steel fist to bang on the ceiling again, a last feeble attempt because I was making no progress with the lock. The activity only made my claws dull.

"It's cowardly to starve someone to death," I said.

Not that I was afraid to die. I would be welcomed into Niflheim with loving arms…or would I? On my one raid I had failed Her. The true Daughters when they died were held in honor, they earned a place at Hel's table. The others? They were nothing more than the rabble of souls wandering Niflheim.

I couldn't die yet. Not before I earned Hel's favor. Then I would be ready, and I would face Her proudly.

I collapsed to the floor of my cage and pulled my knees to my chest. Apart from the saltwater shower, I had not bathed either. I relieved myself in a hole carved into the floor, and as humiliating as that was, I couldn't even be bothered by it. I could think of nothing but food and water. Water and food.

I heard the shuffle step of the thin boy approaching and lifted my chin. He held a plate of food and a small cup of water. He set it down in front of the doors and quickly backed away. I snatched the cup of water and poured it down my throat and then shoved the dried fish in my mouth.

My stomach was not satisfied by it. Instead it tightened into a fist, trying to keep me from filling it. But I forced the food down. I didn't know if I would get another plate like this, and I needed every sliver of my strength.

The boy, though cowering, remained. He sat across from me, watching, and carefully placed his cane against the wall, far out of reach. He sat just outside of an arm's length away as if he had calculated it at some point. His calculations only made me think harder. I imagined ways to kill him even as he sat where he was, while I was behind these bars with none of my weapons.

I had four viable options already. I had trained in killing people for nine years. Did he think a little distance would save him?

I folded another piece of fish into my mouth and ground it down with my teeth. Even with the sound of my rampant chewing and gulping, his wheezing breath reached me.

Gasp, gasp, huff. Gasp, gasp, huff.

It irritated me.

"You would do the world a blessing if you stopped breathing," I said.

While I had been sitting here, starving, I tried to remember my lessons on the Southern languages. By the way the boy clutched the purple bruises on his neck, I assumed I had improved.

"How many did you kill?" he asked.

I thought back to my one raid. There had been the first man, the ignored priestess that should have been my kill, and after Merle and I left the church, I killed three more men while she stood aside and watched. Four. Dagna killed eight on her first raid.

As I thought of my failure, the stone in my pocket seemed to twitch, taunting me.

"Why did you take me?" I asked, choking down another mouthful of water.

"The people of Helvar are murderers and thieves," he spat.

I swallowed another piece of bread. Then I was to be made an example for all of Helvar.

"And when your Emperor conquered the Eastern lands, I suppose he brought cakes and flowers."

His breath took on a new wheeze. Everyone thought they were so righteous until they were forced to look closely at their own reflection. The Southern Emperor had killed thousands more than we in Helvar ever did, but he did it for himself, not for the Goddess. The boy's true issue with the Daughters was that we believed in something different.

I tossed the empty cup back to him. "More water."

He clutched the cup, shaking in what appeared to be some semblance of anger. Even his ire was pathetic and weak and so it gave way quickly. He returned with more water while I thought of a fifth way to kill him through the bars. Unfortunately I couldn't do it, not yet.

We had been sailing for three days, and even in this slow, fat, whale of a ship, that would have taken me further from home than I could sail back alone. The ship seemed to require at least three men to handle it. I would need to keep two of them alive to get the ship back home, and whichever two I chose, they would not likely help me if I killed one of them.

When I escaped this cage, I would have to hold them hostage. Force them to bring me back to Helvar and then kill them. Even better. Their blood would be fresh when I delivered it. The spoils would be new.

Their time to meet Hel was coming, but not now. Not until I was back on the shores of Helvar.

"Why me?" I asked. "Why did you take me as your sacrifice? How did you get to our island? How did you convince Dagna to help you?" Merle would want to know. *I* wanted to know.

He stared at me a moment longer before he stood up and hobbled away. I had pushed too hard. I took another gulp of water and ate the last of my fish. As long as they kept bringing me food, I could wait for answers. I could wait for blood.

CHAPTER 4

✕

The footsteps coming weren't the broken ones. I had been going to the bathroom in the small hatch in the floor and quickly drew up my leggings and feigned sleep. An odor of perfume curled up my nostrils, and when I opened one eye, I saw the tall, rouged man with the curled hair delivering my tray.

He wore a tunic with bloused sleeves, embroidered around the collar with gold thread in a swirling design that looked like tree branches. It was an ornate style common to Southerners, *wealthy* Southerners. On his long fingers hung three rings, two with ruby stones and another with a large emerald in the center. When I killed him, the riches of his life would all be mine in exchange for his soul, and it looked as if he had plenty of riches to give.

He set the tray down in front of me and removed an atomizer from his pocket, spritzing the air with more perfume. My eyes watered.

"It smells like something died in here," he said. "And as much as I have begged to give you a bath, Nik has refused, to the detriment of us all." He sprayed the perfume twice more, blowing it through the bars of my cage.

From his belt hung a sword, a decorative rapier. It was long and thin, gold hilt and three more rubies encrusted into the top. The shame of my capture continued to grow. The only capable man of the three of them was the one who stole my knife, and if I had met him sober, out of this cage, I could have bested him.

I snatched at the bread and gnawed on it while the boy watched, smiling with rosy cheeks. He had thick lashes, almost like a doe, and his brown eyes were lined in charcoal. He was the prettiest man I had ever seen.

"I really cannot stand all of this animosity in the air," he said. "It's terrible for the complexion. I am Flavian." He made a subtle bow. "And you are?"

"Why did you take me?" I asked instead.

He wrinkled his nose. "Well, you see, the Emperor wants to know more about your Northern ways. He is quite tired of you devastating and robbing the port towns. We found you in Brezadine, when you were, ah, selling some of your stolen goods. It was Nik who approached the girl who brought you to us. She suggested we take you, since you are from the South. She seemed quite eager to help us once we offered her proper compensation."

I gnashed the bread between my teeth. Of course she had. I wondered now how much they had paid Dagna for me. Whatever it was, it was too much. She probably would have paid them to take me away.

I was in Brezadine six weeks ago, and these boys were looking for one of us then, plotting and making plans. This was no simple snatch and grab.

"Why didn't you take me from Brezadine?" I asked.

"The girl suggested we wait. She said they would notice if you went missing in the city, but that there would be an end of summer celebration. Everyone would be too drunk to see a small ship in the cove, and she could make excuses for your absence."

Dagna's plan had been well thought and successful. She was cleverer than I could have imagined.

"Your name then? Since I answered your questions." He smiled at me, driving a dimple into his chin.

"Carina," I said. "The Unstoppable."

"The Unstoppable," he repeated and leaned against the wall. "It's certainly a name that captures attention. They might give me the same name--Flavian the Unstoppable. Though it wouldn't be for my prowess with the sword." His smile widened, and I rolled my eyes. My second idea would be my best choice for killing him. Bite off one of the sharp claws on the end of my finger and spit it back into his eye.

"What will it take for you to turn this ship around and bring me home?" I asked.

His smile dropped. "More than you have," he said. "The Emperor demanded we return with one of Hel's Daughters or not return at all. You can see our conundrum." He reached inside his tunic and removed a small bottle. He pulled the cork and drank from it then passed it to me, stretching his hand into my reach, unwavering, unafraid, even though I could cut it off at the wrist without breaking a sweat.

I took the bottle and left his fingers intact. I couldn't be starved again. One sniff of the bottle's contents burned my eyes. I was cautious to drink. I had been fooled before, but they had no need to drug me. I was already behind bars.

The alcohol warmed my throat. I handed the flask back to Flavian the Pretty, and he took another drink before returning it to his tunic.

"I won't talk about my Sisters to your Emperor," I said. "I would rather die."

"That is your choice," he said. "We are only to deliver you. What you do after that is up to you, although I would appreciate if you don't kill yourself until after we have you delivered. It would be such a waste."

Against my will, my taut muscles softened. I despised him less than the other boys. At least he was honest, and now I knew the circumstances. They had to bring one of us back for their Emperor or be exiled. I had to kill them all and take their ship or I would be shamed. Thankfully, I trusted my skill and yearning more than theirs. It was only this cage stopping me.

"What are the others' names?" I asked.

"Nik is our captain, the angry one with the penchant for knife throwing. Mateo is our navigator and resident scholar."

"The sickly boy," I said.

"Yes."

"And what are you?"

He smiled with a string of white, pearl teeth. "I am the funder of this trip. This is my ship. I paid for the food, supplies, and you," he added, as if I were the same as a loaf of bread.

I picked up the wooden plate and flung it at his head. It bounced off his forehead with a dull sound, the sound of a hollowness. He jumped up and pressed his palm to his face.

"Mateo was quite right," he said. "You're not good company at all."

He rushed off in a flurry of perfume, and I smiled. Just because I couldn't kill them yet, didn't mean I had to sit here and listen to their annoying chatter.

After I finished breakfast, I went back to work on the lock, scraping away at it. I knew it wouldn't work, but I preferred doing something rather than sitting here and festering. All the plans I made hinged on me being out of this cage. I could do nothing until I was free of this cell and could face them on equal footing. They had more numbers, but I had been training to kill people since before I grew into my knobby knees.

I would never forget the first day of training. Merle marched me up to the sparring grounds herself, tall and proud with her cloak billowing behind her. I had barely risen to her navel, short and scrawny. In a rare show of affection, she placed her hand on my shoulder and knelt to look me in the eye. I focused on the small scar in the center of her chin, one of her training scars, one of the few signs that she had ever made a mistake.

"The one who succeeds is the one who never relents," she said. "Don't relent, Carina."

Don't relent Carina.

I sat back in my cell and ran my fingers along the hem of my cloak, my shame cloak. Despite it being a reminder gift, it was a fine cloak, flawless stitching. Merle still valued me, believed in me.

I would not relent. I would not be stopped.

However, I took a short rest around mid-day, expecting one of the boys to come with my lunch. They didn't. My plate-throwing incident cost me a meal, possibly more. My fingers cramped from working on the lock. I stretched them out and examined the ends. The tips were almost round now, and I had no whetstone.

I did have a stone, though.

I took out the rune stone and ran a claw along it. It felt more like scraping against glass than stone. It was a strange rock, a perfect circle, no other markings or indents apart from the carved snakes. I couldn't tell what had been used to carve the snakes into the stone, either. A chisel would have made rougher lines. Von had said the ink used was blood, and it seemed as if it had seeped into the stone itself, becoming a part of it.

I closed my hand around it. "Are there any spirits here?"

The ship creaked as it rocked back and forth, but no corpses crawled their way through the slats. I shook my head. Only a legend.

I put the stone away and leaned against the bars, settling into the sway of the ship. I wondered what Dagna told Merle about my absence, if she'd said I'd drowned in the sea or been eaten by a bear. Had Merle wept over me?

No. Merle did not weep. Especially not for death.

On Helvar, we celebrated one's death as a venture onto the next journey. Hel took those when they were ready. She swept them away in a loving embrace, away from the pains of living. I would do the same for these boys once I escaped. Perhaps with a little pain and suffering as retribution for my days of torment.

Dinner was kept from me as well, all for striking a boy with a wooden plate. I wondered where I'd be if I'd taken that dance with Von. He would have marched up to Merle with me, shown her the stone, and Dagna wouldn't have been able to trick me with her poisoned wine. I might still be on Helvar, pushing away Von's advances, suffering judgment from Merle, and taunting from Dagna.

Nowhere was perfect, I supposed.

I fell asleep in my cell and woke when my head slammed against the bars of my cage. I jerked upright, prepared to punch or scream at someone, but there was no one to punch. Rain bleat against the sides of the ship, and the floor tilted angrily up and down.

"Lower the sails!" one voice shouted from above. Nik, the captain. "No, God no. Not like that." Thunder clapped, and a rush of water poured in through the porthole across from me. Aegir, the sea giant, was furious. Was this anger on my behalf? I liked to think so.

Another rush of water poured across the floor, this time reaching my cage. I stood up as it flowed over my toes, and I banged on the ceiling.

"Release me, before I drown."

"Tie the ropes off," Nik shouted. "No, no, tighter."

Oh the perils of going on a sea voyage with a mapmaker and a pretty boy—neither of them knew how to command a ship.

The boat rocked hard to port, and I stumbled into the wall. More water ran across the floor, this time reaching the bottoms of my leggings. I suddenly became afraid that I would drown down here. No. No. No. This was not how I would meet Hel, half-starved and drowned inside a cage. I wanted to die in battle. With respect. I banged harder, desperately, on the wood above me.

"We will all drown!" I shouted. "You cannot manage the storm by yourself!"

Heavy steps charged down the stairs, and when the door thrust open, a gust of wind ripped through the ship. Nik appeared with *my* knife hanging on his belt. He came right up to the bars of my cage and looked at me with a sort of angry disgust.

"You know how to sail," he snapped.

"Better than your crew," I said. My skin tingled. He was going to let me out of this cage, and as soon as I was out, I would never be put back in.

"If we don't survive this storm, you don't survive this storm," he said.

"It takes at least three to sail this ship in fine weather. We need all the hands we can get. I know that." I held his coal black eyes. It was hard not to look eager or justified. I kept my steel fingers tight and fought against the waves threatening to knock me off my feet.

He yanked a key from his pocket and thrust it in the lock. "You're not the only one on this ship who knows how to use a blade. Remember that."

The click of the lock opening was like a breath of air. I stepped out of the cage, and Nik drew back. His eyes widened as if he suddenly realized his mistake. I held up my steel hand and wriggled my claws. He reached for one of the knives on his belt, but before he could grab it, I snatched the open lock from the cage door and pitched it through the porthole. That cursed lock would never torment me again.

"If you touch anyone, I will pitch you over the side of the ship myself."

He jabbed a finger at me, and a laugh bubbled in my throat. I would have loved to see him try. He and his boys had only faced me restrained and drugged, and even then I had gotten the upper hand on one of them.

But now was not the time for laughing or pointing out their mistakes. He especially would have to stay alive if I wanted to get this boat back to Helvar. He was the one most competent to sail.

I elbowed him aside and stalked toward the stairs. "Your ship is going to sink if we don't stop it." What would soon be my ship, once I killed them and stole it, and I wouldn't have it thrashed to pieces.

I splashed through seawater on my way to the deck and thrust the doors open. Heavy wind and rain pelted my cheeks. I closed my eyes and held my hands to the sky. *Bring the storm, Aegir. You set me free.* The rain felt good on my skin. The clean air tasted fresh in my lungs. Days of stink ran down my arms and legs, and I opened my mouth to drink it in.

"Help them with the sails," Nik said.

I opened my eyes and found the two other boys, drenched like rats, struggling to capture the ropes for the mainsail. I stepped toward them and shooed them away with one flash of my claws. I snatched the rope in my steel fingers and started rolling it around my hand. The heavy wind tugged at the wavering sail. I tugged harder, pressing one foot to the side of the ship while I curled rope.

Aegir was furious. I had only seen him this angry once, on the way back from a sailing trip to Brezadine. Black clouds had formed out of nothing, overtaking the sky. Our longship rocked and creaked, taking on more water than it should have. While the women pulled hard on the oars to bring us back to port, Aegir swept two of them into the water and kept them. It was not easy to swim with a steel hand, especially not on angry seas.

This ship was not like our longboats. They didn't use a *styr bord* rudder or oars. It was powered purely by wind and water, a sturdier ship, but a much slower one. In this case, the sturdier part of it could mean our lives.

"Get the other sails," I said to Flavian and the scrawny one. Dumbfounded, they stumbled across the ship to the prow. I wanted to question why the Southern Emperor sent such a useless crew, but now was not the time.

I captured the main sail ropes and knotted them to the pegs on the side of the ship and fought to roll up the thick fabric. It was heavy from water. They left it up too long.

A flash of lightning crashed, and in the light, I saw another wave rise. It was going to break on the deck. I dropped the sail and dug my claws into the rails. I sucked in a breath as the wave crashed. The water swallowed me whole. When it cleared, I rubbed the salt from my eyes and counted bodies. Four, including my own.

In all directions, black clouds overtook the sky. Even this fat, heavy ship couldn't survive indefinitely. We had to steer ourselves toward land and hope the waves washed us ashore.

"We need to go to land," I shouted to Nik.

"There is no land here," he shouted back. He struggled against the wheel, trying to keep us steady.

"There is land here." I pointed to the starboard side, to the solid shadow to the north.

"We can't go there," Mateo said.

"Why not?" Flavian asked.

"It is—"

"I know what it is," I shouted. We were six days south of Helvar. There would be only one island in the waters here--Isla Mortem.

"I don't know. What is it?" Flavian's face paint smeared from the waves and rain. Black tears ran down his cheeks.

"The Dead Isle," Nik called as another wave rose up over the side of the ship.

I grabbed the rails again and took a breath. The wall of seawater felt like a hundred bodies leaping onto my back. It lasted longer this time. My lungs ached and my claws slipped from the rails. When the wave dissipated, I gasped for air.

I shook the water from my face. One, two. Only two figures on deck: Nik the Knife Thief and Pretty Flavian. No sign of Mateo.

"Mateo!" Nik called into the wind. There was no answer, of course. The boy could barely walk. I doubted he could swim. Better to be swallowed by the sea than wither slowly and decay. It was a kind end for him.

"Go swiftly…" I stopped. Five slender fingers clung to the port side rails. Hel's fire, he still lived.

"Mateo!" Flavian called.

He and Nik didn't see the boy. It would be easy enough for me to keep silent. Another wave would launch him into the water soon enough. Possibly the small gift would be enough to get Hel to appease the sea giant, and we could avoid Isla Mortem.

Or the other two could get knocked off the ship, and I would have to command it on my own. No, this death was mine, I had earned it through days of insult. If anyone was going to kill the boy, it would be me.

I yanked my claws out of the wood and started for him as another wave rose. It crested high, and the white knuckles of the sea giant's fist appeared in rolls at the top. I dove for the boy's hand.

"Mateo!" Nik shouted as the ship rocked backward, sucked down from the force of the wave. I grabbed the boy's hand and locked my claws around his frail wrist. I dragged him over the side and held tight while the new wave smashed on our heads.

I hadn't taken a breath. My lungs shrieked for air, and I took it as soon as the wave shattered. The boy sat shivering beside the rails with his eyes wide and his teeth chattering, a rat dredged from a well.

Flavian and Nik stared at me as if I had brought Mateo back to life and not just dragged him onto the ship.

I stood and left the boy shivering and wheezing. "Make for the island," I said. "Before the sea giant feasts on all of us."

I only saved him as part of a greater plan.

CHAPTER 5

✕

egir released us, but not without taking a large bite out of the ship and consuming most of the supplies. My future offering to Merle had been decimated. What remained, we piled on the beach. No fresh water. One crate of water-logged bread and dried pheasant, and the contents of Flavian's wardrobe, which he was happy to see. I was too. The fine fabrics were something. I also had the stone, but would it be enough? I could never forget Merle's face when she caught me sparing the priestess.

The storm might have set me free, but it had a price.

"We need to repair the ship and leave this place." Nik paced the beach at the edge of the trees, not daring to venture into them.

Isla Mortem gained its name because of the creatures that lived here, hairless monsters with claws like knives that walked on all fours and dropped down from the trees like shadows. They were soulless things that could not be killed. They were exempt from Hel's reach, an abomination against the Goddess, against everything. You lived. You died. Those were the eternal rules.

Of course those were only tales because we owned no truths. Supposedly anyone who faced the Sahrimnir never lived to tell the real story.

"It's a clever lie," Merle had said. "Someone told it to keep people off the island."

The Daughters stopped here, to make repairs or avoid storms, but even we did not venture into the trees. We always kept to the beach.

I stood up and brushed the sand from my backside. My already filthy clothes were now filthier, crusted with saltwater and sand. They hung stiff on my skin like armor.

"Where is my sword?" I asked. "Did it sink with the food?"

The three boys looked to one another, sharing silent conversation. They had it. Perhaps stuffed in with Flavian's blousy tunics.

"Give it to me," I said. "Give it to me, and I'll go into the woods for water and food. You can cut down some of these borderline trees and repair the ship." I couldn't get back to Helvar in a broken ship, none of us would make it far without food, and it would be so much easier to kill them with my sword than without.

Another secretive look. They were rightfully suspicious. Flavian nudged Nik to speak. "We can't trust you," he finally said aloud.

"I saved *his* life." I pointed a claw to Mateo who sat limp in the sand, a wet rag wrung out to dry. They didn't need to know it was only a temporary reprieve until I could kill him myself. "And what do you think I'm going to do in the woods? Befriend the Sahrimnir? Take command of them and lead them back here to eat the skin from your bones?"

Flavian winced. "You don't have to be so detailed."

"I'm not doing this from the goodness of my heart," I said. "In exchange for saving your lives, I want you to bring me back to Helvar." This was exactly what I needed, a reason to go back.

"No," Nik said, without conferring with the others, silently or otherwise. "It's six days back. We won't have enough food."

"I can get enough food and water for six days."

"I didn't say six days. I said *sixteen*," he said. "After we bring you back, we'll need to return south, to Brezadine, which will be another ten days from Helvar. Are your fellow murderers going to stock our ship with supplies before we go?"

No. They would not. And it wouldn't really matter because these boys would be dead as soon as I no longer needed them. But I couldn't say that.

"We go to Brezadine from here," Nik said.

I sat back down on the sand. "Then I guess you'll all die of thirst." I picked sand from my claws. "I'm used to being denied water. I'm of strong, good health. I'm not so sure about all of you." I pointedly looked to Mateo. He would be lucky to survive the afternoon.

"It could rain," Flavian said.

"It could," I agreed. "But it won't rain rabbit or pheasant."

"We can fish, then." Flavian wrinkled his nose while he eyed the water.

It was obvious he had never fished in his life. Good fish would not be in water so shallow, and we had no hooks or nets. What he found near the shore would be scales and bone.

These boys were more useless than I thought. Why, of all the capable soldiers the Emperor could have sent to Helvar, did he choose these three?

"Why did you come for me?" I asked. "Why not someone else?"

Another look, another secret.

"Give her the sword." Mateo tossed a handful of sand. "Let her go." A pointed subject change.

"She could kill us all with it," Flavian said between his teeth, as if I couldn't hear him.

"I could kill you with this if I wanted to." I held up my steel hand. "But I will need my sword to face the woods, and I need you alive to sail the ship." At least two of them.

"Take the sword," Mateo repeated. "Get the food, water, and we will leave you in Brezadine as long as you vow not to kill any of us on the way." He lifted his head and looked directly at me.

It wasn't the deal I wanted. It would extend my journey with them by days. But he said nothing about killing them as soon as we reached Brezadine. I could sell Flavian's expensive tunics and hire a crew to help me sail back to Helvar from there. It would work.

"You have my solemn vow on the Goddess Hel Herself, that from here to Brezadine, your lives will be your own."

"Take the sword." He nodded to Flavian's crate of clothes.

I dipped my chin and stomped through the sand to the crate.

"I didn't agree to this," Nik said.

"It's done," Mateo said.

Digging through bloused sleeves and gold trimmed tunics, I found my sword and breathed a sigh of relief. Gut Spiller was unharmed, as sharp and shiny as it had been the last time I'd held it. I was whole again, unstoppable. The Unstoppable Carina.

I also found my cloak and silver arm band. The arm band I slid over my wrist. The grand cloak would only slow me down in the woods. I pointed to it and turned on Flavian.

"Keep this safe," I said. "One tear, one stain and I will hold you responsible."

He sucked in a breath and pressed his hand to his chest. "I would never deign to let such a fine garment come to harm."

I believed him, despite the smudges of black under his eyes from the waterlogged charcoal liner. He had a penchant for detail and fine things.

Before I left, I grabbed a water bag and another satchel for game and wrapped them around my belt. Only one thing was missing, and it winked at me from the belt of Captain Nik. I marched directly toward him, waiting for him to flinch, but he didn't. I stood in front of him, nose to chin as he was taller than I was, and snatched my knife from his belt.

"This too is mine," I said.

"You will die in there," he said. Not concerned, just stating what he thought was fact.

"No, *you* would die in there." I turned toward the trees. "Fix the ship," I shouted over my shoulder. "I'll be back before sundown."

Just before I disappeared into the woods, I took a breath, hoping no one noticed my hesitation. Then I moved into the cover, crunching on leaves and broken twigs. A fluttering overhead, a flash of red. I stopped and pulled my sword as a red bird flitted to the next tree and landed on a branch.

I shook my head. The Sahrimnir were a story—like the one of me storming through Frisia to kill priestesses. All exaggerations and bold-faced lies.

This was an unexpected setback, but I still had everything in control. I would get the food, the water, they would fix the ship, and I would slaughter the boys in Brezadine. Wouldn't Dagna be surprised to see me rise from my watery grave? She would be more surprised when I jabbed my claws in her chest and marked her like she had marked me.

The trees grew close together. I used my sword to clear a path, looking for signs of game. I only needed food and water for four days if we were to go to Brezadine. Six rabbits, or four rabbits, four fish, and some greens. A simple stew could last with small portions. No one said we needed to eat well, only that we had to *not* die. I had survived three days without food and water, and I liked the idea of watching them go to bed with near empty stomachs like I had. It would make them weaker, easier to kill once we reached Brezadine.

I heard another rustle, lower to the ground this time. I backed up against a pine and pulled the small fish knife. The bush rustled again, and I thought about the Sahrimnir, and the tale the *skalds* sang.

With eyes of red and teeth of green,

The Sahrimnir go unseen,
On Isla Mortem they do hide,
Waiting like the ebbing tide,
Face them bravely if you dare,
With sword and bow and knife and spear,
Kill them once, kill them twice,
You may even kill them thrice,
But they'll come back for number four,
And you'll meet Hel before the morn.

A small brown rabbit emerged from the shrubs, and I nearly jumped out of my leggings. I regained my senses before it escaped, drew back the knife, and lodged it in the rabbit's side.

He let out a squeak before he fell to the leaves. I picked him up by the ears and examined him and his two, long front teeth.

"Are you what has the whole world terrified?"

He was hardly dangerous and not at all frightening. I shoved him into my bag. If I found three more like him, I could be done with this hunting trip.

I kept clearing a path east, to avoid wandering. It would be easy enough to follow the sun back to the beach if I got lost. I found two more rabbits, and then I heard another sound—water. I cut away a few more branches and found the source, a bubbling brook that ended in a shallow pool. Kneeling by the edge, I scooped cool water into my mouth and swallowed a mouthful of dirt and grime.

It ran off my fingers in streams of brown. Standing up, I took a long look at the surrounding trees for signs of movement. Even if the Sahrimnir were false, bears were very real. I didn't want to be caught by one unarmed. Once I was certain the land was clear, I removed my belt, sword, and silver arm band. I untied my leather armor and hung it on a welcoming branch and stripped out of my boots, tunic, leggings and undergarments.

The water was cold but clean. I rinsed my clothes out as best as I could and hung them in a patch of sun to dry. Then I sank my body into the cool water and tried to scrub days of filth and seawater from my skin and hair.

It felt good to be clean again and under trees and sky instead of behind bars. I traced my finger over my newest scars, the ones from my fight with Hild. Apart from the one on my stomach, there was another on my back, my calf, my right arm, my left arm, my right wrist and two on my left thigh. Sometimes the battle took longer to win. Sometimes you had to take a few marks. Like this trip. I had to suffer these boys for a little while longer, then I would have my success: Merle's approval and Dagna's destruction.

I laid back in the water and stared up at the trees, the patches of sunlight and the birds fluttering by. I was glad no one came into these woods. They were peaceful, untouched. I closed my eyes and floated on the water, letting my hair splay out around me.

Suddenly, my peace shattered. I turned upright and caught another flash of red in the trees—two flashes. Eyes?

With eyes of red and teeth of green.

No, it was only a story. It had to be two birds, flying extremely close to the ground.

Unconvinced, I crawled out of the water and sat on the bank, letting the droplets roll from my skin while I squeezed what I could out of my hair. I twisted it into a quick braid and redressed in my damp clothes and filled the water bag. I had enough rabbit. I would pluck a few greens on the way back and paired with the dried pheasant we saved from the shipwreck, we would have enough. I only hoped the boys held up their end of the bargain and fixed the ship. We needed to be on our way.

I retraced my steps to the beach. I saw the white light breaking through the trees and heard low, suspicious voices.

"We can't let her go," Nik said.

I crouched down and breathed slowly, quietly, as if I were stalking more rabbits.

"We can't bring her back to Fortis," Mateo said. "Have you seen her? She's disgusting. I'd rather let a rabid tiger loose in the city."

My lip curled. I was disgusting? Me? Then it was only because I had been left to rot in a cage for days.

"You're not the only one who made the vow to bring her back," Nik said.

"That's right, Mat. We all promised," Flavian said.

What promises had they made to the Emperor? What did they owe him?

"I have more right than you do to make the choice," Mateo said.

"That's not fair," Flavian said. "We all—"

"Shh," Nik said. "I hear something"

Hel's fire. He was more astute than I wanted him to be. I stood up and pointedly broke a large stick to make my presence known. Once I stepped onto the beach, I dropped the bag of rabbits on the sand and acted as if I hadn't heard them debating my imprisonment.

"Three rabbits. Clean water. It should be enough to get us to Brezadine."

"What about the monsters?" Flavian asked.

I shook my head. "Not here, or if they are, I didn't see them. How is the ship? We should get into the water before dark." The sooner we left here, the sooner we reached Brezadine.

I pulled my sword, and both Flavian and Mateo took a step back.

I ran the length of the blade between two steel fingers, drawing sparks. "I want it known that if you were to break your end of the bargain, I would be exempt from mine." If they tried to betray me or imprison me again, I would kill them all and find some way to sail the ship on my own, propelling it with pure ire and stubbornness if necessary.

Flavian gasped in horror. He looked on the verge of swooning.

"No one is breaking the bargain," Mateo said.

"Good." I couldn't really sail the ship by myself. Not a fat, cog ship like this one.

I moved to replace my sword in my belt when the trees behind me came alive. Four feet, running fast. I turned as a large, brown, hairless beast dove from the woods, long yellow claws reaching for my chest.

I swung my sword in a full arc, catching the beast across the neck. My Helvar-made, sharp-as-Hel's-hand blade barely cut through the skin, and there it stuck tight while the creature howled and sprayed blood onto the white sand.

It kicked furiously while I tried to wrench my sword free. The howl it made pierced my ears.

"Get away from it," Nik shouted.

"I'm trying. There." I finally got my sword free, and the beast limped back to the woods, leaving a trail of blood on the sand. The Sahrimnir weren't undead. They were just extremely hard to kill, skin like leather armor.

"Get to the ship," Nik said.

"Is it fixed?" I asked. My hands shook. I had faced the Sahrimnir and survived, but I preferred not to do it again.

"Yes," Flavian said. "Let's go." He put an arm around Mateo's shoulders and helped him toward the ship. I picked up the bag of rabbits and froze when I heard a chorus of howls, five at least, just on the other side of the trees.

CHAPTER 6

✖

I slung the bag of rabbits over my shoulder and ran, tearing through the sand toward the ship. The Sahrimnir moved fast. Their pounding feet echoed through the ground. Their howls cut me to the ribs. Flavian and Mateo were a few steps ahead of me, and I fought to reach them. The bags of food and water slowed me down.

"Take these." I tossed the bags at Flavian. "Get to the ship!"

None of us would survive without the food, and now that I had faced one beast, I knew better how to kill them.

I spun around as the leader of the pack lunged. He was no larger than Horrible Hild. No more menacing than Merle. It was only his thick skin that made him a worthy foe. With both hands on my sword, I thrust as he lunged and jabbed him in the center of the chest. My sword cut through leathery skin.

Blood sprayed from the wound, and he collapsed with a whimper, legs twitching. I had done it, a shot straight through the chest...except my sword was stuck again. Hel's fury. The next beast reached me before I grabbed my sword. It leapt for me, jaws open, teeth bared. I punched it in the eye with my steel fist. The beast shook off the strike easier than I shook it from my fingers. The pain raced from my wrist to my shoulder.

The beast caught my steel hand and tried to bite through it. My arm twisted painfully. I cried out and tried to kick it free, reaching for my sword with my other hand. My fingers brushed the hilt---not enough. I grabbed the fish knife from my belt and jabbed it into the creature's eye.

It let out a piercing howl and released me. I rolled through the sand and

41

grabbed my sword, this time freeing it from the dead beast's tough skin. I moved to stand when something struck me in the back. It pushed me into the sand and stole the air from my lungs, otherwise I would have screamed. Sharp claws sank into my shoulders. I scrambled through sand, trying to break myself free and then the weight lifted.

I rolled onto my side and found the three remaining creatures all wrestling over a mound of blood and fur—one of the rabbits.

"Run!" Mateo called. He held the bag of rabbits. He had given one up to save me.

I grabbed my sword and stumbled toward them. Warm, wet blood ran down my shoulders. I buried the pain and burst up the gangplank. The one rabbit had not lasted long. Two of the creatures raced behind me.

I skidded onto the deck and stopped at the edge of a large hole. Flavian grabbed the back of my tunic and kept me from tumbling into the lower decks.

"We used the deck planks to fix the hole in the side," he said.

I could see that--now. Nik wrenched the gangplank up and yanked on the sail ropes to winch the mast. I grabbed the other side to help him, fighting against the ache in my shoulders. Flavian and Mateo sat by the rails, useless. Frozen in shock and terror.

The white sail dropped over the ship, and nothing happened. No wind. Something lodged into the ship with enough force to rock it. One of the Sahrimnir clung to the side, sharp claws stuck in the wood. Nik yanked a crossbow from a hook on the rails.

"Aim for the eyes," I said. "The skin is too tough to pierce with that."

He nodded and pressed the crossbow to his cheek, squinting one eye. The bolt flew and hit the creature in the center of its right eye. It howled and dropped to the water. It sank below the surface with its mouth open, clawing at the sea to no avail.

They couldn't swim. Thank the Goddess.

Five more of the beasts howled from the beach, at the edge of where the water curled up to shore. I pressed my hands to my head and tried to muffle the sound. I would never forget it, and I would never, ever set foot on Isla Mortem again. I would drown first.

"You're hurt," Mateo said. "We should stitch your wounds." He reached for me. If he dared touch me, I would cut off his one good leg.

"I can take care of it myself," I snapped and pulled away from him. "You wasted one of our rabbits."

"To…to save you."

"A competent person could have done it without wasting the rabbit. It should come out of your share." I hated that he had helped me. That I hadn't been able to defeat the Sahrimnir on my own.

"You would have died," Flavian said.

"I'm not afraid of Death," I said. "She is everyone's end."

"Yes," Mateo shouted. "But that doesn't mean we should rush to get there. Or that we need help to do it. We are all plenty capable of dying on our own." He used the railing as support to hobble away from me.

It was only four days to Brezadine, but that would feel like a lifetime stuck with these boys. When I made the bargain, it had seemed easy enough—just don't kill them immediately. Now I worried this would be my most difficult challenge, even harder than earning my claws.

Unfortunately I'd given them a vow, their lives would be their own until Brezadine. I swore it on Hel too. I couldn't go back on that promise, however, I had been careful. I said their lives would be their own. If they fell off the ship and drowned on their own, I couldn't be held responsible.

"I'm going below decks," I said.

I struggled to keep my chin upright as I plodded down the stairs. Each step drove a new pain through my shoulders. Below decks, in the galley, I found a flint stone and burned the scraps of a broken crate to get a small fire going. Stripping out of my leather armor and tunic, I set my knife in the fire until it glowed red hot. Then I pressed it to my shoulders to seal and sanitize the bleeding wounds.

Horrible Hild had shown me this method of healing when I'd been eight. I had been struck with an arrow, one that should have been blunt-tipped. They were practice arrows. The older Daughters-in-training fired them from the tops of the climbing walls while the newer Daughters tried to breech the defenses. Dagna had been one of those outfitted with a bow, and she "accidentally" grabbed a sharp-tipped arrow from her quiver when it came my turn to practice the siege.

It struck me through the shoulder with a dull thud. I heard the sound before I registered the pain. Thankfully Dagna hadn't yet possessed the skill or strength to pierce it through my chest. I collapsed to the field, and Hild plucked me from the grass.

Without warning, she yanked the arrow from my shoulder and pressed her burning knife to the wound.

"Get up. Keep going. If you don't, you'll meet the Goddess sooner than you'd like."

What a fool I'd been to take Dagna's extended hand, to believe she wanted to make amends. From day one, she had been showing me how badly she wanted me gone and how far she would go to do it.

Well, she had failed in killing me then, and the Sahrimnir failed in killing me now. I was unstoppable.

I drove the hot blade into my skin and sealed the Sahrimnir wounds closed with a fiery burn. I bit my tongue and held back the scream. I pulled the hot knife away from my skin once the burning ceased and the blood stopped running down my arm.

"Get up. Keep going. If you don't, you'll meet the Goddess sooner than you'd like."

That was the only way I knew to succeed.

My tunic, however, couldn't be repaired with a hot knife. I wondered if Flavian had some twine, or I could steal the thread from one his bloused shirts. He owned plenty of them.

Poking through the beehive of rooms below the deck, I found the captain's room that Flavian had clearly taken for himself. His perfume hung in the air and his crate of clothes sat in the corner. My cloak was laid gently over a wooden chair, carved with armrests that looked like horse heads.

There was a large bed in the center, nailed to the floor, dressed in cream-colored linens and four feather-stuffed pillows. In his drawers, I found a wooden box filled with coins and two bottles of vintage wine. More for my Sisters once I took his life. The drawer below held a second wooden box. I opened it, expecting more riches, and only found a small, soapstone carving of a man, a good-looking man with high cheekbones and full sculpted lips. He sat with one leg pulled to his chest and his chin resting on his knee. He smiled as if he had a secret to share.

Who did Flavian keep in his drawer? A brother? A lover? A friend? And more importantly, why did I care? The carving was fine but wouldn't be worth taking. I shoved it into the box and found what I was looking for, a small sewing kit.

I did my best to stitch the holes in my vest and tunic. I learned to sew by stitching wounds, and as such, each tear through the leather looked like puckered skin once I was done with it.

I slid it over my shoulders and poked round in the other rooms of the ship. I found the washroom with empty tubs for bathing and waste. Much more dignified than my hole in the floor and the seawater dumped on my head. I also found the bunkroom, with four bunks, clinging to the walls. Two on either side.

The lower bunks were occupied, and it was easy to see which was which.

Underneath one were stacks and stacks of books. I took one out and ran my clawed fingers across it. I couldn't read it. It was written in the Southern characters, where each one made a separate sound, and together they made words. I knew how it worked, but it seemed like a waste of paper to have so many characters when a rune could tell a story with less effort.

Under Nik's bunk was another wooden box, blackened from age and oil. I took it out and flipped the latch. Inside were more small, carved figures along with a collection of carving knives. So I had found the sculptor. I took out one of the carvings, a little dolphin rising from the waves. I ran my finger down its smooth back and across the tiny teeth inside its nose. This was the finest carving work I had ever seen. It might be worth some money in trade, at least the knives would be.

I replaced the box under the bed. Thinking of carvings, I took my own stone from my pocket, the rune stone. Thank the Goddess I hadn't lost it on the beach. Now that I had taken stock of the ship and the contents, the offering didn't seem as grand. There had been so much more in the ship before the storm. I wondered if it would be enough, and as I thought of Merle's face when she caught me in the church with the priestess, I didn't know.

I also supposed it didn't matter. I had heard their conversation. I had to kill them in Brezadine, otherwise they would take me to their Emperor. The only one adamant about not taking me to the Emperor was Mateo. But how much authority could he really have? He was their navigator. But on the island he said he had more right to decide my fate than they did. How?

I sighed and climbed onto one of the empty bunks, the one above Mateo's. I stretched out my tired muscles and aching shoulder and stared at the ceiling. Everything about this kidnapping was so strange. These boys were so ill-equipped, and they let me out of the cage too easily. I couldn't help but worry there was something else, something I didn't quite grasp, and until I did, I would have to be cautious.

I fell into a half sleep, waking every now and then to make sure no one was planning to put me in shackles again. The eighteenth time I woke up,

I couldn't go back to sleep. My hunger growled at me.

I crawled down from the bunk. My shoulders throbbed, stiff from being cut then burned. I stretched my left hand, five metal fingers. I combed the claws through my hair and followed my stomach to the galley where the fragrant smell of rabbit and wood smoke wafted into the hall.

When I poked my head inside, I found Mateo and Flavian seated at the table, and Nik hovering over the stove, stirring a pot of stew that smelled surprisingly good for what little we had.

"Feeling better, Carina?" Flavian said.

"I *am* hungry."

"Then have a seat." He patted the bench beside him and smiled.

While I had slept, he had changed into a fresh red tunic and black leather vest, eyes re-lined in thick charcoal and a very potent fresh wash of perfume. If he walked into the woods with that odor, every animal in the area would run for safety.

Rather than sitting next to him, I sat opposite, next to Mateo who shied away from me as if I were the one emitting a rotten stench.

"Here." Nik dropped a wooden bowl in front of me and set two more down for Flavian and Mateo before sitting with his own.

We all stared at the stew without moving. The boys kept their hands in their laps as if they were waiting for something, for me to eat it perhaps. I would not be drugged and shoved in that cage again.

"Is something wrong?" Nik finally asked.

"Why aren't you eating?" I asked. "Is something wrong with the stew?" I made a promise not to kill them on the way to Brezadine, but the promise had not been mutual.

"In the South," Flavian said. "It's customary to let a lady take the first bite."

"So you men can make sure it's safe before you try it?"

I knew how other places were. They treated women like property, servants, made them parade around in uncomfortable dresses much like Flavian's, with sleeves that would catch in a bow or a sword and long skirts that would tangle their feet. A woman's only purpose was to be beautiful and marry well and apparently taste food first.

"It's meant to be polite," Mateo said. "Something you obviously don't understand."

After he spoke, his wheezing breath rattled in my ear, and I closed my steel fist. I ached to slam it down on his bony fingers. Breaking a hand wouldn't go against my promise.

"Oh for God's sake." Nik dipped his spoon into the stew and shoved the bite into his mouth. "Happy now?"

"Yes," I said and switched my bowl for his and ate the soup he already tasted.

It was good. Good for anyone. Better considering I had only given him a few scrawny rabbits and herbs to cook with. Or perhaps I was just so hungry, dirt in water would have tasted fine.

"How is your back, Carina?" Flavian asked.

"Much stronger than yours," I said. "Have you ever used that sword at you belt?" I nodded to the jeweled staff. Another prize that would be mine soon enough, although it was more of a decoration than a weapon.

"Oh no, never. I leave the fighting and killing to much more skilled people--like yourself."

I cracked a smile. He was a charmer, no denying. He was also obviously rich and pampered, and at home, he probably didn't have to lift a finger to dress himself. It would make him easy to kill.

I dipped my spoon into my bowl for more soup and came up empty. I stared at the bottom of the bowl for a moment, hoping it would refill.

"I know," Flavian sighed and rested his rouged cheek in his palm. "Nikos is a magician when it comes to food. He can make a five course meal out of a handful of fish and a few raw potatoes. I suppose that comes from—"

"Quiet." Nik stood up and snatched my empty bowl. "We're on rations until port." He threw the bowls into a pot of seawater and stomped from the room.

Mateo followed shortly after with less of a fit, except he still made noise. His cane tapped on the floor angrily as he dropped his bowl in the seawater and shuffled across the floor. Scrape, drop. Scrape, drop. I couldn't decide which sound was more infuriating.

As soon as he hobbled up the steps, Flavian pushed his bowl toward me. A few bites of stew lingered on the bottom.

"I'm trying to watch my figure," he said. "And you did more activity than I did today."

Thank you. The words sat on my tongue, and I couldn't say them. Or wouldn't say them. This act of kindness couldn't erase the days I spent in a cage. It couldn't save him from Death. I filled my mouth with his last bites of stew.

"What were you going to say about Nik?" I asked when the silence turned too long.

"I think he made it clear that he doesn't want it said."

"You know, while you had me in the cage, starving me, I spent my time thinking of ways to kill you." I couldn't explain why I said that. I supposed I did not want them to trust me. I wanted to make it clear I was a force to fear because they didn't seem to fear me enough at the moment.

"No doubt." Flavian leaned his cheek on his palm, unperturbed. "How many did you come up with?"

"Seven," I said.

"That is quite a few, however, if you killed me now that would make your bargain with Mateo moot, and Nik is more likely to cut me than you at this point."

"Are you certain about that?"

He paused. "No, I'm not. But I'll make a bargain of my own with you." He reached into his pocket, and I held up my claws.

He stopped. "Do you think I would honestly draw a weapon on you?"

I didn't know. But if he tried to cut me, I would remove his hand at the wrist before he could. He seemed to realize that too. I lowered my claws.

"Right." He drew out a bundle of leather, tied in a roll. "We all have our skills, Carina. I prefer to get what I want through charm and flattery. I've always been worthless with a sword, but I don't need it. I excel at two things: love and games." He unrolled the leather bundle, and out fell eighteen small round stones, nine white, nine black. "Do you know how to play?"

"No." I scratched one of my claws absently on the table, to keep them in view.

"It's simple. I'll give you black; it seems to be your color." He slid the nine black stones across the table to me. "The point of Nine Men's Morris is to get three of your pieces in a row. If you do that, you can remove one of mine. The game ends when one player is reduced to two. Would you like to try? I can explain more as we go along. I'll go first." He set one of the white tokens onto a black dot on the piece of leather. It consisted of three squares placed inside one another bisected by two lines. At each intersection, there was a dot.

I set one of my stones on another dot.

"Oh good, you're a quick learner."

We went back and forth. Once I lined up three of my stones, I was able to take one of his.

It was more of a strategy game. Not like the games we played on Helvar. If the game didn't end with a black eye, no one wanted to play. As soon as the pond froze, the *Knattleik* battles began. We had teams and a ball and had to kick it across the ice to breech the other's defenses. No one ever walked away unharmed, and then we would all go to the longhouse, the *skalds* would sing songs about the victories and losses, and we would drink mead warmed on the hearth fire.

I took another one of Flavian's tokens, and won the game.

"Very good, Carina." Flavian clapped his hands. "And in exchange, I will give you a secret. The reason Nik is so skilled in the kitchen is because when Mateo and I met him, he was an orphan, living down on the docks, eating rats and rotten fish. The only man I know who can make a decent meal out of garbage."

I shook my head, confused. I hadn't wanted to know that, and now I did. I couldn't give it back.

"Why are you telling me this?" I asked him as more questions arose. How had Nik been orphaned in the South when he had the look of someone of the East? Had his parents died on the voyage south? Had he been kidnapped like me?

"This is how the game is played." Flavian picked up one of the white stones and rolled it over his fingers. "You win, you get a secret. I win, I get a secret. Shall we play again?"

"No," I stood up. This was a more dangerous game than *Knattleik*.

"Oh come now, Carina. Are you afraid?"

"I won't tell you the secrets of my people." This was his way of getting treasure back to his Emperor.

"Fine then. I won't ask you any questions about the Daughters. They will all be specifically about you, and in exchange, you cannot ask me about the promises we made with the Emperor."

I hesitated.

"Are you still afraid?" Flavian raised an eyebrow. "You have so many personal secrets, Carina? How about this, the game will end when you say it ends, and anything we say to one another will not be shared with those above." He nodded to the ceiling.

I went through the details of his arrangement, finding no benefit for either of us. "Why?" I asked. "Why do you want to know about me?"

He shrugged. "I'm dying of boredom. I have been on this ship with those two for near three months, and I'm on the verge of jumping ship and talking to fish for some decent company. You are the first interesting thing to set foot on this ship since our last stop in Brezadine so please, I beg of you, do me this favor?" He pushed the black stones toward me and fluttered his eyelashes.

He made a point. The journey to Brezadine would be tediously long without some entertainment. I sat down. If I didn't want to answer a question, I would end the game. Or I could always lie. It would be good to know more about these boys even if I couldn't ask about the Emperor. Merle would want to know why he had such an interest in us, and why he chose these three to fetch one of us. She would want to be ready in case the Emperor tried to come for one of us again.

We played again, and this time, I lost miserably.

Flavian leaned across the table and licked his lips. "Tell me Carina, did you leave a broken heart behind on Helvar?"

"No," I said, my mind instantly turning to Von.

"Well that is a blatant lie." He slapped the table. "This game is no fun if we both lie to one another. What can it hurt? This is between you and me, and I can promise you, I will never go back to that island again. I have no intention of meeting your goddess so soon. So, again, tell me Carina? Is there a heart swooning over you on Helvar?"

He made a valid point. He would be dead long before he could tell anyone about Von.

"Yes," I finally said.

"Oh." Flavian pursed his lips. "Who is he? Or she?"

"That would be two questions. You must win again." I festered over the rules enough to know that.

"Fair enough." He cleared the board and gave me back my black tokens. Minutes later, they sat in his hands, and I owed him another answer.

"I want a name," he said.

"Von."

"Von the what? I know you all give more definitive names than that."

"Von Whalehunter," I said.

"Oh." Flavian sat up straighter. "I like the sound of this immensely. Is he handsome?"

I shrugged.

"He is then," he said. "And you are not at all interested in him? Pity for this poor young man."

I opened my mouth to argue, to ask how he knew that, and changed my mind. I was beginning to see that Flavian was as skilled with his words as Dagna was with her axe, beheading truths with expert force. To beat him, I would have to be more cunning. I won the next game, barely. We both only had three tokens left in play.

"Why is Mateo in charge of this journey?" I asked.

Flavian's eyes flashed, but in accordance with the rules, I had not asked about the Emperor.

"He's in a well-to-do position in Fortis, one of the lead mapmakers," Flavian said.

"How?" I asked. "When he's so young and frail?"

It was the combination of the two that put me off. The elderly and frail on Helvar were still sought after wells of knowledge. They were revered and respected. But the young and frail? They hadn't had enough time to earn their position and lacked the strength to take it. One could gain a solid place in farming or as a storyteller, but they wouldn't have been sent on an important journey. That was reserved for the strongest. The fiercest. The Daughters.

"I suppose that's what made him so well-to-do. He had the blue plague as a child and as such, spent two years of his life in bed. He learned to read. He studied books, stars, maps. He practiced drawing. Since he couldn't go anywhere with his legs, he travelled far and wide in his mind." Flavian smiled with a sort of pride.

The boy escaped Death once before then. Very few survived the blue plague. It was a skin rot. It started from the surface and dug its way deep, devouring bodies from the outside in. The Death Goddess had been very displeased those years. She claimed many lives. To complete their raids to protect their own people, the Daughters travelled south more often. I had been claimed during the outbreak, possibly saved.

It also explained the wheezing. The disease probably hadn't stopped at his legs. That boy was already living on borrowed time. If I didn't send him to Niflheim, he would find his way there on his own soon enough.

Flavian won the next game and continued his questions about Von. "Why is it you don't return this young man's affections? Is there someone else?"

"No," I said, growing more uncomfortable.

These were questions I asked myself. What everyone on Helvar would have wondered. Why didn't I go with Von? I enjoyed his company. There was no better whaler. He was handsome, and as part of my initiation I drank Hel's poison. Willem Steadyhands mixed the secret elixir, and I gulped it from the bed of a silver chalice while my newly burned hand healed into the steel claws. The elixir ensured that I would never have children of my own. My body, in its entirety, belonged to Death. It could never give life. I could have spent my nights with Von with no consequence, just as he wished.

But I didn't wish it.

"The game is over." I pushed the leather board and the small stones aside, exercising my right to quit.

"Well, you lasted longer than I thought you would." He collected the pieces and re-rolled the board. "I want it made clear that every match I lost was on purpose."

I raised an eyebrow.

"Don't look at me like that. It's true. All part of the strategy. You have to think you're winning to keep playing." He tucked the leather wrap into his pocket. "I'll just have to make my own speculations about this Von Whalehunter, and I'll assume that despite being dreadfully handsome, he is rude, or foul, or very poorly endowed."

"He is not rude, and I know nothing about his endowment."

"See, you're already telling me more without telling me. Now I know this is an unrequited love. On his part. Not yours. If you had asked the same question of me, I would have told you about Arturo," he sighed. "The most handsome man in all of Fortis and foolish enough to spend his nights with me."

Arturo must be the subject of the sculpture he kept in his drawer. "Is he rude or poorly-endowed?" I fired the insulting question back.

"No, on both counts." He winked. His eyelashes were impossibly long. Had he put charcoal on those too? "He's just a boy," Flavian said. "And my father is the most old-fashioned man in all of Fortis. He insists I must settle down with a woman, an important woman. Have you met the wealthy women in Fortis? No, I doubt you have. Take my word when I say if you think Nik can be a bit stuffy, they are much, much worse. If I were to be with a girl, she would have to be more like you--wild and unpredictable, but even you cannot hold a candle to my dear Arturo."

"I'm devastated."

"Well." He rubbed his chin. "If you ever feel like playing a different game, I am quite skilled at that one too and very well-endowed." He leaned toward me, suffocating me in a cloud of perfume.

"You wouldn't be once I was done with you." I raised my steel claws and snipped them together.

His face went still before he burst into laughter. "I do like you, Carina. It will be sad to say our farewells in Brezadine." He sat back in his chair and folded his hands behind his thick black curls.

I liked him too, or at least despised him less than the others. But I jabbed down any nagging feelings about sparing him. Death did not release the jovial or amusing, either. This was why we didn't speak to the villagers we raided. It was better not to know them before we slit their throats.

CHAPTER 7

✖

Steel fingers were not as resistant to the salt air as fingers made of flesh. Rust crept into the joints. I couldn't make a fist without something grinding or creaking. On Helvar we used an oil made of beef fat to protect them from the elements. Dagna hadn't dropped any of the oil in my pocket when she'd dragged me off the isle. She probably assumed I would be dead long before my fingers rusted.

The thought of her face when I returned to Helvar with the ship she'd sent me on, made my chest swell. I would be sure, when I sailed the ship into the island docks, to watch for her, to focus hard on her expression, the wideness of her eyes and the curve of her lips. To take it with me to bed every night for the promise of sweet dreams.

But I continued to worry. What would Merle see when I arrived? A dilapidated ship? Three incapable sailors sent to the Goddess as petty offerings? A Daughter of Hel who had been tricked into drinking poison and held captive for days, who had a few carvings, some fine clothing, and a rune stone in her pocket? Would it be enough?

I rubbed my rusted fingers together.

On the horizon, the port of Brezadine appeared, rising out of green water. Sandstone buildings draped with bold red awnings dotted the waterfront city. They were strung with wooden scaffolding and arched tunnels decorated in patterns of blue and red tiles.

I checked the sword at my waist and the knife beside it. As Brezadine neared, so did the fulfillment of my vow not to kill them. I had to kill them or face whatever plot they had to get me to the Emperor. As far as offerings to Hel, I could figure something else out once the boys were gone and the ship belonged to me.

"Drop the sails! Ready the anchor!" Nik shouted, awakening Mateo and Flavian from a dazed stupor.

I grabbed one of the mast ropes before Mateo could reach it. He backed away quickly, either in fear or because he knew I could wheel it in quicker.

"Lower the anchor," Nik shouted, and Mateo and Flavian fumbled with the crank to get the anchor into the water.

Nik knowingly made the call earlier than necessary. The ship was still gliding into an open dock. By the time the two boys got the anchor into the water, it was time. It dragged along the ocean floor until it caught, sidling us up against the wooden dock.

I tied off the ropes and pushed the gangplank over the edge. The smell of spices mixed with the sounds of bleating goats, chimes, and sitar music. I closed my eyes and smiled. It was something familiar, if not entirely familiar. The Daughters came here frequently to barter their gifts from Hel for more usable things.

During my training, I travelled with Merle and the others on these trips. On my second visit, Merle had bought me a honey cake with some of the bounty we'd earned from the trade of goods from their latest raid.

"When the Goddess of Death is satisfied, She provides for all of us," she'd said.

I repeated these words as I pulled on my sword. Killing these boys was not my personal vengeance. Their deaths would serve all of Helvar. Their blood could mean my life spared.

Mateo stood the closest. I yanked my sword and swung it at his neck. A wooden crate struck my arm, and my sword clattered to the ground. I reached for it with my claws and couldn't wrap my fingers around it. They were immovable. Bound by rust.

"Don't move."

I yanked my fish knife and straightened. Nik stood across from me with one of his knives raised and his mouth pulled taut. Flavian and Mateo stood to the side. Flavian flushed with shock, Mateo with the words, "I knew it," on his lips.

"We had a deal," Nik said.

"That deal has ended."

Nik narrowed his eyes. "Do you want to go back into the cage?"

"You will never get me in that cage again." I lunged for my sword. Nik threw his knife. It caught the sleeve of my tunic and pinned it to the ship. He had another knife in his hand before my next breath.

I threw mine, and the small fish knife lodged into his forearm, sticking out of his flesh like a thorn. He did not drop his knife. He did not flinch.

"You're not the only one who can fight, who is willing to take a hit."

He removed my fish knife and held it in his other hand, dripping with his own blood. I was slightly impressed. He had the strength and fervor of a Son of Hel, which would make this more difficult.

I unpinned his thrown knife from my tunic and readied to pitch it at back him.

"The next one won't strike an arm," I warned.

"Neither will mine."

"I am not going to your Emperor!"

"You're not leaving this ship!"

We both swung our arms back until Flavian stepped in between. His cloud of perfume stung my eyes, ruined my shot.

"Everyone calm down," Flavian said.

"Move, Flavian," Nik growled.

"No, you'll kill each other. What no one has suggested is that we tell her the truth."

"Don't," Mateo warned. "It won't make a difference."

"What is the truth?" I demanded.

"It's time," Flavian said to Mateo. "Otherwise we go home emptyhanded."

"I don't care," Mateo huffed.

"Mat," Flavian pleaded. "It's her dying wish."

The grimace on Mateo's face softened. Who was *she*? As far as I knew, the Southern Emperor was a man, Basil the third I believed. It was hard to keep track. If the Emperor died, they simply placed another one in his throne and dropped a crown on his head.

But never a *she*.

"Go ahead then," Mateo finally said. "You'll see it won't matter."

"Thank you." Flavian exhaled. "Carina," he paused, "we know your mother."

My heart stopped beating for a moment. At the word, "mother," my mind went to Merle and her glinting, silver tooth. Then someone else appeared in my thoughts, the blurry image of a softer face, the sound of humming in my ear...but that woman was dead. If she didn't die before the raid then someone had surely killed her during it.

"I have no mother," I said.

"Yes, you do," Mateo said through his teeth.

"She wasn't on Orsalia when the Daughters attacked," Flavian said. "She was on Fortis...on other business. When she returned home, she found her husband and neighbors slain, her daughter missing. She's still alive.

"We came here for you," he continued, "specifically you. We waited for you here, and when the Daughters arrived, someone told us the girl you call Dagna would be more than happy to get you to us. We're just trying to bring you home."

"No." I refused to believe that the woman they called, "mother," had survived. To do so, she would have had to abandon her own child with a coward. She would have left me for dead. "You're taking me to the Emperor, as punishment."

"No, we're not," Flavian said. "The Emperor doesn't give a whit about you, to be fair. He is so pompous, he sees you and your Daughters as nothing more than a nuisance, and more of a nuisance for King Charles up north than you are for him. If we delivered you to his chambers, he would most likely offer you gold and riches to double your raids, for you are the enemy of his enemy."

"I think that's enough," Nik said.

Flavian waved his hand in a flourish. "I'm only trying to prove that we're being forthcoming."

"Why weren't you before?" I asked. "Why lie at all?"

"Well, we thought you might be more unlikely, or unwilling, to believe the truth versus a lie," Flavian said, "and we were all trying to keep from finding that steel hand around our necks."

"It doesn't matter," Mateo said. "I don't want to bring her back. Nyssa can't see her like this."

Nyssa? Was that her name? I kept learning things I did not want to know.

"That's not your decision to make," Nik said. "She asked this favor of us all and I intend to do it, no matter what it takes." He shook his knife in warning.

"I'm not going," I said. He could wave his knife all he wanted.

"It's her dying wish, Carina. You can't give a sick woman her dying wish?" Flavian asked.

I was about to say, "no," when Flavian stepped closer. "Come on, Carina. Take a trip with us, see her for a minute and then I will personally deliver you back to your island. Fortis isn't a bad place to stay. Good food. Good wine, and I have some influence there." He twisted one of his fine rings as proof. "You'd be my personal guest."

I paused, watching the gold ring curl around his finger. Last summer, a convoy of ten ships returned from a voyage to the Southern Isles, claws clean of blood. No offerings in tow.

"They had a blockade of ships, waiting for us," Greta Goldenrod had said as she tossed her yellow braid. "We had no choice. We had to turn back."

Merle patted her on the shoulder. "Then we have no choice, Sister. We must, for the time being, abandon the Southern Isles until we can find a way through their defenses." She clicked her claws together as she spoke, her brow knitted in rage. No one kept the Hands of Hel from making their claims…but the Southern Emperor had.

Until we find a way through their defenses.

With his outstretched hand, shimmering with rings and jewels, Flavian offered me a way through the Southern defenses. If I went with them, I could kill them and others on their home shores, deliver their souls to Hel, and bring back the wealth of the Emperor's kingdom. That would be more than enough to prove my worth to Merle. This was a gift from the Goddess, one I couldn't deny.

But if I agreed too easily, they would know.

"I want my knife." I pointed to Nik. "And three hundred in gold coins once we arrive."

"I could arrange…"

"I'm not finished. Hel demands blood. I need a life. That woman's life." I would take more than that, but they didn't need to know.

"You mean to kill Nyssa?" Flavian's cheeks blanched.

"You said it yourself, she's dying. That woman owes me a life since she stole mine. She abandoned me with a fool."

"She didn't abandon you," Mateo said. "She needed to leave."

I shrugged. "And I need to offer up a life."

"No, absolutely not." Nik shook his head. "I knew this was a mistake. I'm putting her back in that cage." He moved for me, and I flashed the knife. I'd cut off his nose before he locked me up again.

"Carina," Flavian shouted. "It's the end of summer. You do not need to make any more offerings this season. Let your goddess take Nyssa in her own time, and I'll send you back with five hundred in gold."

Everyone froze. Five hundred pieces was more than the stone in my pocket, more than Dagna claimed on our raid, and it was only a fragment of what I would gain.

"I want your word on your god," I said. "I come with you, see this woman, you send me back with five-hundred gold."

Flavian pressed his hand to his chest. "My word on God, my wine, and my dear Arturo. This is all we want."

"Then I accept," I said, trying not to look too pleased. The fool would pay me himself before I killed him for more.

"We can't trust her," Mateo said. "Do not let her go."

Nik looked me square in the eye. "Now your turn," he said, "You make a vow on your goddess. Make a vow that you will not harm any of us, ever."

Hel's Fire. He would ask something like that. "I vow on the benevolent Goddess Hel, that I will not harm any of you," *until Fortis*, I added in a silent prayer to the Goddess. I could break a promise to them. Not to Her.

Nik exhaled and wiped the blood from the fish knife on his pants. He flipped it around and handed it to me hilt first, and I returned his knife to him.

"There." Flavian grinned. "Isn't that nice? It will be a much more pleasant trip now that we're all friends."

Nik, Mateo, and I all glared at him. I made no bargains about "friends."

"Alright, well." Flavian puffed his chest outward. "Why don't we see about restocking the ship and having someone see about this hole in the deck? Carina? Mat? Care to venture into town?"

"I'll stay here," Nik grumbled and dabbed at the blood on his arm. I wondered if he was this sore all the time, or if it was all because of me.

"I need some things in town, too," I said. Oil for my fingers. A new tunic. I picked up my sword and slung it on my belt.

CHAPTER 8

✖

We made a slow trek to the market, walking along the docks at Mateo's languid pace. He kept plugging forward and I appreciated how he never asked for a rest. He continued step by step, breath by breath. Since we had made our arrangement, and they had purchased their safety to Fortis, I could look at him as just a boy now. Not a kidnapper. Not a soul to offer to Hel. Not yet, at least. For the time being he was simply a young man, another living victim of the plague.

"Why you three?" I asked Flavian as we walked. "Why did this Nyssa ask you to come get me?"

Even though the Emperor hadn't sent for me, it still seemed like a poor choice of crew to go to Helvar. I understood the timing. The urgency. She was dying...even though she'd had thirteen years to come for me. Nothing like waiting until the last possible moment.

"She trusts us," he said.

"Why?"

"We love her."

I noticed Mateo kept strangely quiet, apart from the wheezing.

"She was my governess," Flavian continued. "You can rest assured I would be a much more scandalous cad if she hadn't intervened. My sister would probably be the subject of some very unflattering gossip too. Our parents were always incredibly busy. It was Nyssa who took the time to make sure we turned out all right."

"Was she Nik and Mateo's governess too?"

"In a way," he said as we arrived at the market.

The strong scents of harissa and honey dates, the bleating of goats, and the vendors making deals in clipped, Eastern voices hung in the air.

This language I knew well.

"Dates for you?" A vendor shoved a basket of them under my nose, and I snatched one. The Daughters were very well respected here. Despite this being one of the Emperor's territories, his presence here was minimal. What mattered in Brezadine was trade, and the Sisters had it, bountiful goods from the North that could only be swapped here.

This was our mutual space, where the North, South, East and West could collide. Everyone with coin or goods were welcomed ashore, and in exchange for their welcome, the Daughters always eliminated the Eastern city from their raid route.

We stopped at a food tent, and Flavian greedily filled bags with smoked goat meat, potatoes, rice and grain. I slipped a vial of goat fat into the bag, using it to oil my fingers first. My salt-stiffened metal fingers came back to life, curling into a tight fist. Much better.

Flavian stocked up on wine next, sampling each bottle before he bought it. He seemed to have an endless supply of coins, paying errand boys to run the supplies to the ship while he filled another bag. He was practically begging to be robbed.

I supposed if someone tried, I'd have to cut them. Those coins would be my coins eventually.

We wandered into the goods section of the market, and Flavian stopped at a booth selling jewelry.

"Does he really need more rings?" I muttered aloud.

Mateo shrugged.

I leaned against the stone wall while Flavian shopped, wondering if I should return to the ship or not, but at the moment, I did not want to spend any unnecessary time with Nik. I fingered the hole in my tunic, the one he made with his knife. When he'd thrown it, the blade had been a blur. I would have to watch that one. He had more skill than I thought.

I took my rune stone from my pocket and rolled it in my fingers. When I did, I thought of the priestess with Merle's dart in her throat, blood running down her white robes.

"What is that?" Mateo asked.

Before I could speak, the jewelry vendor pointed to it. "May I see that?"

I dropped it back into my pocket. "No."

I had been foolish to drag it out in public. If it truly was Rorik's stone

Merle would want to find the right buyer for it, someone who dealt in rare collectibles. Not some street vendor.

Flavian wandered off to a booth selling silk scarves. I scanned the booths for someone with tunics. A young boy racing through the market crashed into my elbow. Before I could scold him, he disappeared between a set of robes, a flying red sash.

I rubbed my elbow. The market had seemed less chaotic when I marched through it by Merle's side with forty other steel-handed women behind me. People had been more respectful. It was if they knew I was a fraud who couldn't even kill one priestess.

"Can we leave?" I asked Flavian as he wrapped a blue scarf around his neck.

"In a minute. Patience, Carina. How much for this one?" he asked the merchant.

I reached into my pocket and ran my thumb across the stone. The instant I did, I knew it was wrong. I yanked it out. These carvings were rough. Handmade. This wasn't my stone.

The boy. That little worm picked my pocket! But how did he know what I had?

The jewelry merchant.

I stomped back to the booth, claws grinding.

"Where are you going?" Mateo shouted.

I ignored him. This insult could not be suffered, even if I was a lone Hand of Hel in the market. I knocked the merchant's table to the side. His baubles and bracelets spilled to the cobblestones. I grabbed the vendor by the neck, five steel fingers in his throat and shoved him against the wall, proving to myself and everyone here, I did not need a horde of women behind me to be an imposing force. I deserved these claws.

"Where is my stone?" I hissed.

"I…I don't know."

"Liar." I dug a claw into his windpipe, drawing blood.

"Good God," Flavian called from behind me. "I turn my back for a minute and here you are, trying to kill someone."

"This is none of your concern, Flavian. Give it to me," I said to the merchant.

"I don't have it," the man gasped.

I stuck another claw into his neck, drawing more blood and a tear from the man's eye.

"The boy took it," he said.

"Where is he?"

"That is all I will tell you."

"I could kill you," I warned, prodding a third claw into his skin.

"Then you would break the trust that binds us. Your kind would no longer be welcome here."

He was right. The true police here were the Jaysh Aldam, a gang of loyalists. They kept the peace. They enforced the laws. They allowed the Daughters to come here and freely trade because we did not draw blood on these shores. If I killed him, I would break that pact for all of the Daughters, for generations to come. It would be an offense less forgivable than sparing the priestess.

"Carina." Flavian placed his jeweled hand on my arm. "I think we have reached the end of our questioning, especially since we have decided there will not be any killing, yes?" He smiled at me.

"Killing, no," I said. "But it will be hard for him to examine his jewelry if I cut out his eyes."

Flavian balled his hand to his mouth and gagged. "Please, Carina. Not so graphic."

"There are things worse to fear than your sharp claws," the merchant said.

I uncurled my fingers, one by one, and let him fall. The merchant collapsed, wheezing.

"Now, sir." Flavian twisted one of the rings from his finger. "What would it take to lead us to the boy?" He held the ring in front of the man's nose.

"More than you have," the man said and bent down to scoop up what jewels he could salvage, wrapping them up in the folds of his robes. He scurried off like a rat, and I made a move to chase him.

Flavian caught my arm. "A precious stone you must have owned, Carina."

"I will have it back," I said. I would not tolerate this robbery.

"Yes, you will," Flavian agreed. "And I intend to show you that things can be done without threats and violence. Come with me." He slid his ring back onto his long finger and marched down the thoroughfare.

CHAPTER 9

✖

lavian led us to a small café that overlooked the harbor. It was nice.
The tables bore fresh flowers in glass vases and long drapes hung in
front of the open windows. We sat at a small round table in the
corner, away from the open air awning that looked out over the sea. I
tapped my steel fingers on the table. I ached to know how eating lunch
would bring me my stone.

"You stay here," Flavian said. "I'll order for us."

My stomach growled at the scent of spiced harissa and sweet honey
dates. Flavian went to the counter and spoke closely to young woman on
the other side. From behind the folds of her veil, I caught a small smile.

"How much time have you spent here?" I asked Mateo. Flavian seemed
to know his way around.

"We were here for a few weeks, waiting for your people to come." He
shifted in his chair, from the discomfort of the conversation or of his leg,
I didn't know.

"What drew you to Dagna" I asked.

He shook his head. "I'm not sure we should be discussing this."

"Why? I want to know." Mostly I wanted to know so I could give the
details to Merle, how Dagna turned against one of her own and opened our
island to weakness.

Mateo pressed his lips together in some semblance of defiance.

Flavian sat between us. "*I* found Dagna," he said. "I used the same
tactics I am going to use to get your rock back. Flattery works much better
than threats, enough to find out which of Hel's Daughters might be willing

to betray another. Or who in town would deal in stolen stones."

Ah, I understood…he paid for it.

A young man emerged from the kitchen, carrying a tray of steaming bowls and a carafe of wine. He was as pretty as Flavian in a different way. Blue tunic tied tight at his slender waist with a gold sash, and instead of a clean shaven jawline, he boasted a short, neatly-trimmed beard.

He plucked the bowls from the tray and set them on the table then leaned forward to pour the wine. When he did, his lips brushed Flavian's cheek.

"What can I do for you?" he asked.

"Now or later?" Flavian ran his fingers through the tip of the man's beard.

For someone so devoted to a man named Arturo, his affections seemed to leap onto whatever body stood closest.

"Meet our friend, Carina," Flavian said as I stabbed a date from the bowl with my claw.

"Greetings," the man bowed. "I am Samer."

"Carina has experienced a bit of trouble in the market," Flavian said. "A boy took a rather important bauble from her, and she would like it back."

"Hmm." Samer rubbed his chin. "Can you tell me more about this boy?"

I swallowed another date and thought to the boy, racing through the market. "He was small," I said. "Young. No more than eight or nine, and he wore a red sash."

Samer's eyes flared. "Then you should consider your jewel gone."

"I'm afraid Carina does not let go that easily," Flavian said.

"Of course not." Samer bowed. "But we cannot speak here. Meet me in private. Upstairs. I will tell you what I know." He ran his fingers across Flavian's neck. "Come alone."

Flavian cleared his throat and snatched the bowl of dates as I was reaching for another. "I won't be long…too long. You eat, and I'll be back with your answers."

"Are you after my stone or Samer?" I asked.

"I am exceptionally good at multi-tasking," Flavian said and winked.

Samer held a curtain aside that led into a set of sandy stairs. Flavian placed a date on Samer's tongue before they ascended. I shook my head and grabbed a bowl of porridge. At least there was food.

"Why is the stone so important to you?" Mateo asked. He took a deep breath after, as if the one question left him breathless.

"Because it's mine."

"And that is the only reason?"

"I don't need another reason." Although a worth of three-hundred gold pieces made it more appealing.

I sprinkled salt into my porridge and continued eating, trying to ignore him, but that whistling breath drove stakes through my temples. I pushed the bowl aside and made my way to the patio.

The air here was still warm. Up north, the chill would be coming soon, the leaves would be turning. My new plan to spill blood on Fortis would ensure I couldn't return until after the first frost. Would I be forgotten by then?

Even if I was, they would remember me when I returned with the riches of Fortis. Merle had yet to name an heir to the whalebone throne. Dagna was most likely, but with her disgrace and betrayal, and my upcoming prize...it could be me.

I imagined myself in-between the massive ribs of the whalebone throne, draped in furs, claws raised. The entire island of Helvar at my command. No one would question me again.

Shuffle, clop. Shuffle, clop. Mateo crept up behind me, interrupting my dreams.

"I keep thinking," he said. "About when you pulled me back onto the ship during the storm."

I rolled my eyes. As tempted as I was to tell him I didn't want his death to go to the sea giant, I had to lie. "I was trying to convince you to take me home. I thought preventing you from drowning might help."

"I thought that too," he said. "But then..." His voice trailed. "Death spares lives as easily as she takes them."

Was he trying to find hope? He of all people should know it didn't exist. "No," I said. "She does not spare anything. Eventually She takes us all."

I looked down to his leg when I spoke. Time was our only weapon against Death, and sometimes it was more of a burden than a gift. Painful suffering was cruel. It was the burden the Disgraced bore for failing their final test, that I bore for knowing the weakness of my father, and Mateo bore in the fight against his own body.

"You were brave," Mateo said softly, "when you fought the Sahrimnir.

I could barely look at them, and you stared them in the face and killed them."

My frown softened. Flattery always helped. "It wasn't a bad idea with the rabbit, either," I said. "Considering you had no other options."

He snorted. "I don't think that's a proper 'thank you.'"

"It wasn't meant to be."

If he expected me to grovel at him for pitching a dead rabbit at a monster, a rabbit that I had hunted and killed, he would be waiting an eternity for it.

"What is taking Flavian so long?" I asked and regretted the question as soon as I said it. I really didn't want to know what he was doing upstairs. "I mean, if he's so in love with this Arturo then what is he doing with Samer?"

"He told you about Arturo?"

"Against my will, yes."

Mateo leaned against the rails, and the salt air ruffled his dark air. "I suppose he's afraid. His father is an important man in Fortis. He expects great things from Flavian. Flavian knows he's going to have to eventually do what his father wants, which will mean giving up Arturo. I think he's trying to act as if the relationship isn't serious so that when it ends, he won't be hurt."

"Who is his father?" I asked. "Is he the Emperor's son?"

"No," Mateo said.

That was unfortunate. Apart from killing the Emperor himself, offering Hel his son would be a worthy sacrifice.

"I suppose your Nyssa supports Flavian's true love?" I said.

"Yes, she does. She's a very loving and accepting person," he said wistfully.

I snorted. A loving woman who married a coward and abandoned her only child with him. So far, I was not impressed.

"Ah well." Flavian finally strutted from the café with his dark curls mussed, his rouged cheeks redder than ever, and a thin sheen of sweat on his skin. "I have the answer to our problem." He leaned on the rails between us, smelling strongly of harissa. "The boy in question, the one who took your stone, is property of the Jaysh Aldam, Blood Army."

I made a face. Of course it would be the Aldam to take my stone.

If I started a skirmish with them, they would consider our trade agreement moot. They would claim any Daughter of Hel who walked this land, and not just kill them. Not right away. The Blood Army liked to torture their victims. They turned death from something final and peaceful into a long, painful experience. They were no friend to us. The peace we made was tentative at best, based solely on gold.

I would have to let the stone go, which made me feel sick.

"Fret not, Carina," Flavian said. "It makes your face look like a dried prune. There may still be a way to your stone. We will talk to Nik."

"Nik?"

"He is from Brezadine. He used to be in the Army."

My mouth fell open. It made sense, somewhat. Nik hadn't batted an eye at caging me, starving me, and it would explain the skill with the knives. Nik had been trained and hardened like me. But he was cut with a different sort of steel.

"We can't ask Nik," Mateo said.

"It will just be a question," Flavian argued. "But first, let's go the inn and get rooms for the night. I am in desperate need of a warm bath." He clapped his hand on Mateo's shoulder. "Are you coming, Carina?" he asked. "Even you can't be above a soft bed and a hot bath in the most comfortable inn in Brezadine. I am buying, of course."

No, I was not above it. My salt-crusted skin ached for a bath, and I had no qualms about using some of Flavian's coins in advance.

He led the way along the docks toward the Almasa Inn, which was the finest inn in Brezadine, located on the eastern side of town with an unhindered view of the ocean. The archway over the entrance was encrusted in gold tiles. They must have paid a fortune to the Blood Army to keep them from being pried from the roof in the night.

"Ah, Mister Katrakis, glad to see you have returned to us." The man at the door bowed low in deference to Flavian. He wore blue satin robes and silver slippers that curled up at the toes. "I see you have a new guest." The innkeeper eyed me cautiously, pausing at the tips of my steel fingers.

"We'll need three rooms for the night." Flavian dropped a small stack of gold coins into the innkeeper's palm.

"Very good, sir. Our best rooms." He bowed his head.

Flavian paid for me to have my own room with a bed draped in red and gold silken linens and gossamer curtains on the windows. A tub sat in the center of the room, filled with warm soapy water with a basket of various oils beside it. A young serving girl emerged from the closet with an armful of towels.

"Would you like me to help you, miss?"

"No, go."

She set the towels down on a wooden bench and ducked her head. I had been bathing myself for as long as I could remember. I wasn't about to let someone do it now, especially someone paid for by Flavian.

I sank into the tub and closed my eyes. The serving girl returned with a pile of clothes she set on the bed. After she left, I climbed out of the tub, leaving a ring of dirt and grime around the edge. I patted myself dry with one of the towels and wrapped another one around my hair before I examined the clothes.

Flavian must have sent someone for them, and they were well chosen. It was exactly what I would have picked for myself. They were of Northern stock, I recognized the smooth brown leather and beige linen. It must have been something we brought down here once and traded.

With the fine room, warm bath, and even finer clothes, I enjoyed a taste of the bounty I would receive at the end of this journey. I wondered what Dagna was doing at this very moment. Probably cutting fish, covered in bloody scales. I grinned.

I clasped my belt around the new tunic and leggings, and someone knocked on the door.

"Carina?" Flavian said. "Can we speak with you?"

Here was the only downside, my traveling companions. "Come in." I yanked the towel from my hair and let the dark tendrils fall slack on my shoulders. Flavian entered the room with Mateo and Nik flanking him on either side.

Flavian had also bathed and washed himself in a fresh dose of perfume. Mateo wore a clean tunic with his dark hair sleek with water. Nik had done nothing to improve his appearance whatsoever. He still wore the salt-crusted tunic and dried blood on his arm, four mismatched blades hanging from his belt.

"Good God, Carina, you look fantastic," Flavian said. "Who knew all it took was a bath and a set of fine clothes to make you stunning."

I crossed my arms over my chest. Flavian's eyes dipped too low. "What do you want?" I asked.

"Well, we've convinced Nik to help you."

"No they haven't," Nik said. "They only convinced me to leave the ship. If the Aldam took your stone, they want it. They won't want to give it up."

"Neither do I."

"If you confront the Aldam, they will cut off your fingers one by one and shove them down your throat," he warned.

I held up my steel hand. "I would like to see them try and cut these off."

"You might be surprised."

I rolled my eyes. "Can you help me or not? If not, I will go on my own."

He scratched his neck. "If I help, you do this my way. No arguing. No going rogue."

I swallowed. These were difficult terms.

Nik shrugged. "Then I guess you don't get your rock back."

I sighed. "Fine, we'll do things your way."

He dropped his arms. "Then let's go see an old friend of mine."

CHAPTER 10

✘

Nik led me into a part of Brezadine I had never seen before, through dark alleys and thin passageways. He moved in shadows, bouncing from stone to stone. It was obvious he knew the city and knew it well.

"How long were you a part of the Aldam?" I asked in the Eastern language.

He laughed derisively. "I don't know if you would say I was a part of it. I was a possession, a slave, like the boy who took your stone. I was orphaned at five and sold to the Aldam as an errand boy. I escaped three years later. Stowed away on a ship bound for Fortis. This is the first time I've set foot in the city since."

"But weren't you here before? When you found Dagna?"

He pressed up against a wall. "I didn't leave the ship."

"Should I feel privileged that you left it now? For me?"

He snorted. "I did not leave it for you. I'm here for Nyssa. If you went after the rock on your own, you'd get killed."

"I am not afraid of death."

"I don't care what you are afraid of. Nyssa saved my life. She was the one who found me by the docks when I arrived in Fortis. I'd been eating boiled rats and rotten lettuce. She fed me, clothed me, taught me the Southern words. She taught me to read. She arranged a position for me with the dock master, which granted me a chance to sail. I owe her everything, and she only asked me for one thing. You. It would be poor repayment to let you die."

He owed her everything. I owed her nothing. How easily she'd cast her own child aside and picked up all of these orphans instead.

"I don't need a caretaker."

"This way." He darted left.

We reached the inner depths of the city. The smell of salt and spices did not linger here. The air reeked of filth and sickness, the quiet disturbed with moans and coughs. A little boy and girl leaned up against one another, hands open and resting on their knees. Flies buzzed around their heads. I thought they were dead until the girl's knee shifted.

My steel finger twitched. It would be a great mercy for me to send her to Death now.

"You might as well do it," Nik said. "When I was a boy, I wished a thousand times for Death to take me, and She never came." He sounded bitter.

I could easily take this girl's last breath and didn't. The Daughters did not kill in Brezadine. We had a pact.

"Let's go." I kept walking, not looking back at the girl, but I silently prayed to Hel that She would come for this girl soon.

Nik turned the corner and went up a pair of wobbly, wooden stairs. They creaked and shuddered with every step. At the top, the wooden landing leaned far over the alleyway.

"Who is this friend we're visiting?"

"An old connection to the Aldam." Nik knocked on the door three times, rested and knocked twice more. Nothing happened and so he tried again.

This time the door flung wide open. "The knock has…" The girl who shouted at us went quiet, her red-painted mouth dropping wide. She wore a blue silk headscarf with a chain of golden coins wrapped around her head. She was lovely and seemed out of place in this bleak side of the city. She belonged closer to the coast, in the glimmer and light of the market.

"Rahim?" she whispered.

Rahim?

The girl grabbed him by the arm. "Get in here." She tugged him inside and I followed, closing the door behind us. She wrapped him in a tight hug. Nik, or Rahim, returned it after a long moment, easing his chin to her shoulder.

I picked at my claws, waiting for this moment to pass.

"What are you doing here?" the girl pulled back and clasped his hands.

"I thought you were dead."

"Good. I want them to keep thinking it." He turned to me. "This is Carina. The Jaysh Aldam have taken something from her. I owe her mother a debt, and I was wondering if you could help us get it back."

The girl blinked twice. "One of Hel's Daughters." She released Nik and came to me, absorbing every fold of my tunic, every hair on my brow. "I've never met one of you in person. I am Fahima." She clasped her hands and ducked her head.

"Carina, the Unstoppable," I added, wishing I could stab the words from the air as soon as they left my mouth. Did she need to know that?

"Carina the Unstoppable." She ran a finger over her lips. "In another life, I would be one of your women warriors. May I see the hand?" She reached for my steel fingers.

I jerked my arm back. "I just want to get my stone." I didn't want to be a spectacle.

"Of course." She wandered across the room, stepping over satin cushions and piles of books. The apartment was nothing like I expected, like an egg. Plain on the outside, rich and golden on the inside.

Fine silk curtains hung from the windows in deep blue, adorned with sparkling gold coins, and under our boots was a hand woven wool rug. Fahima sat on a settee and pulled a book from her shelves.

"What kind of stone did they take from you? Ruby? Diamond?"

"It was a rune stone," I said. "Something called Rorik's stone."

"Rorik's stone?" Her eyes went wide. "But that is only a legend."

"What is Rorik's stone?" Nik asked.

"A rune stone, from the North. It can revive the dead." Fahima went for her books.

"It cannot do that," I said. If it could, it would be an abomination, a trespass against Hel.

Fahima pulled down a book and set it on her knees. She flipped to a page with a drawing of my stone

"The stone comes from Perdita," Fahima said. "Rorik was a soldier. When he returned from war, his family was dead. He carved the stone in their blood and was able to resurrect them." She showed the book to Nik. He squinted at the page.

"The Aldam have a keen fascination in legend and ancient relics," Fahima continued, "especially ones that can undo the most final of circumstances. Rahim here is an excellent carver. I am sure he can make you an almost perfect copy. You would never know the difference."

"I go by Nikos now," he said to her. "Nik."

"I see." Fahima tapped her finger on her lower lip. "I might have some stones around here like the one you lost." She reached for a wooden box, and inside were various rocks, ranging from small, red rocks to large, white rocks. It seemed she was a collector of many things, from books to pebbles and all else in between, like the insects pinned to a board on the wall and rolls of parchment stacked in the corner.

Fahima selected a gray rock in the same oval shape as the one in the book. "How about this one?"

I took it from her and examined it closely. It was the same shape and color, and I had seen Nik's carvings. He could make a better recreation than the one the boy tried to pass me in the market. What did it matter if it was the real stone or not? Neither one raised the dead. If I could gain the same coin from a fake, the value did not lessen.

Except, I would know it was wrong. I would always know I had been robbed, fooled.

I dropped the rock in Fahima's palm. "I want my stone. Not some copy."

Nik sighed as if he expected that answer. "What can you do, Fahima?"

"If you can make the copy, I can go to the den and try to make the switch. I cannot make any guarantees, though. If Mahmod has it, I won't be able to touch it."

Nik took a step back, afraid of the name, "Mahmod."

"You must stay here," Fahima grasped Nik's hands. "I don't want them to find you." She ran her thumb across his knuckles.

"I can't let you go alone. No one will recognize me."

"I recognized you," Fahima said.

"Because you actually looked at my face. The others never looked me in the eye." Beads of sweat dotted his nose.

"I'll go with her," I offered. I couldn't leave the recovery of my stone to chance.

"You cannot go into the den," she said to me.

"We'll wait outside, in the shadows," Nik said. "No one will see us, but we'll be close enough."

Fahima squeezed his hand. "If they find you--"

"I'm not a boy anymore," he snapped.

"Very well then."

She gave him the stone and another box with small chisels and knives. Nik sat down at the table, pushed aside yet another stack of books to make space for himself and only left the one open with the picture of my rock. He scratched at the replacement stone, flipping his head back and forth between the stone and the book, making small, intricate lines into the surface of the stone, as intricate as the little teeth carved into the dolphin under his bunk.

"When did you learn to carve?" I asked.

"They don't give you toys in the Aldam," Nik said. "I had rocks and knives. I did what I could." Was I supposed to feel sorry for him? I didn't have toys either, apart from a small wooden sword. Von and I used to whack each other's knees with them, then we would walk through the woods with a hand-carved bow in search of small game.

I missed Von. That Von. Not the one who tried to kiss me. I missed being a child with Von. I missed the age when he had no requirements of me.

"Rah...Nik, is being modest," Fahima said. "He used to do a great deal of business selling his trinkets here. His father was a carver."

"Don't talk about him." Nik said. "Here." He handed me the rock. "How is this?"

I laid it on my palm and ran my thumb over the markings. They were rough, as they should have been, and too clean, too perfect. The ones in my stone had been weathered and blurred. I supposed if the Aldam had not gotten a good look at the stone, it would pass.

"It's fine." I handed it to Fahima for inspection since she was craning over my arm.

She held the rock in her fingers and compared it to the one in the book. "It's perfect," she said.

"Then let's make the switch."

Fahima gave Nik and me simple linen cloaks to wear. I draped mine over my head and pulled my steel claws into the sleeve before we followed Fahima down the creaking stairs into the streets. She dropped a handful of coins to the sick children without stopping, as if she were throwing bread crumbs to birds. The coins clattered against the stones, snatched up by quick hands.

Fahima turned down another alley, where the men lit the torches on the walls in a race to beat the fading sun. Even with the sunlight, the corridor was dim, the perfect place for thieves.

"This is it." Nik caught my hand. He tugged me into an alcove while Fahima continued on, to a building made of yellow stone marked with the sign of two knives dripping with blood. We had a perfect view of the entrance, and I had a feeling Nik knew we would.

Fahima disappeared into the building in a flurry of blue silk.

"Why can she come and go as she pleases?" I whispered. A rat scurried across our toes with a piece of flatbread in its teeth.

"Her mother is one of the Blood Wives. She belongs to Mahmod," Nik said.

"Then Fahima is his daughter?"

He shrugged. "He would never officially claim her, but yes."

"Why won't he claim her?"

"When you deal in torture the way Mahmod does, you don't want to claim things that people can take from you. As long as Mahmod is content with her, she'll be taken care of. Even when the Emperor took the Eastern lands, those in service to the Aldam remained untouched by the Emperor's soldiers. The same can't be said for those who hid under the caliph's protection. Fahima will be fine unless she's caught."

His fingers danced over knives on his belt. None of them matched. One bore an ivory hilt, another steel, another carved from wood, stained with age. I could picture him snatching them randomly from unwatched belts like he had taken my fish knife. What a hypocrite. He despised me and the Daughters when he was no better. Worse, because he served no one...no one apart from Nyssa.

I wondered what she thought of his knife thieving.

Footsteps approached. Nik pulled me deeper into the alcove. I closed my steel hand and pulled the hood farther over my head, watching the man from under the folds.

He was tall and broad, the male, dark-skinned version of Horrible Hild. A thick beard sprouted from his chin, and his dark eyes flicked back and forth. A hunter's eyes. He missed nothing, which was why he stopped in front of us.

"What are you two doing here?" He bent in half, trying to steal a glimpse under my hood. I hid deeper under it, smelling the alcohol on his breath.

"You have a coin to spare for the poor?" Nik asked in a strained, high pitched voice.

"No." The man said. "Now clear out of here." He raised his hand in the air to strike, the motion so smooth it was obvious he had driven his knuckles into many cheeks.

Nik ducked his head and grabbed my wrist. His hand was cold and clammy on my skin.

"Wait," the man said. "Let me see your face." He reached for the hood of Nik's cloak. If he saw him, he would know him, and he would kill him. He would kill us both.

I spun and caught the man's arm at the wrist. Five sharp claws prodded into his skin. "Don't touch him," I hissed. This was my life to take. My stone. This man wouldn't take it from me.

"One of Hel's Daughters." The man rolled the words on his tongue. "What are you doing here? I thought we had an agreement. You keep to your business, and we keep to ours."

He moved to lift his other hand, and I sank my claws so deep into his arm, they disappeared. "Don't move." I held his gaze. *I am Carina the Unstoppable.* "This *is* my business."

He kept smiling at me, an eerie smile of pointed teeth, and moved his other arm regardless of my warning.

"I'll take your hand," I said.

"Not before I get your head, Little Girl." He grasped the hilt of his sword, a long, curved scimitar and swung it toward my throat, stopping just as the edge kissed my flesh. "Now tell me, what are you doing here?"

The name, Little Girl, nipped at my heels. Even when I had been a little girl, no one called me that. The men did not disrespect women on Helvar--even when they were small. I ached to kill him simply for that, except I'd let him take the advantage. If I sank my claws any deeper into his arm, he would slice through my neck.

"My friend here told me if we waited long enough," I said, "we would see the largest horse's ass in existence. And here you are." I smiled back at him, and his grin disappeared into a thin line. His scimitar bit into my skin, and I wrenched back on his arm. Who would be faster? If I took his arm, he would be in too much pain to slice off my head.

"Stop," Nik said.

The man turned to Nik, finally seeing him, and the man's jaw dropped, as if he were looking at a ghost. Nik wore same expression. His eyes widened to the red rims, and sweat rolled down the lines of his forehead.

"You are not one of hers," the man said. "You are one of ours. Rah…" His chin dipped to his chest before he finished, to the knife thrust in his stomach. My knife. It was embedded in his gut up to the hilt, where blood stained the ivory.

Nik gasped and yanked the knife back. The man dropped in a heap of bloodied linen, exhaling the last of the air from his lungs. I pried my claws from his flesh and left behind five, very distinct marks. We would have to hide the body, otherwise one of my Sisters, or I, would be blamed for the kill.

"Go swiftly to…"

Nik dropped my knife into the pool of blood and fell to his knees. He pressed his palms to his face and burst into heavy cries. My body went stiff. I had never seen a grown man cry. Or a grown woman for that matter. Tears on Helvar were reserved for children.

He needed to stop this. Someone would hear.

"Quiet," I hissed. "One of us was going to have to kill him."

Nik raised his head. His eyes were rimmed in red. "You don't understand. I wanted more than that for Javad. I wanted pain and suffering. He went too quickly." Nik spat on the man's corpse.

Whoever this man Javad was, he had been cruel. The Sisters dealt in death; the Aldam dealt in pain and power. I tried to imagine all of the horrible things this Javad could have done, what the Army were notorious for, and my stomach turned. I doubted my imagination even reached the extent of it.

"Hel will make him pay for his crimes."

"Not enough," he snapped.

Quick footsteps shuffled toward us. Someone heard his outburst and now we would have more Aldam to kill. I plucked my knife out of the blood and held it tight. Fahima's slippers skidded across the stones. She stopped a hair's width from the river of blood leaking from Javad's open mouth.

"What happened?" Her nose flipped from Javad, to the blood, to the inconsolable Nik.

"I need to hide the body," I wiped the blood from the knife on my cloak and returned it to its rightful place—my belt.

Fahima swallowed. "The well. It's not far from here."

The well would work. A long drop might damage his skin enough to hide my marks, and if it didn't, then the water would complete the task in a day or two. Fahima pointed me to it, and I latched my claws around the top of Javad's cloak.

As I dragged Javad across the stones, I heard Fahima quietly whispering to Nik. He finally went quiet.

Javad's head lolled to his chest as I tugged him step by step to the well in the center of the square. Behind us, a trail of blood marked our way. I would have to clean that up too, or someone would find him sooner than I wanted. Hiding bodies wasn't one of my greater skills. On the raid, we left the corpses where they lay. Our job was only to deliver their souls to Niflheim, not deal with the parts they left behind.

After I leaned Javad up against the well, I reeled in the bucket. I dumped the water on the stones, washing away some of the blood, not all, but we didn't have time for me to scrub blood from stones. Someone could appear at any moment, another member of the Army.

I heaved Javad onto the edge of the well, and his robe pulled back to reveal a fine dagger with a serpent head hilt and emerald eyes. I would have taken it if it had been my kill, but it wasn't. It was Nik's, and I had the feeling he didn't want any mementos. I gave Javad one last shove, and he and his fine dagger tumbled into darkness. Thud. Thud. Splash.

"Go swiftly to Niflheim," I whispered. *Go swiftly and let Hel decide your eternal punishment.*

When I returned, I found Nik in the crook of Fahima's arm, staring at the blood on the stones.

"Javad was a horrible man," Fahima said as she ran her fingers through Nik's dark hair. "Rahim saved me from him once. He was going to…well, let's just say that Javad did not let Rahim go unpunished. There will be many who are glad he is dead, and many who will be angry as well." She kissed Nik's cheek. "You have to go. Before they find the blood."

Nik nodded and stood on wavering legs, like a puppet hanging by strings.

"Here is your stone." Fahima handed me the rock.

A strange calm crept over me when I touched the stone. A tingle raced up my arm. This was *my* stone. Unquestionably.

"You should both leave the city tonight," Fahima said. "I will wash away the blood and seal the well. The water will be undrinkable with Javad's poison in it."

"I owe you a debt," I said, and it wasn't with a light heart I said that. When the Daughters owed a debt, they paid it.

"No, I owed Rahim a great debt."

"This is my debt. Not his." I dipped the tip of my knife in the blood, and with it, I drew the runes for gift and Daughter on the sleeve of my cloak. I tore off the scrap and gave it to her. "If you give this to any of Hel's Daughters, she will grant you a favor."

"I'll take it then." Fahima folded the fabric into her sleeve. "I'd be a fool to refuse a favor from such a strong warrior. Now go." She kissed Nik one last time. "I will miss you my sweet, Rahim. But I would miss you more if you were dead. Go." She pushed him toward the pier, and his feet shuffled forward.

I hooked my arm through his elbow and pulled him beside me. He stumbled at first, then his boots fell into a copy of my pace.

When we reached the marketplace, I slowed down to blend with the crowd, not easy to do with the blood smears on my cream-colored cloak. Even in the flickering lantern light, curious eyes found me. I kept my head down, not sure if it would be worse to remove the bloody cloak and show my steel hand instead. I couldn't let the Daughters be blamed for this. I just had to keep moving.

At the docks, I dragged Nik into another run, aimed for the fat cog ship.

"We have to fetch Flavian and Mateo," Nik said, as we stumbled up the gangplank

"No you don't," Flavian said, emerging from the belly of the ship. "We were testing the supplies." Flavian wore a red wine moustache over his lopsided grin. "Oh God." His smile dropped. "Why are you covered in blood? What did you do, Carina?"

"She didn't do it," Nik said. "We're leaving."

"What happened, Nik?" Mateo asked.

"I don't want to talk about it. Raise the sail," he shouted. I took one rope while he took another.

"I find it impossible to believe you had nothing to do with this," Flavian said to me.

I pursed my lips. I did have something to do with it, but it wasn't my story. It wasn't my kill. I wouldn't say a word about it, in part because it seemed to drive Flavian mad to not know.

Nik grabbed the wheel and turned it hard port. The wind billowed in the sails and pushed us away from the burning torchlights of Brezadine. Toward Fortis. Toward glory.

"The women from the North came with a naval force, like stinging hornets, and spread on all sides like fearful wolves. They robbed, tore, and slaughtered until there was nothing but blood."

Captain Moller, Vinya Army

CHAPTER 11

✗

I sat on the deck of the ship, the salt air whipping though my hair and took the stone from my pocket. I rubbed my thumb across the runes, and a shadow appeared beside me. I gasped as I saw the priestess in her bloody robes, reaching out toward me.

I shook my head and dropped the stone in my pocket. It was a reflection of the sun on the water, a mirage. Nothing more.

Mateo's telltale shuffle crept up behind me. My shoulders curled around my ears. I thought he had been down below, making maps. I wished he had stayed there. We were only four days from Brezadine with weeks to go. My patience would surely be tested on this venture. But I could not kill them until Fortis. I needed Flavian to take me into the city, and then I would strike, like a serpent inside a rabbit den.

Mateo leaned against the rails beside me. "Nik still won't tell us what happened."

"Then perhaps it's none of your business."

"Why do you have to do that? Why do you have to be so foul all of the time?"

I spun on him. "If I recall, you were the ones to take me. If you don't like it, perhaps you should have left me on Helvar."

He leaned against the rails and stared at the sea. "I thought you would be different."

"Different how?"

"I don't know." He scuffed the boot of his good foot on the wood.

"When we get to Fortis and you meet her…can you try to be polite?"

"I will be however I want to be." I ran my claws together, trying to bury the sound of his irritating breath.

I wasn't sure if I would be able to avoid this meeting with Nyssa. They would likely drag me from this ship straight to her bedside. If that happened, I would not be polite. I would stand at the foot of her death bed, tell her what a horrible mother she was, how much I despised her, and then I would wish her a pleasant journey to Niflheim. She could rot there with the rest of the rabble. When I died, I would be at Hel's side, one of Her chosen warriors.

I scratched my claws into the wood railing. "Why are you so dedicated to her anyway?" I asked Mateo. "I know she saved Flavian from his own foolishness. Nik from starving, but what about you? Why did you sail to Helvar for me for your beloved Nyssa?"

Mateo scratched the back of his neck. "I had the plague when I was young. She nursed me back to health and looked after me since."

"Oh, I see." This woman adopted every wounded orphan she could find and added them to her collection. No wonder she had such devoted followers. She had given them all life, and now Death was coming to take her.

Life and Death were not without a sense of irony.

"She thought about you," he added. "Always."

I snorted. "She probably should have thought about me when her village was raided--instead of abandoning me in Orsalia with that disgusting man they called my father. Did you know he tried to trade me? He tried to pass me off like an old pair of shoes to save himself. Merle saw right through his cowardice."

"Is that what they told you?" Mateo asked.

"Have you heard otherwise?" I challenged.

"No," he admitted. Because no one besides the Daughters left the Orsalia raid alive that day. And what reason did they have to lie to me?

"She always regretted leaving you."

"Did she?"

"She had to."

"Why?"

The three boys pinched their lips and shared their secretive look. I didn't even care. I didn't care why she left or that she had regrets. Everyone did. Hers would be over soon enough when she passed into

Niflheim, and then I would never think of her again.

"Do you care nothing for love or family?" Mateo asked.

"Yes," I said. "I care a great deal about it. Enough to kill to keep my family fed and well-tended. The people of Helvar picked me up after the woman you love so much left me discarded. They carried me. They fed me. They taught me. That is family, and when you stand there, wheezing, judging me for being cold and cruel, just remember that everything you despise about me is because of her. Your precious Nyssa made me this way."

He closed his fist, and his sallow cheeks turned pink, flushed with heat and anger. I thought he might hit me. I would have been proud if he had. I would have slapped his hand away like a bug before he touched me, but I would have had a bit of respect while I did it.

As it was, though, he uncurled his fingers and shuffled away from me, hobbling downstairs.

"That was cruel, Carina," Nik said under his breath. The insult coming from him stung. The boy who survived the Aldam thought I was cruel? I shouldn't have cared, but I did. And I hated myself for it.

"I'm tired of being treated like an abomination," I said. "You were the ones who came for me. You took me. If I wasn't what you wanted then you should have left me where I was."

Truly, the Goddess was testing me, making me suffer this torment to reach the Southern riches. The more I suffered, the more bountiful my offerings would be. I had to remember that.

"Come now, Carina," Flavian said, dampening the burn with his velvet voice. "Not many of us have interactions with the Daughters, and those of us who do, don't normally live to tell about it. Your, ah, persona does take some getting used to."

"Persona?"

"I rather like it," Flavian said. "In fact, I was hoping you could teach me a thing or two." He drew the thin bejeweled rapier from his belt and held it toward me in weak arm and a clumsy stance.

"You want to teach you how to use that? To do what? Sew?"

"Very funny," he said. "I'm not completely useless. I did take fencing lessons for three years. I might not have paid complete attention, but I'm paying attention now. So teach me something. If not for advancement in my technique, then for the pure simplicity of having something to do. I'm bored." He waggled his sword at me in a taunt.

I drew my sword, flicked my wrist, and swatted the thin blade from his hand. It arced across the deck and planted itself in the mast.

"Lesson one," I said. "Hold onto your sword."

Nik smiled as Flavian tried to remove his sword from the wood. "You need to give a man a moment to—"

"Lesson two." I swatted Flavian on the backside with the flat of my sword. "Stop talking."

Flavian huffed and straightened his vest, and Nik burst into laughter. I raised a brow. It was the first time I had ever heard him laugh. It was a more pleasant sound than the wailing he'd done in Brezadine.

"I'm ready to try again." Flavian stood across from me with his sword held like a fishing rod.

I swatted it out of his hand without even looking.

"You were not ready," I said.

Dagna had done the same to me when I'd been given my first sword. She smacked me repeatedly with the blunt side of hers, forcing me to drop it. She hit me over and over again until my fingers turned purple. I bandaged them together and kept standing in front of her, determined to hold my sword until one time, I did.

I used a much more gentle strike on Flavian when I swatted the sword from his hand for the one hundred and eightieth time in four days, or something like that. I'd promised not to "harm" him on this journey. I was only trying to pass the time.

The jeweled rapier spun three times before lodging itself into a crevice between deck boards.

"We can't move on until you master lesson one." I yanked his sword from the floorboards, pockmarked with holes. Not as big as the one by the stairs, covered loosely with a sheet. There hadn't had time to repair the deck hole in Brezadine. We were too busy running from the Aldam.

"Fighting with a twig like this, you'll have to be faster." I clutched the thin rapier sword in my steel fingers and slashed it through the air. "Stand still." I pointed the sword at the center of his chest. "Heart, lungs, stomach, spleen, liver, kidneys, groin." I moved the sword across his chest and down as I recited the rhyme we learned on Helvar. Helvar children would chant it when skipping across the stones in the river.

"That's a lovely song," Flavian said. "Is that what they sing to send you to sleep when you're a babe?"

"Yes," I said, "and I would have pleasant dreams about cutting open foolish boys who couldn't hold swords."

His face went slack. "Good God, Carina, was that a joke?"

I didn't answer him. It wasn't that I didn't know how to laugh or enjoy myself, I simply couldn't do it with them.

Across the ship, dangerously close to the sheet-covered hole, stood Mateo. He watched us with puckered lips, always looking like he had eaten something bitter. He'd been souring over the insults I'd slashed at his precious Nyssa, probably stewing up some retort behind his glassy eyes.

I ignored him. "They are the best organs to strike for a kill," I said to Flavian. "With a sword this small, your advantage is being able to slip through the ribs without having to angle your blade." I touched the tip of the sword to the center of his chest, right over his heart, and held it there.

His breath hitched, and all signs of his mocking grin disappeared. It was that easy, a thrust of this sword, and it would plunge into the center of his heart, turning spoiled, arrogant Flavian into nothing but lifeless flesh and bones.

"I am tired of this." Flavian backed away. "You should give it a try, Nik." Flavian waved at Nik across the deck.

"No." Nik curled his hands tight to the wheel of the ship. "I like a bow or a knife well enough." He, rightfully, didn't trust me. But I had no intentions of killing them now.

"Then you, Mateo?" I offered the sword to our pinch-faced navigator, expecting him to refuse. I waited for him to tell me my deadly organ rhyme was monstrous, or his usual, snort once and hobble back downstairs to his books.

Instead he said, "Alright," and limped toward me.

He leaned the cane against the ship rails and took the sword from me, nearly tumbling forward when he shifted his weight. He used the sword as a makeshift cane before leaning on his one good leg and letting his injured leg hang behind him.

"Alright." I lifted my sword. Before I could get it in position, Mateo jabbed at my stomach. I caught the sword with my steel hand before it sunk into skin.

"Spleen, right?" he said.

"Yes." I released the sword, and he drew it back. He had been paying attention. I decided to see how much he had learned and swung out toward him. He shifted the sword between his body and my blade, and the two swords clanked together. He blocked the strike but lost his balance and fell against the railing.

"Not so hard, Carina," Flavian said.

I hadn't used my full strength. If I had, Mateo would be short one head.

"No," Mateo said. "It's fine." He swung out again, and I blocked the strike with the flat of my sword.

"Good," I said before I could stop myself. "I mean, it's better than Flavian."

"That can't be a hard thing to do," Nik said, while he straightened the ship wheel to even out the deck, perhaps to help keep Mateo steady on his feet.

"I take insult to that," Flavian said.

Mateo took another strike, and I blocked it, of course, but let him keep swinging at me. It seemed to help with the purse of his lips and the sourness of his complexion. The red flush spread from his cheeks down to his chin. I imagined him how he might be if he'd never had the plague. Tall and strong, with thick black hair like Flavian's and a wide grin. He could have been a formidable foe. Even in his current state, with some modifications to his stance and continued practice, he would be adequate.

I twisted my arm to deflect his next swing. Crash! Our two sword collided in sparks.

Alright, perhaps he would be more than adequate.

Of course, I was only blocking his strikes, not fighting back. It would be easy enough to beat him. He put all of his weight on that one leg, his one support. If I cut it once, he would fall and never get up again.

He swung again, and this time he stumbled before he could complete the strike. He fell to his knees, and sweat rolled off his thin crop of hair.

"That was a much better showing than mine." Flavian knelt to help him up.

"No." Mateo pulled himself up on the rails and shuffled to his cane. I flipped Flavian's sword upright and grasped it by the end.

I extended it to Mateo. "Now you should work on blocking."

"I think that's enough," Nik said.

"Can Mateo not speak for himself?" I turned to Mateo. "You should work on blocking." I stretched the sword further toward him.

His breath heaved in and out while he stared at the gleaming tip of the sword. Nik and Flavian flocked around him like two mother hens. No doubt this Nyssa had done the same, perched him in a library and coddled him. It might have been his hatred of me that pushed him to take the sword, but hate and stubbornness could go a long way. I wanted to see how long it would carry him.

Mateo snatched the sword from me and righted himself. Sweat rolled down his cheeks in rivulets.

"Good," I said. "Now keep in mind, you will always have a disadvantage, and people will abuse it. They are going to swing for your legs first. You'll have to be ready to block. But that will only be a distraction. As soon as you're guarding your legs, they're going to aim for your organs. It will be all in your wrist." I showed him with my own sword, twisting my arm to guard my legs, then flipping it immediately upright to protect my center. I realized this could come back to haunt me when I moved to kill him later. I also had faith that I would still be able to best him.

The first few times, Mateo didn't flip the sword fast enough to block the second strike. He dropped the rapier once and fell once. "I think you've done enough," Flavian said. Mateo ignored him and stood up, red-faced and drenched in sweat as he held the sword in front of him.

He was persistent. He just might continue to stay one step ahead of the Goddess…until I took him.

"Ready?" I asked, and before he could nod, I swung for his legs. Crash! The swords met. I drew back and swung again for his middle. I went for the front of his tunic, and the tip of my sword hit the tip of his.

The sword fell from his fingers, and he collapsed to the deck.

"I can't do anymore." He broke into a coughing fit, and I agreed.

"Not today." I nudged the sword to him with my boot. "Practice when you can. I don't think Flavian will need the sword."

"It did look rather nice on my belt," he said.

Mateo grasped the sword and fumbled for his cane. It took him several long moments to get to his feet, and he made a sound like a choking gull while he did it. Except his breathing didn't bother me as much as it normally did. He had earned the extra gasps.

"Did you enjoy learning of this?" he asked between breaths. "Or did you just do it because that's what they told you to do?"

My spine stiffened. "I had a choice. I could have been a wife or a farmer or a hunter. I could have built ships or learned the smelt. I chose this."

"You didn't answer the question." His gaze pierced me from under his fringe of sparse lashes.

"Yes, I enjoyed it."

Most of it, I thought. There had been long days and even longer nights, nursing wounds and rubbing mint oil on sore muscles, only to get up and do it all over again, putting blister upon blister, ache upon ache. It had all been worth it in the end, though. I earned my claws. I earned my place, and I would keep it.

CHAPTER 12
✖

The door to the church was ajar. I crept toward it, sword in hand, my pulse beating in my ear. When I kicked open the door, there was only one woman inside: the priestess draped in her long robes. She didn't turn or shift when the door slammed against the wall. I cleared my throat to make myself known. Still not a shift, a flick of a finger, or even a sigh.

I moved deeper into the dimly lit church. The only light came from the candles, flickering on the altar. The air inside the church hung like a blanket, pressing on my chest. I struggled to breathe and made a wheeze like Mateo's.

The closer I got to the priestess, the warmer the air turned. Were the candles giving off that much heat?

I cleared my throat again. "I am here in the name of the Goddess Hel," I said, my voice wavering. What was wrong with me? I shouldn't be afraid of a single priestess. I was a chosen warrior of Death.

The priestess did not move or speak.

I touched her shoulder, and it felt crinkly, like a piece of parchment. She tipped backwards and fell flat on the floor. Her white robes were stained red down the front, and two black holes plunged into her face where eyes should have been.

Her lips were caught in a slight smile, two wrinkled worms, and her cheeks collapsed to deep hollows. A storm of black beetles poured from her open mouth, and I stepped back, repulsed.

A dry laugh echoed off the stone walls. I frantically searched to see who was laughing when the dead priestess sat upright.

The black beetles continued to drip from her mouth and now, her eye holes. The bugs streamed down her cheeks like tears.

"You will pay for what you have done to me," she said.

I backed away from her. "I did nothing. I didn't kill you."

She crawled to her knees, twisted bones snapping back into place. I choked down a scream.

"You are one and the same," she said. "We are all the same. One of us is one of you, and soon you shall be one of me too." She reached out for me with bone fingers. The flesh curled back to the knuckles.

"I did not kill you," I said again and opened my eyes.

The small cabin was nearly pitch black apart from the stream of moonlight on the floor. I clutched my chest. My heart pounded against my palm like a drum, and my skin was sticky with sweat. The sound of Mateo's soft breath was almost a comfort. Something touched my skin, and I twitched to shake it off, imagining the black beetles. It was only the corner of my blanket, brushing my leg.

I hadn't suffered nightmares like that since I first came to Helvar. I used to wake in the night, screaming, and when Merle or Von asked me what I had dreamed about, I had no answer. I couldn't remember. This nightmare, though, I remembered clearly. I could still see the beetles crawling from her empty eyes.

I hung my legs over the side of the bunk and rubbed the heel of my hand into my eye, trying to grind the image away. Nik's bunk was empty. I wondered where he went. I decided to find out versus going back to sleep.

I slid on the linen cloak Merle had given me and reached into the pocket of my leggings. I removed the rune stone and ran my finger over the carvings. What if the legend held some truth? What if the dead priestess came back in my nightmares?

I shook my head. No, I was using magic and legend to explain away bad dreams. The nightmare was my guilt for sparing the priestess's life, and I wouldn't shake it until I made my mark and claimed the souls of Fortis.

On the deck, the cool wind blew off the water, cutting through my cloak. I drew it tight around my chest and stepped toward the moonlight. There Nik stood, staring into the blackness. We dropped sail at night. He didn't have to stay awake to keep watch. But after sharing a bunkroom, I knew he slept fitfully. More than once I'd woken up to find his eyes on me.

"I couldn't sleep," I said in the Eastern tongue.

He didn't respond, and my mouth went dry. Please, not another nightmare. "Nik?"

This time he turned. "Sorry, I was thinking about something."

I had a flash of the priestess again, her deep black eyes. "What?" I asked to distract myself from my own worries.

"Nothing," he said. "Why are you awake?"

"No reason."

He sighed. "This is going to be a poor conversation if we both lie. I was thinking about Javad."

"Ah." I nodded. So we were both consumed by the dead.

"I feel guilty."

"For killing him? You shouldn't. He would have killed us if you hadn't struck first."

"No." He shook his head. "I feel guilty for waiting so long. He hurt me. I ran away. I left Fahima and all of the others behind. God, I can't even think about all of the horrible things he must have done between now and then. He was Mahmod's right hand man. Any horror Mahmod dreamed, Javad made it happen. I should have killed him in the middle of the marketplace and hung his head on a post for everyone to see. I should have ripped him limb from limb." He nodded to the stairs, toward Mateo and Flavian. "They wouldn't understand."

But I would. Because I had drawn blood before. "Dead is dead," I said. "It doesn't matter how. We all end up in Niflheim whether we are stabbed or drowned."

He leaned on the rails. "I just wish things had gone differently. That's all."

"I understand," I whispered. The priestess was dead, but it did matter to me how it happened, by Merle's arrow. Not my sword. "I failed," I said. "I couldn't kill her."

"Who?"

I gripped the railing and looked north, toward the leading star, toward Helvar. "The priestess. It was my first raid. She was alone in the church. An old woman. I didn't even like her. She was unarmed. I could have choked her with one hand, or stopped her heart with one strike, and I didn't do it." I opened my mouth and now all of my worries spilled from my lips. I couldn't bring them back.

"You feel bad for not killing someone?" he asked.

"It was a raid. That's what we do. We are the hands of Hel. The living plague. If I can't deliver death, then I can't be one of them." My shame splattered on the deck like vomit, but it felt good to talk about it. I couldn't tell anyone the truth on Helvar. Not without outing Merle as a liar. She told them all I *had* killed the priestess.

He crossed his arms over his chest. "You know, Death spares people too."

"She does," I said. "But I can't."

"Why not?"

"Because I have tan skin. Black hair." I tugged on my loose tendrils. "I am not of Helvar blood. That man, my father, you know what he did? He offered me in exchange for his life. Merle took me and killed him, as proof that you can't make deals with Death. I was a punishment, a trick. The others can falter. I can't."

He turned to the water and run his thumb across his knuckle. "When I was a boy, and the Daughters would come to Brezadine, the other boys and me...we would hover in the marketplace like flies. We were there on Javad's orders, to make sure we got the best of what your Sisters brought. But I liked the show. We had never seen women so strong with gold and red hair like that.

"On one trip, after a rough meeting with Javad, I found one of them in the market and I begged her to kill the Aldam. I asked her if she would go into their den and slaughter them all. She said to me, 'We don't hunt on these lands.'"

"Because we need them for trade," I whispered.

"Is that your goddess's rule? Or yours?" he asked.

Ours, I didn't say. Indiscriminate Death would not forgo an entire city because She needed the wool. *We* did that, and I never questioned it until now. I was taught alongside all of the other children of Helvar the ways of the island. We hunted, farmed, sewed and fished. What the island or sea didn't provide, could be gained from the sacrifices to Hel. But some of the gifts we received in exchange for the offerings had no value to us beyond trade, and we couldn't trade with towns and cities we had formerly raided.

"It's the way things have always been," I said. "Death will take them all in due time."

"Not soon enough," Nik said. "Not for the slaves of the Jaysh Aldam or those they kill."

"What do you want me to do about it?"

"Nothing I suppose," he said. "But you shouldn't feel guilty for sparing one life when so many others are overlooked." Nik took a knife from his belt and flipped it in his fingers. "When Nyssa found me, I was so angry and mistrustful. Then I met Mateo and Flavian. I hated them too at first. They were naïve. They'd never seen anyone flogged, or raped, or slit across the throat. I envied them."

"You shouldn't envy someone for being naïve."

"I don't. Not anymore. Now I feel like it's my job to protect them from things like that, like you."

"Dragging me onto your ship was probably not the way to do that."

He laughed. "No, probably not." He flipped the knife in the air and I realized it was my knife, missing from my belt.

"Give that back."

"Here. It's a nice knife." He twisted it around and handed it to me by the tip.

"Did you rob me in my sleep?" I snatched for the blade and returned it to my belt.

"No, I took it while we were standing here, talking. I learned a few useful things from the Aldam. Did you carve that yourself?"

"No, it was a gift." I ran my finger down the length of the short, curved blade and the fish-carved ivory hilt. I hadn't thought of Von in days, and it had been blissful not worrying about him catching me by the woodpile and grabbing my waist to steal a kiss. "Here." I handed the knife back to Nik. "Keep it. It will save you the trouble of stealing it from my belt."

"I couldn't," he said as he practically drooled over it.

"It belongs to you. You drew blood with it. Even if you killed Javad a little later than you would have liked, he is dead all the same. Don't forget that."

He took the knife from me and added it to his mismatched collection. I would have it back anyway, once I killed him.

"Thank you, and thank you for not telling Mat and Flavian about what happened in Brezadine, either."

"My pleasure." I liked watching them itch, aching to know. "Goddess help you if you breathe a word of the priestess to either of them."

"I won't."

Nik and I both leaned against the rails and stared at the moonlit water. I supposed it was not my wisest move to tell him my deepest fears, but they would die with him when he went, and by sharing my secrets, I seemed to improve his trust of me. The more they trusted me, the more leeway I would be given on Fortis.

The piece of this I dreaded was meeting with Nyssa.

"Are you ashamed to bring me back to your Nyssa?" I asked Nik, stirring the silence.

"No," he said without pause.

I raised an eyebrow. "You won't ask me to act a certain way, or be polite? If I stand in front of her dying bed and call her an awful mother and a disgrace, you won't try to stop me?"

"Is that what you're planning to do?"

"I might."

"You are a horrible mother. You left me with a coward, and then came for me thirteen years later. You, whom everyone loves, left me to die, and it was a dealer of Death who took me under her wing. Now you must face the Goddess for your crimes."

"You all think she's this wonderful woman," I continued. "It's an insult. She left me, and now that she's dying, and suffering from long held guilt, she sends you to disrupt my life and drag me back. It's selfish."

"It's selfish," he agreed. "And I'm sorry that you and I don't know the same woman. But she wishes that things had turned out differently too."

I rolled my eyes. "She certainly wished for a long time before doing anything about it."

I leaned my cheek in the palm of my steel fingers, and the aroma of goat fat and fish wafted up my nose. It would be nice to tell her all of the hateful things I had to say, claim the lives of her three boys, and then let her suffer with that for her last few days. But even that hardly seemed fair. She left me for thirteen years.

I scratched my claws into the railing while the ship bobbed up and down. The sea was calm, the sky clear. Nothing of note except for a black shadow in the distance, moving quickly toward us.

"Someone's coming," I said.

Nik narrowed his eyes. "It's not one of ours."

"One of ours?" I raised an eyebrow. It certainly wasn't a Helvar ship. It was too large and sailing alone. The Daughters never left the isle with less than four ships.

"It's not from Fortis." He exhaled. "We didn't really have permission to take this ship," he explained.

"I thought this was Flavian's ship."

"It is, but it was a gift from his father, who never expected Flavian to take it out of the harbor, let alone to Helvar and back."

"And who exactly is Flavian's father?" I crossed my arms over my chest. This secret had gone on long enough.

Nik pursed his lips. "It's none of your business."

"I think it is if we're being followed. I won't fight unless I know why I'm fighting."

"We don't know that we're being followed."

"On Mateo's routes?" In addition to having the will of an ox, Mateo had earned his well-to-do position as mapmaker. I had peeked at his maps. He didn't follow standard routes. He made his own. They veered around the merchant paths, running through deep and shark-infested waters many others wouldn't dare test. Somehow, though, he found the way.

Nik pressed his fingers to his forehead. "Flavian's the consul's son." He went for the wheel and his spyglass. He held it to his eye and ran to the bow to examine the other ship while I devoured this new fact.

I should have known. Flavian was more spoiled and pampered than any wealthy merchant or lord I had ever seen. Being the consul's son was like being Mahmod's daughter. The Emperor governed the Empire; the consul managed the city. Flavian's father was the eyes and ears and fist of the local happenings in Fortis.

I could already see Merle's silver smile as I brought back the bounty from the consul's son. It was as close as I could get to the Emperor without gutting him. I would bring Hel right to his front door where She could not be ignored. Truly I was blessed.

"I can't tell what kind of ship it is." Nik came back to me, and I erased all signs of joy from my face. I could not look pleased about being followed.

"It's not yours. It's not ours, and it's not from Brezadine," he continued. "It might just be a merchant ship, sailing the same route. But to be safe, wake the others. When you get back up, help me with the sails."

I nodded and went down to wake Flavian and Mateo. I couldn't decide if I wanted a fight or not. After days on this ship, sparring with Flavian and Mateo, I welcomed a terse and sweaty sword fight. But now I knew who I traveled with, and I could not risk losing Flavian to someone else.

I woke Mateo first.

Gently, I nudged him. "Mateo."

He jerked awake, pushing himself upright. "What's wrong?" he asked, blinking away sleep.

"There's a ship behind us."

"A ship?" He rubbed a fist in his eye. "On my route?"

"Yes. Bring the sword." I gestured to Flavian's bejeweled rapier and took my own longsword from under my bedsheets. When I stopped at Flavian's cabin, I woke him less gently.

"Get up, Flavian! Get on deck!"

"Good God," he sputtered and rolled out of bed

The consul's son. I shook my head. The consul's son had been sitting under my nose this entire time, a ruby-encrusted sheep waiting for slaughter.

I returned to the deck, tiptoed around the hole we had not yet fixed, and helped Nik winch the mainsail back into position. Mateo hobbled onto the deck followed by Flavian with his dark curls mussed and his bloused tunic untied.

"I hope there is a good explanation for this," he said.

"There is," Nik said. "We're being tracked." He pointed to the mystery ship, looming ever closer. Had we been in one of my longships, the tracking ship would be only a memory by now. But in this slow, fat ship, we were like a beached whale, ripe for the taking.

"By whom?" Flavian sputtered.

"We don't know," Nik said.

"Does your father have enemies?" I asked, hardly a question that needed to be asked. Everyone in power had enemies. The more power, the more enemies.

Flavian blinked. "Oh God, Nik. You told her?"

"She has a right to know," Nik said.

"Not everything," Mateo said through his teeth, making it obvious there were other secrets besides my near-dead mother and Flavian being a few steps away from royalty. I was sure I would get those soon enough. These boys seemed incapable of keeping secrets for long.

Escape from the mystery ship didn't appear to be an option. Our mainsail sat flat, no wind to push it. The other ship had either caught a wind or rode on momentum while we'd been idling here.

"It looks like a merchant ship to me," Flavian said and handed the spyglass back to Nik.

"Perhaps they're in need of aid," Mateo suggested

"Ships in need of aid do not cut through the water at high-speed on direct course for the *consul's* ship," I said. Flavian and Mateo's naivety was showing.

"Keep a cool head," Nik said. "No raised weapons until we know what they want."

Flavian and Mateo crept closer to Nik and me, as if we could shield them from arrows. Mateo's breath washed over the back of my neck, and I cringed. This would not have happened to the Daughters. No one would dare touch us.

The shape of the ship appeared in full now, illuminated by the moonlight. It was a non-descript ship with a white sail, stained yellow from age, and no figurehead on the mast. It was a fat cog ship like this one with a raised forecastle and poop deck. They launched ropes from their deck to ours. The hooks pinched to the railing with sharp claws. I dropped my hand to my longsword, tight to the hilt, but kept it sheathed for now. We were sorely outnumbered.

In a quick pass, I counted twenty on deck, and no one would be foolish enough to show their entire crew. There had to be at least five to ten more below deck. In all my training, I had never fought more than five at a time. Also, to win the fight, I would have to keep Mateo and Flavian alive. Nik could handle himself. Or not. I needed at least two to crew the ship back to Fortis, and I needed to be the one to send Flavian to Hel.

The other ship reeled us in like a dead fish. The men were all dressed in rusted chainmail with dented and blackened helmets, suggesting they had been in a few fights before this one. Underneath their armor, the colors of their tunics varied from dull gold to moss green. They didn't have anything to unify them. Or identify them.

Once our ship was close enough, they bridged the gap with a piece of wood and four of them came across, dropping onto our deck. My steel fingers twitched. I focused on the leader, a tall figure, the same height as Nik. His face was shadowed under the dark night and the cover of his helmet.

"I am Nikos, captain of this ship. How can we help you?" Nik clenched his jaw as soon as the question was out, and his fingers played with the top of one of his knives.

The lead soldier removed his helmet...her helmet. Now I could see her sharp nose and green eyes. Her amber hair was cut short, almost to the skin, flattened by her helmet. I thought Helvar was the only place where women were recognized as the superior soldiers. I was glad to be wrong. I would have been happier about it if this woman did not appear to want to cut me as badly as I wanted to cut her.

"We came for the stone," she said in a Northern tongue, an unusual variation of it. I didn't recognize the accent.

Flavian nudged me in the shoulder blades. This had nothing to do with him and everything to do with this ridiculous rock.

"What stone?" Nik asked in a fairly convincing, unknowing tone.

"Rorik's stone," she hissed through her teeth. "We are those loyal to Perdita. The stone was made by us and belongs to us. Our spies in Brezadine pointed the finger to you." She raised her finger to my nose. I clenched my steel fist to keep from clawing off her hand.

"Perdita?" Flavian said. "There is no Perdita."

Which was probably why they looked as if they scrounged their ship and clothes and armor from the scraps that washed to shore. Perdita had been defeated by Murus, absorbed into the other country over eighty years ago.

"There will always be a Perdita as long as there are those loyal to it." She flipped her hand, palm side up. "Now give us the stone."

I dropped my hand to my pocket, eliciting a few swords pointed in my direction while I drew the stone out of my tunic. The woman exhaled a long breath when her eyes fell to it, as if it were an old friend she hadn't seen in ages.

The stone was mine. I should fight for it. Merle would fight for it…because she was Merciless. I was unstoppable. The real prize wasn't the stone. It was in Fortis with Flavian. If I fought, I would be stopped. If I gave up the stone, I could reach the win. This was just another scar on my way to victory.

"Take it." I tossed it the stone to the woman, and she snatched it from the air.

"Thank you," she said and smiled cruelly, the way Merle smiled right before we launched ourselves on Frisia. I had made an awful mistake. "Now kill them," the woman said to her men as she walked away with my stone. I drew my sword.

CHAPTER 13
✖

The three men lunged for us. Flavian disappeared, not surprisingly, and I sliced one man across the stomach, under his ill-fitting chainmail. His blood sprayed across the deck, and I barely had a chance to whisper his prayer to the Goddess before another soldier launched at me.

Nik slashed at a man with his knife, catching him under the neck. Mateo vomited on his boots when intestines spilled across the ship. But despite that, he managed to block the attempt to cut off his legs, and the second attempt to slice through his ribs, long enough for me to sever the man's leg from behind.

When the man collapsed, I kicked his body over the rails.

"Go swiftly to Niflheim," I shouted into the water as Mateo caught his breath.

This had not been my plan, but it was incredibly satisfying, fighting people with skill like I had done in my training. This was what I thought the raid would be, something of a challenge, where my heart beat wildly, and I knew, if I stopped moving, I would die. These were worthy offerings to Hel.

The woman climbed back to her ship and sent more men after us. Twelve, I counted quickly as the others crawled up from the deck. Still, no sign of Flavian--coward. Nik pulled his crossbow to his chest. Mateo held his jeweled sword, shaking uncontrollably. He'd only learned to use a sword earlier today. He was not ready for battle.

I wanted to tell him to go below and hide wherever Flavian was hiding.

Mateo's life was mine to take, and when I took it, I would be merciful. A quick stab to the heart and immediate silence. He did not deserve to be cut apart piece by piece by pirates.

But we needed every sword we had. "Just keep them distracted as long as you can," I said to him and balled my fist to strike a man across the jaw. His helmet twisted to cover his face, I slit his neck, and pushed him into the water.

"Go swiftly to Niflheim!"

Someone aimed a crossbow at me. I ducked as he fired, and the bolt soared over my head. Nik returned with a bolt of his own, lodging it into the shooter's right eye. I turned over my shoulder and gave him a nod.

On the prow of the ship, Mateo remained on his feet, managing to defend himself from another Perditian. He blocked low, then high, and then the man made a fatal flaw. He left his side exposed.

"Nik," I called, hoping he would see the opening and take his shot. But Mateo found it first. He jabbed the tip of the jeweled rapier directly into the man's kidney. Blood pooled out of the wound, and I was about to shout out congratulations when Mateo vomited again.

A hardened warrior he was not.

I was on my fourth or fifth kill; I lost count. To me they were only obstacles to pass to reach the woman from Perdita, the one who had my stone. I wanted it back. If she had taken it and left, I would have let her have it. Now, I would send her to Hel and reclaim my prize.

"Excuse me, Fellows." Flavian waved a handkerchief from the other side of the ship. He had dug out some armor from his things, thick chainmail that came over him like fish scales and a helmet that drew down over his nose. "I think you have the wrong stone." He held up a rock that looked somewhat like my rock, at least from here, in the dark. He was either a fool or a genius. We would all find out soon.

"Go get it!" The woman snapped, and her men shoved me aside to chase after Flavian...who stood conveniently on the other side of the sheet-covered hole in the deck. Had it been daylight, there was no chance they would have confused it for solid ground, but under the moonlight, it looked like nothing more than a puddle of water.

Three of them tore through the cloth and collapsed to the deck below where Nik leaned over the edge and fired three crossbow bolts.

Flavian laughed and threw the stone over the side of the ship. "Go get it if you want it."

Two more men raced to the railing and dove after the falling stone, leaving one man behind for Nik to slice open with a knife. The remaining Perditians scattered across our ship, which left the woman unguarded on hers.

I leapt over the gap and held up Gut Spiller, stained red with the blood of the woman's men. Her mouth drew tight, and she raised her sword between us.

"I will take my stone back now." I waved to her with one my steel fingers.

"What are you doing so far from home, Daughter of Hel?" she asked. "If you are an outcast, you can join me and my men."

"Your men are dead."

"We are more than this," she said. "And with the stone, we will bring up the kings and queens and soldiers of old. Perdita will rise again, an unstoppable force." Her face twinkled with the imagined glory of what it would be like to have an army of soldiers brought back from the dead.

I laughed at her. "The stone doesn't work. Your men have died for nothing."

"You think because the stone doesn't work for you, it doesn't work at all? You're the fool, Daughter of Hel."

I frowned. No one called me a fool. "Give me the rock!" I shouted.

"No." She raised her sword over her shoulder and swung out. I deflected the strike with my steel hand. The strength of it rattled through my bones. I swung back with Gut Spiller, and the Perditian's sword met mine in the middle. I could see how she gained command of this ship. She was good.

I fought the temptation to do what I would normally do. Go in with claws and sword raised and suffer a few minor wounds for the sake of the killing blow. She was not one of my Sisters. She would not spare me. She also wasn't an untrained villager.

I used some of the lessons I had given to Mateo on defense, blocking her strikes instead of forcing my own. This was how we had done things in training, one on one, sword against sword. Then into small groups and teams. We always had to be ready for the people to rise up against us. It was human nature to rally against Death, even when staring into Her eyes. It was the look this woman had now, and I felt sorry for her.

I didn't know how long she had been seeking this stone, the promises she made to her people, how many of them were scattered through the former lands of Perdita, hoping to regain control of their name and their country.

The only advantage I had was youth. She had clearly studied and practiced, trained for hours on end until her hands blistered. If she were ten years younger, I would have worried. But she was tiring. She stumbled, sweat running from her brow, and she dropped her sword. I let her pick it up and face me again. A little longer. Let her go in glory.

I knew what it was like to be a stranger in a strange country, fighting for acceptance. I couldn't take that from her yet. Hel would not begrudge me giving her a few more minutes.

The next time our swords clashed, hers slipped from her fingers and skittered across the deck. She didn't even move to chase after it. Her shoulders dropped, and she raised her eyes to mine. She looked defeated. But what could I do? I couldn't spare her. I didn't think she would have it anyway. She was a fighter. She lost. It was her time.

"Go swiftly to Niflheim," I said and swung my sword across her neck.

She dropped to the deck, gone. It was the fastest way to take someone apart from jabbing into her heart, which I would have done had she not been wearing chainmail.

I lowered my sword and took a deep breath. My muscles ached in a way they hadn't in weeks, with a tiredness I'd almost forgotten. I breathed in the salt air, the sweat, and the blood. I felt strong, satisfied, and regretful. Killing the villagers had been one thing, a necessary sacrifice to defend our island. But I could not feel proud over the death of the Perditian pirate.

Bending down, I reached into the woman's coat pocket and took the stone. I also kept her sword. She had nothing else of value to give—apart from her life, which had been a worthy gift. They all had been. Hel would be pleased, proven by the sunrise cresting over the water. Red glow in the sky meant death the previous night.

I dropped the stone into my pocket. The familiar weight felt like an embrace. I had missed the stone without even knowing I had missed it. The plank connecting the two ships had fallen in the water. I leapt from one side to the other and as soon as I hit the deck, my stomach dropped.

Something was wrong. Very wrong.

"Mateo."

I leapt over fallen Perditian soldiers and pools of blood to find Mateo perched up against the rails with Nik and Flavian hovering over him, his two mother hens.

Mateo looked like a half-melted candle. His shriveled, bony leg was soaked with blood. The Perditians had done exactly what I said they would do—exploited his injury.

"Are you hurt anywhere else?" I squeezed between Flavian and Nik, one more clucking hen. It would have been better for the pirates to kill Mateo versus leaving him wounded.

"No," he said.

"We should get him downstairs," Nik said.

He and Flavian picked him up and carried him to the stairs. The deck was slick with blood and bile. Flavian gagged while he held Mateo aloft.

"Let us take him to my cabin," Flavian choked. "It will be more comfortable."

Weaving around trunks of clothing and wine, they managed to lay Mateo down on the bed where he sank into the feather-stuffed mattress.

"Let us see how bad it is." I reached for the tattered shreds of his leggings, and he jerked away.

"No, I don't want you to see it."

"Don't be difficult. I guarantee I've treated more sword wounds than either of these two." As proof, I lifted my tunic to show him my stomach, riddled with scars. His face changed. Was that pity? I dropped my tunic and reached for his leggings again. This time, he didn't fight me.

I focused on keeping my face still as I peeled back the bloodied fabric. I thought I had seen grave wounds. Ulf once returned from a fishing trip where he'd nearly lost a battle with a walrus. It gored him in the thigh, and even after that, his leg had not looked this bad. Now I knew what Mateo did not want me to see. The wound itself wasn't grave. It was deep and probably hurt. But in comparison to the others, it was a small scratch on a leg that had already been gnawed on by dogs.

There was more scarred skin than new skin, all wrapped tightly around withered muscle and bone.

"I can stitch this up," I said as calmly as I could and held out my hand to Flavian. "Give me your flask of alcohol and leave us."

Flavian stripped out of his chainmail and recovered the flask. He handed it to me before he and Nik made for the door. I took out the needle and twine from Flavian's drawer and found a box of chocolates beside it. He must have gotten them in Brezadine and hidden them from us. The chocolates hadn't been in the drawer the first time I searched his room.

I uncorked the bottle of alcohol and held it over Mateo's leg. "This is going to hurt, quite a bit," I warned.

"If you haven't noticed." He balled the sheets in his hands. "I've done this before. Several times."

I nodded. I'd been stitched before too, but I couldn't compare my scratches and nicks to this. They called the plague the blue plague because it came in through the sufferer's skin, eating the victim from the outside in. After three days of infection, their skin turned a pale shade of blue.

The only chance of survival was to catch it before those three days and remove as much of the infected skin as possible. Doctors stitched together scraps and hoped that was enough, that they reduced the infection to the point that the victim could suffer it. Mateo, while his leg would have been healing, would have been bed ridden, waiting for the remaining poison to finish attacking his heart, liver and lungs. By the end, there must have been enough left for him to survive.

For a time.

Had Merle not taken me from Orsalia, I might have caught the plague too. It ravaged all of the cities. Hel only spared us death because we made our sacrifices to Her as usual.

I poured the alcohol on Mateo's leg. He arched his back and dug into the sheets as the liquid ran over his wound and washed away the blood. Once his body relaxed, I set to work closing the wound. With each stitch, I wondered why I was doing this. He only had a few weeks to live as it was. As soon as I was settled in Fortis, I would kill him.

But this was something more deeply ingrained into me than my devotion to Hel--my devotion to my Sisters, my fellow warriors. Mateo and I had fought and won a battle together. I couldn't leave him like this.

"You did well for yourself out there...despite the vomiting," I said while I stitched.

"That sounds like a compliment...almost," he said through clenched teeth.

"It is...almost," I said. "You also let yourself open for attack."

"Sorry, I haven't been trained as a murderer. This is all new to me."

His lips puckered. I could see his imagination working, me slaughtering people everywhere I turned, as if that was all I did. All I was.

"I am not a murderer," I said.

"You killed plenty of people today."

"So did Nik. So did you. Would you have preferred I let them slaughter us instead?"

He sucked in another breath as I tugged skin together. "What about the villagers you kill? They aren't attacking you."

"Death needs to make Her claims. I merely steer Her eye in the right direction."

He snorted.

"What? The rest of you might prefer to leave things to chance, but I don't."

"I would rather die than live with blood on my hands."

"Then why didn't you sacrifice yourself to the Perditians?"

"I was trying to protect us, this ship."

"Exactly," I said. "I kill to protect my people."

I pulled the last of the wound closed, pulling it taut until the skin puckered, almost as tightly as Mateo's lips. I washed the wound, bandaged it, and cleaned the needle. I scrubbed my hands and liberated Flavian's hidden chocolates. I stabbed one with a claw and handed the rest to Mateo.

"Eat. You'll need your strength."

He held the chocolates in his lap. "Did you get your stone back?" he asked.

"Yes." I took it out of my pocket to show him.

"Do you really think it does what they said it does?"

"Raise the dead?" I examined the intertwined snake drawings and thought of the Perditian's last words. *You think because the stone doesn't work for you, it doesn't work at all?* "No. It's just a legend. Those pirates were deluded." I rolled the stone in my fingers and caught a flash of the dead priestess, beetles crawling from her wrinkled lips.

I quickly returned the stone to my pocket. *Just dreams.*

"I appreciate that you would have been willing to give it up for us," he said.

"It wasn't for you." I cleared my throat. It would not be a good idea to tell him it had been a trade, the stone for the chance to kill him and his friends later. "I mean, I'm tired of being hassled. I just want to go home."

His lips pursed at my mention of, "home." "Why do you love them so much? What have they done for you?"

I frowned right back at him as I stood up. "They raised me. They taught me how to sew, fish, and fight, and you should be grateful they did because those lessons helped you today too. Without them, you would have been cut deeper than your leg."

"*She* loves you too."

It always went back to the horrible Nyssa. "If abandoning someone and sending kidnappers after them means 'love,' then I don't want it."

I left the room and popped the chocolate on my tongue, wondering why I hadn't let him bleed to death.

CHAPTER 14

✕

When Hel is satisfied, She provides.

She was very satisfied with the Perditians' sacrifice that day.

Before we cut the marauding ship loose, we raided the stores. Despite their shabby appearance and rusted armor, they had been traveling with crates of untouched swords, books, and clothing from the former Perdita. Including a painting of the famed Rorik who made the rune stone. In my mind, I had pictured him to be tall and handsome, as most people of legends seemed to be. In reality Rorik had been somewhat portly and squinty-eyed.

"We shouldn't take these things." Nik picked up a vase painted with images of birds on the rim.

"Would you rather sink them into the sea?" I asked. "This could be the last there is of the former country of Perdita. If we don't take it, it will all be lost."

"Carina makes a valid point," Flavian said, already running his fingers over a fine, fox fur trimmed cloak. "We would be preserving it, not stealing it."

Nik had been outvoted.

We moved the crates from their ship to ours and cut the other ship loose. It drifted aimlessly into the water, and we set to work cleaning up our ship and hauling out the bodies that Flavian had tricked into the hole.

"It was a clever move," I said to him. I could say that now…since it worked.

"I know." He grinned, and my mouth returned the grin until I made the mental note to quash it. This was a temporary alliance. I couldn't let it deter me from killing him in Fortis once he led me to his wealth.

We scrubbed the last of the blood from the deck, and Flavian and I went to bed. He took Mateo's bunk and spent twenty minutes complaining about how hard it was and how drafty it was until the exhaustion of complaining finally carried him to sleep. Good thing too, because I was five minutes away from cutting out his tongue, promise be damned.

I rolled onto my side, and the stone jabbed into my hip. I pulled it out of my pocket and ran my fingers over the runes. If it did work, how? Did it require a chant? Or did it only work during a full moon? Everyone wanted the stone. No one seemed to have instructions.

Merle would want this, and more for the possibilities than the coin it could gain. I would have to keep it more closely hidden.

I tucked it in my pocket and closed my eyes. In sleep, I found myself in a longboat, rolling up to the shores of Frisia, however the boat was being pulled by the bloodied corpses of the Perditian pirates we had just slaughtered. Their female captain sat at the back of the boat with her innards spilling onto her boots.

"Row! Row!" she chanted and smiled at me with a peeling grin.

The boat hit shore, and I leapt onto the sand. The ghostly pirates pulled on the oars and drew the longboat back to sea. I climbed the hill to the village where more specters lingered. The smell of rot rose up from the ground. Limbless villagers wandered aimlessly, moaning, reaching for me. I hurried past them to the safety of the woods, where the lights of the church beckoned me.

I stopped outside the doors. They were partially open. Candle light flickered on the other side.

"Come in, Carina." The priestess's voice wrapped around my waist like a rope and tugged me inside.

Again, the old woman stood alone by the altar, except this time she was moving, lighting another flickering candle. I sighed. No bugs appeared to be dropping from her dead eye sockets. No flesh peeled from her bones. She looked as she had in the moment before Merle shot her.

"Do you want me to apologize?" I asked. "Is that it?"

"Like you said, you have nothing to apologize for. You did not kill me." She set the candle on the table and walked toward me. As she moved from flickering candlelight into the shadows, her skin turned gray and waxy. The edges of it peeled from her jaw.

"You are in the unique position of being unattached." She took another step, and a piece of flesh dropped from her chin. "You can act without orders from your leader." Her ear turned black and dropped to her feet. "You can think for yourself for once." As she spoke, the odor of rot seeped into the room.

I covered my nose with my arm. "What do you want of me?" I asked in a muffled voice.

She stopped right in front of me, and I closed my fists. Underneath her gray skin, black lines crossed her cheeks and her chin. She smiled, and her lips peeled back to reveal rotting gums and green teeth. I wanted to scream or push her away, and I could not seem to do either.

"I want you to see the cost of death," she said in a low voice. "I want you to see the true price that we pay for your clan to rob and pillage us." She raised her arm and the doors swung wide.

Outside, the ghostly villagers waited, bearing torches and severed limbs. They moved on me like a slow-moving swarm of festering bees.

"No, this is only a dream." I backed away, and the priestess caught my arm with a firm grip.

"You cannot run this time."

I sat upright in the bunk and struck my head on the low ceiling. Sweat coated my forehead. I ran my hand down my arm, and my skin burned hot apart from a patch on my forearm. Cool to the touch. Where the priestess had grabbed me.

A shiver rolled through me and I patted my hand on my pocket. The stone. Was this the way it worked? With nightmares and rotting priestesses? I did not know. I only knew I did not like these nightmares or visions or hauntings or whatever they were.

I heard footsteps overhead and crawled out of bed. Our bunkroom was empty. As I made my way up the stairs, I heard Mateo on the deck.

"They have a map book from old Perdita," he said. "We don't even have one of these in the Fortis library."

Of course that would be his first choice of the spoils, a book of maps. But if he had the strength to flip through old map books, then his battle wound must be improving.

I stepped into the open air. Nik and Flavian were digging through the Perditian crates like children grasping at a basket of sweets. Nik seemed to have forgotten he had been staunchly against taking their things. He twirled two new knives in his hand crafted with silver hilts decorated with lines of ivy.

"Carina." When he saw me, he hastily tucked the blades into his belt.

"Why did you let me sleep all day?" I muttered. It would have been nice for someone to wake me up before that nightmare. I grabbed a tin of dried fish and stabbed a piece with my claws.

"We thought you had earned the rest," Flavian said. "Apparently you could use a bit more."

I sneered at him and took another piece of fish. When I killed him I would be doing the world a favor by silencing his annoying voice. The cost of his Death would be endless moments of peace. A blessing more than a curse.

I ate another piece of fish and glanced at Mateo. He sat on a crate with his injured leg stretched before him and the map book on his lap. A thin sheen of sweat coated his pale cheeks and bruises sank under his eyes. He should still be resting. If he continued to push himself like this, he might die before I could kill him.

"Oh dear God," Flavian exclaimed and dredged a massive pile of red velvet, lace, and pearls from one of the crates. When he held it to his chest, I recognized it as a dress, one that seemed large enough for four people, yet only bore two sleeves.

Flavian picked up the skirt and turned around. "There's another one in here," he said. "A blue one. It would look so fetching on you, Carina. What would it take to get you out of that wool tunic and into one of these gowns?"

I snorted. "I'll wear one of those gowns when you do." I said it without thinking, wishing I could take it back. But it was too late.

"Done," Flavian said and smiled.

***

I really had no problem with dresses. Sensible dresses. Plain dresses. As children on Helvar, we often wore oversized tunics and linen dresses in the summer to keep our legs bare for splashing in the surf or running through mud.

But as soon as training began, we swapped our skirts for leather armor and leggings. Wearing a dress was a quick way to get stabbed. It only took once for me to learn that, when Dagna stepped on the back of one of my cotton dresses, held me in place, and jabbed her knife into the back of my arm. We were six.

This dress had the chance of killing me even without Dagna in the area. It was a cage made of velvet, incredibly heavy and stiff. If I fell over the side of the ship, I would drown. But if I refused to wear the dress, I would never hear the end of it. Flavian would annoy me to the point where I had no choice but to stab him, and then I would never reach Fortis.

Begrudgingly, I held up the heavy skirts and trudged my way back to the deck, knocking over a pitcher of water. Flavian was already there, dressed in the red gown with a fresh splash of perfume on his skin and pink circles of rouge on his cheeks. I had not examined myself in a mirror, the only one was in Flavian's rooms, but I did not need a mirror to know that he looked far better in his gown than I did in mine.

"Oh Carina." Flavian placed his hand to his cheek. "I didn't think it was possible to look so glum in such a fine gown, and somehow you've managed it."

"Then perhaps I should take it off." I turned for the stairs.

"No, absolutely not. Not until we have a dance." He plucked a flute from one of the crates and tossed it to Mateo, who didn't get his hands up quickly enough to catch it, and so the flute skittered across the deck. Nik recovered it and placed it in Mateo's hands.

He flipped it a few times in his thin fingers before drawing it to his lips. How he intended to play it in his current state, I had no idea. But then low, even tones poured from the end of it followed by the brisk twitter of more high-pitched notes. He was as gifted with it as some of the *skalds*. I didn't even know he could play.

"Here we go." Flavian grasped my hand. The heavy skirts tangled around my legs while Flavian pulled me to the center of the deck, away from the gaping hole. I looked to Nik for help, and he clapped his hands to the beat of the music and smiled as if to say, "You did this to yourself."

Flavian curled his fingers around mine, and I placed my steel hand on his shoulder, prodding a claw into his back.

"Carina, I am not a pin cushion."

"You could be," I said, and he laughed.

He wouldn't be laughing when I truly did make him a pin cushion.

"Just this one dance," he pleaded, "and then you can take off the gown. I'll even help you if you like." His smile widened.

"No, I do not like," I said. "One dance then."

I'd noticed the longer I refused or ignored him, the more persistent he became. As he spun me, I imagined all of the gifts the consul's house would hold when I sent Flavian to Hel, how Merle and the others would applaud me when I returned with things they could only dream of taking. This dance was a slash to the ribs. It would leave a mark, but it wouldn't kill me.

"Wonderful." He tightened his hand on my waist and spun me around the deck. The stars overhead turned to streaks of light, and our two dresses together made a crinkling sound.

"This is ridiculous," I said. "Do you really enjoy wearing that dress?"

"It's not so bad."

He spun me out to the length of his arm and pulled me back. I slammed into his chest and he placed his hand on my lower back. "I'll admit. It's a bit heavy. My sister's dresses are much lighter and airier."

"So this is not the first time you've danced in skirts?"

"No." He spun me again and twirled me back. "For someone who spends her days in tunics and armor, it shouldn't be a sin for a man to wear velvet."

"It's not," I said. "It's your god who is so concerned about behavior. I couldn't care less."

"Then why do you look so sour?"

"Because I'm wearing a dress, being forced to dance."

"Is it really that terrible?" He spun me again, and before I reached the end of his arm, he caught me by the waist and tipped me backwards. I took a moment, inhaled the salt air, the sounds of Mateo and his flute, the blur of stars in the clear sky, and no, it was not that terrible.

In a strange way, we were celebrating the spoils of victory like we had on Helvar. Except here, I didn't have to hide from Merle's judgmental gaze, or Von's unwanted advances, or Dagna's attempts to kill me.

Oddly enough, in this motley crew of the map maker, the orphan sailor, and the beautiful son of the consul, I felt less anxious than normal. I was a wolf among sheep instead of a dog amongst wolves, and the sheep were somewhat entertaining. For the moment.

"Play something faster," Flavian called, and with a whistle, the music stopped.

Mateo pulled the flute from his lips and bent over his knees, gasping. Flavian dropped my hand, picked up his skirts, and rushed to Mateo's side.

"Are you feeling alright, Mat?" Flavian pressed his hand to Mateo's cheek.

"Just tired," he said. "Sorry to ruin the dance. I should get some rest."

"You didn't ruin anything." Flavian put his arm around Mateo and helped him to his feet. Nik took the other side. While they carried him downstairs, I rubbed my metal claws together.

I did not question Her. The Goddess had Her reasons for taking souls, and for leaving them. But it felt…unnecessary to make Mateo suffer so much for so long.

I took a breath and the dress closed around my ribs. I couldn't breathe. With my claws, I slashed it open and inhaled deeply once the heavy folds of velvet fell from my body. I picked up the wads of fabric, dropped them over the side of the ship, and watched fifty coins worth of velvet sink into the black water. Dressed only in my boots and undergarments, I went back downstairs for my tunic and leggings. I paused just outside the door to the main cabin.

"I'm fine," Mateo said. "Just tired. You don't have to look after me."

Even his argument sounded exhausted.

I continued past them into the smaller bunk room where I redressed. As I slid my tunic over my head, the rune stone dropped to the floor. I reached for it, a hitch running though me when I brushed the side. I caught a flash of the priestess, standing in the corner of the room. I gasped, and ran my thumb over the stone again, watching the same corner. It remained empty as it should.

This ridiculous stone. If this was it working, it was as unpredictable as Egil One Eye with a crossbow.

"Are you here?" I whispered and waited for an answer, another vision. Nothing.

I dropped the stone in my pocket and tied my hair into a braid. I couldn't sleep, not after sleeping all day, and I couldn't stay in this room waiting for ghosts to appear or not appear.

I made my way to the deck for some air, and Nik was there, sealing up the Perditian crates.

"It looks like we'll be getting some rain." Nik nodded to the haze of gray clouds moving across the yellow moon. "Not a storm. Just some rain."

"I know what storm clouds look like." I picked up the dropped flute and pressed my fingers over the carved holes. "When did Mateo learn to play?"

"Nyssa taught him." Nik closed the lid on another crate. "She has a gift with music. A lute-player. She's played for the Emperor himself."

I set the flute down. "Is there nothing this woman can't do?"

"Fight," he said and nodded to me. "I'm glad to see you back in your regular clothes. You looked like a trussed up doll in that dress."

I smiled. I appreciated that he appreciated me as I was meant to be. "Tell that to Flavian."

"I have. You know he only plays these games with you because you get so aggravated. If you ignore him, he'll get bored and stop." He went to close the last crate and reached inside first, removing a ceramic jug. He pulled the cork from it, inhaled the contents, and curled his lip upward. "Perditian wine." He took a swig. "It's sweet. Do you want to try?"

I crossed the deck and took the jug from him, our fingers grazing in the pass. I tilted the jug back, let the wine run across my teeth, and almost gagged on the sweetness.

I handed it back to him. "I thought you were against taking the Perditians' things."

He replaced the cork and tucked the wine back into the crate, sealing it shut to defend against the rain. "Last night, with the Perditians..." he sighed. "I hadn't been around that much violence since my days with...as property of the Aldam. That was what they would do. Take what they want and kill someone to get it. I didn't want to be that person. But now I see that things are much grayer than I thought."

"Grayer?"

"Complex," he said as a breeze blew off the water and pulled a dark hair loose from the tie that held it behind his neck. "If you hadn't taught Mateo how to defend himself, he wouldn't be here right now. We've been holding him back...Flavian, Nyssa and me. You're the only one who cleared the way."

"Too bad it wasn't enough," I said, and I truly was sorry. No one had ever said, even when Death comes for Her due, we couldn't feel badly about it.

"Mateo will pull through," Nik said. "He always does."

I didn't say anything. Even if Mateo beat the plague, he wouldn't be able to beat me, the Hand of Death.

Another gust of wind rolled off the water and pulled one of the mast ropes free. We both dove to catch it, nearly crashing into one another. I stopped myself and let Nik wind the rope back into place. The sails were down. Everything of value had been stowed. We were as prepped for the rain as we could be.

"Who do you sail for in Fortis?" I asked.

"Captain Giannes of the Wren. Or at least I did. I'll see if I still have a job when I get back. We've been gone about three months now. We snuck off in the night. Nyssa and Flavian's sister, Helene, were the only two people who knew where we were going. Helene wasn't supposed to tell anyone until we were a few days away. That is why Mateo isn't taking us along the standard routes. We're worried the consul might send a ship after us."

"It would have served you better to bring a stronger crew."

He shook his head. "We couldn't ask anyone to go with us into Helvar. The three of us are the only three who care about Nyssa enough to do it."

Cared enough? Or were foolish enough? "If you hadn't found Dagna," I said, "you wouldn't have been able to get within sight the island without being speared and sunk into the sea."

"Then I guess it's good for us that you tend to make enemies." He smiled.

I did not. It wasn't my fault that Dagna hated me. "I'm about to make another one."

Nik put his hand on my wrist. "It was a joke, Carina."

I pulled away from him. "You should work on your delivery. It's impossible to tell what should be funny and what is annoying prattle."

"You need to stop being so defensive." His fingers flew toward me and snatched a piece of hair that the wind pulled from my braid. He twisted it in his fingers, examining it. "I used to think you were nothing more than a heartless killer, like Javad. Now I see you're human, just like the rest of us. Scared and confused." He tucked the hair behind my ear, and his fingers stayed there, lingering on my skin.

My heart stopped beating. An itch crawled under my skin, different from the feeling I had next to Von. The same in that I felt like something might happen, like Nik might close this distance between us, and different because I wasn't sure I would push him away.

Nik wasn't handsome like Von, or charming like Flavian. He wore a salt and sweat stained tunic, and had a crooked, hooked nose, and the most captivating stare.

But he was a sheep. One I would have to slaughter soon. He dropped his hand and turned away from me, and I let out a long slow breath, only now aware that I had been digging my claws into my leg. I was relieved, of course. What right did he have to try and kiss me anyway? I was sure, if he had, I would have stabbed him in the stomach and then I would have had to kill Flavian and Mateo immediately after and all hopes of taking Fortis would be gone.

He was lucky he came to his senses first. The senses that reminded him I wasn't worth kissing. That he despised me.

But, of course, the precious Nyssa was worth sailing into Helvar and back. No one despised her.

Hel's fire, I hated that woman. I hated this ship. I hated these infernal boys.

"I'm going to bed," I said.

The first sprinkles of rain splattered from the sky as I made my way down. I laid down on the bunk. The room was empty. Nik stayed on deck in the rain, and Flavian must have been with Mateo.

I dropped my arm over my eyes and saw Nik's dark eyes moving closer to mine. His long hair whipping in the wind. With my mind so ravaged like this, I was going to lose my patience and slaughter them all before their time.

Something banged on the wall. I sat upright and there stood Flavian, cheeks flushed, mouth drawn. What now?

"It's Mateo," he said. "Hurry."

My stomach dropped.

CHAPTER 15

✖

heat radiated from Mateo's skin. His face burned crimson, dotted with sweat, and when we peeled away the bandage from his leg, an angry, purple welt appeared. His shriveled leg swelled to twice its normal size, so much that the scraps of flesh I had sewn together pulled at the seams. He did not open his eyes. His chest barely rose and fell with breath.

Why hadn't he said something?

Why hadn't I cleaned the wound better?

"We need to get him to a doctor," Nik said. "We're only a few days out from Ignus. I'll change course and head east."

Ignus. My lip curled at the mention of the island. It was a religious sanctuary for those devout to the one god. Inhabited by pious priests and priestesses who dedicated themselves to the healing arts. It probably held riches even I couldn't imagine because Hel's Daughters did not go there. In addition to making potions and cures, the Ignusian priests had also stumbled across a rare poison—Ignusian Fire. If a drop of it touched your skin, your flesh would burn away in minutes. It was a deadly enough compound to scare even Death's Daughters away from the isle.

"He won't make it," I said. With a fever like this, for someone like Mateo, three days was a lifetime. It would be more of a mercy to kill him than let him suffer.

"We're going to try," Nik said. "We'll sail through the night, take shifts on deck, sleeping, and looking after Mateo."

"I slept most of the day. I'll stay with Mateo," I offered.

Nik hesitated. "No, I'll stay with Mateo. Flavian, you rest, Carina, you take the helm. And I'll know if you change direction."

Even after almost-kissing me, he didn't trust me with Mateo. Or the ship. He wasn't wrong, either. I *did* want to put Mateo out of his misery and avoid Ignus. But to get to Fortis and my ultimate prize, I had to play their game. Like Flavian said, "Let them think they're winning."

I climbed to the deck, already slick with rain while more poured down from the swath of gray clouds overhead. I winched the sail and changed direction, heading east, toward Ignus. The stone in my pocket pulsed, as if it were laughing at me, as if the priestess found it hilarious that after raiding her church, I was now off to beg for help from another church.

I stayed on deck until the morning, keeping the ship pointed toward the rising sun. At least the sea giant granted us smooth waters, despite the rain. The sun broke the clouds when Nik came to relieve me.

"Go rest now." He slid his hands to the wheel.

"I'm not tired yet," I said. "I can sit with Mateo."

"Flavian's with him. You know I need you on the deck as much as possible. We can't give Flavian control of the ship for long. Go get some sleep." He gave me that captivating, dark glance, and my cheeks burned. I backed away.

On my way to the bunkroom, I stopped at the cabin doors and leaned my ear to the wood. I heard Flavian reading to Mateo. Through the thin crack between the doors, I saw Mateo laid on the bed, sinking into the sheets. I couldn't tell if his eyes were open. I couldn't see his chest rising with breath, but I heard the soft wheeze. He clung to whatever scraps of life his body had left.

Mateo was a fighter. He managed to stay one step ahead of Hel all this time, and it had been my stone and my poor stitching that put this added burden on him. Would this count as taking his life if he died as a result of my mistakes? And what if he lived? What if the Ignusian priests could heal him? He would have a few more weeks at most before I killed him with my sword. If I could do it now, I would be giving him long-deserved mercy.

Flavian dropped the book suddenly and bent over Mateo's form. The consul's son broke into high-pitched whining sobs.

"You can't leave me like this. I'm positively useless without you, Mat. Hold on, old friend. Promise me, you'll hold on."

A knot formed in my throat. I retreated from the door.

I went to my bunk and tried to snatch at sleep. The priestess appeared twice in my nightmares, spewing insects and terror in my dreams. I gave up on sleep after a few hours and crawled out of bed in search of something useful to do: either to help Nik at the helm or put cool cloths on Mateo's forehead with Flavian. I went to the cabin first and pushed open the door. Mateo was alone, the chair beside him empty.

No hens hovered over him now. This could be my chance.

Cautiously, I stepped inside. I approached Mateo, wrinkling my nose. The smell of rot and infection and death hung here like a thick fog. The sheet draped over Mateo's chest was soaked through with sweat, clinging to his ribs. I didn't hear the wheeze. If he passed on his own, I had no need to be here. He would be in Hel's arms now.

Then he took a slow, stunted breath. I sighed, both relieved and disappointed. I did like Mateo. He had admirable qualities. He was an excellent navigator, and he had a strong will. But like and dislike didn't matter in the eyes of the Goddess. Death was indiscriminate.

Except when it comes to Brezadine, I thought, sick with myself for thinking it.

I picked up the discarded book from the floor and smoothed the pages.

"Read," Mateo said in a thin whisper.

I jumped. A second ago I thought he was dead. Now he was talking.

I squinted at the pages of the book. The black lines on it blurred together. "I can't read it," I said.

"Then tell me one of you stories," he said. "A nice one."

"Alright." I sat down in the empty chair. I thought back to all the songs and stories the *skalds* told. Most of them ended with a severed head or a river of blood. I didn't think that was the kind of "nice" Mateo meant. Victorious. But there was one that he might like. Merle told it to me when I'd been a child.

"There was a man named Baldur," I began as she had. "He came from Hebrides, and he was somewhat like Flavian: joyful, generous, and he loved dancing. Everyone in his village adored him." I paused. "And then he died." I omitted that he had been killed during a raid, an offering to Hel. "It was a very painless, swift death," I said instead. "And he found himself in Niflheim, greeted by the Goddess Hel.

"Like everyone else, She was struck by his good looks and charisma and took him on as a lover. 'I will name you my prince of Niflheim,' She said to him. 'Together we shall rule the underworld for all eternity.' Baldur accepted Her offer, slept in Her bed each night, but as the days passed, he became more and more despondent.

"Hel finally asked him what was wrong, and he admitted he loved someone else, a girl from his village named Ulla. Hel turned angry, removed him from her palace, and sent him to the mines to slave with the other tortured souls as punishment for preferring a human girl over her. But She missed Baldur, and his good nature, and his smile and songs, and knew there was only one way She could return the joy.

"Late in the night, She crept up to the mortal realm and back to the village of Hebrides. There She found the girl Ulla, as beautiful and sweet as Baldur had described. Hel raised Her dagger, cut it deep into the girl's heart, and when her spirit climbed from her lifeless body, Hel took her hand.

"'Come with me,' Hel said. 'Someone is waiting for you.' Hel delivered Ulla to the underworld where she was reunited with Baldur. The two lost souls embraced, and Baldur's cheer returned. The vast caves of Niflheim filled with Baldur's song, and Hel returned to Her castle alone, vowing never to love again."

I sighed, feeling the ache in my chest that I had felt as a child. Baldur should have chosen Hel. He was wrong to pick the human girl over the Goddess.

"That is an awful story," Mateo said.

"Why?" Did he feel sorry for Hel too?

"She killed the girl. Why not bring Baldur back?"

"Because you can't come back from Death," I said, feeling another tug from my stone. "It's impossible. The only way to reunite Baldor with his love was to bring her to Niflheim. The Goddess did him a great favor at the cost of Her own happiness. The point of the story is to show how selfless Hel is. Can't you see that?"

"No." He tangled his fingers in the sheet. "I'm scared," he whispered. "Of dying."

He released the sheet and reached for me, a hand to hold. I didn't know what to do. His hand lingered there, so I pressed my palm to his. "You don't have to be afraid," I said. "You've lived a good life. Hel won't send you to the mines. Your soul will glide gently down on Baldur's music."

"Perhaps Mother will be there too," he said, and a thin smile touched his lips.

"Perhaps," I said, not knowing if he meant his true mother or Nyssa, the dying saint. It had to be Nyssa. He had never spoken of his true mother.

"I think I'm ready to die then," he whispered. "It won't hurt?"

I swallowed. Was he asking me what I thought he was asking? "You're ready to go now?"

His chin tipped in a gentle nod. "I am so tired of being tired." As a show of his failing health, he broke into a gasping cough. "Please," he managed to sputter out. "I beg of you." His eyes opened a sliver, enough to make contact with mine, enough to know he was serious.

I stood up and leaned over him, his sunken cheeks and yellowed skin. I made a promise not to harm him, not until Fortis, but this was not a harm. This would be a service.

He continued coughing, and I removed the sweat-soaked pillow from behind his head. If I used my sword, Nik and Flavian would know I was responsible. This way, they would think he had passed on his own. We could change course back to Fortis.

The coughing subsided. He closed his eyes and went still. Tears burned behind my eyes for no reason. This was a mercy killing. The absolute best I could offer him. I held the pillow over his face and tried not to think of Flavian breaking into sobs earlier in the night. *"You can't leave me like this."* This would be a kindness, like Hel taking Ulla for Baldur.

I lowered the pillow onto his face and pressed down. I looked away. Mateo didn't even struggle. I had to do this. If I couldn't put a sick boy out of misery, I could never call myself one of Hel's Daughters.

The door burst open.

"God, Carina, No!"

Nik dropped the bucket of water in his hand, and it tipped across the floor, soaking into the wool rug. I released the pillow. Nik lunged for me, catching my middle. We both fell over the chair and rolled to the wet rug. He pinned me, arms and legs stuck to the floor.

I was glad he had. I was so glad he stopped me.

"What are you doing?" He spit in my face.

"He asked me to," I gasped. "He is in so much pain."

"He's delirious from fever! God, I thought you had changed. I thought you liked him."

"I do," I said. "Enough that I don't want him to suffer."

"You don't even know him," he shouted. "This is *his* life. Not yours. You have no right to it."

"It's not yours either," I argued. Mateo was so sick, he sat at the edge of Hel's fingertips. He only need a gentle push to reach her.

"I promised Nyssa," he said.

"Nyssa," I spat, always the wonderful, perfect Nyssa, controlling them like puppets even from a thousand leagues away. "Nyssa isn't here," I said. "You don't owe her any promises."

"I do! I promised her before I left, I would keep him safe. I promised I would bring back her son."

"You mean daughter." I shook my head. "You came for me."

He didn't retract his statement, and I suddenly realized that he had not made the mistake. I had.

I wriggled free of his grasp and kicked him off my legs. "No," I said. "There was only me. That awful man only had me with him when the Daughters raided."

They all told me the tale, Merle, Odda and Thora, about the coward who would have killed his own child to save his life. They never mentioned another.

"Because Mateo had the plague," Nik said. "Nyssa took him to Fortis for medicine and left you behind because she didn't want you to get sick too. The Daughters raided a day after she left. She didn't get the news until much later, when a ship made it to Fortis. By then, she knew you were long gone, and Mateo was too sick to leave behind."

This was the reason she left me—for Mateo.

"She took a position as a governess for Flavian and his sister," Nik said. "She had nothing left on Orsalia." He flicked his eyes to the limp figure on the bed. "She has so many regrets. She wishes she had taken you too, or that she never left. God, Carina, why can't you see that other people love you."

A thousand emotions swirled through me. It was like trying to catch a fish with bare hands to settle on just one: disgust, fear, sadness, joy…they all wriggled by me. I had a brother. It was hard to see on the surface. The plague stole so much from him, but in my mind, the image of the Mateo who had not been desiccated by illness, had my dark eyes and hair, my infrequent smile, and the same sharp, nose.

We were the same, only divided by chance. The line between Mateo and me was one sickness.

"We're too close in age," I said, searching for excuses. "He can't be more than a few months younger…or older than I am."

"He's a year older." Nik rubbed the back of his neck.

Not only did we share blood. Mateo claimed another year over me. Like Dagna.

"Why didn't he tell me? Because he was ashamed," I answered my own question and looked to him, lying motionless on the bed. I wondered if he was listening, forming judgments as he had when I told him about Baldur. Or if he had slipped into unconsciousness.

"He thought you would be ashamed too," Nik said.

Was I? Yes. But perhaps not for the reasons I should have been. I was ashamed for being ashamed. None of this was Mateo's fault. He wasn't the one who left me. He wasn't the one who offered me for sacrifice. He was a victim too.

"Please," Nik said. "Two more days. Let us get to Ignus and see what they can do for him. If he can't be cured. If he still wants…you can do it." He nodded to my sword.

Nik was giving me permission to kill Mateo. But could I now? Knowing who he was?

We were not supposed to pick and choose victims. We killed at random. But the Daughters of Hel always looked after their own, and Mateo was now mine, by blood, by battle. I could not, would not kill him. It was in the Goddess's power now. She would choose when Mateo left this world for Hers. I would never lay a hand or blade to him.

"You have my word," I said. "I will help you reach Ignus. I will help you save him."

He held my gaze for a long moment before nodding.

"Nik!" Flavian burst into the cabin. "Dear God, what happened?"

Nik and I both turned to him, silent.

"You told her," Flavian said.

Nik slowly stood up. "She had a right to know." He held out his hand to me, mentioning nothing about how he caught me with a pillow pressed to Mateo's face.

I brushed off my knees, ignored his hand, and stood on my own, pushing stray hairs back into my braid.

"What do you need, Flavian?" Nik asked.

"Someone to control the ship," he said. "I have no idea what I'm doing up there."

"I'll be right there."

"What about Mat?" Flavian asked.

"Carina can sit with him," he said, driving that hard gaze into me.

"Come on. We have to find a strong wind. Mateo's turned worse." He clapped his hand on Flavian's shoulder and led him out of the room, leaving me alone with Mateo.

I watched him in his sweat-soaked sheets, barely breathing, and searched his face for hints of mine. On Helvar, I had always wanted there to be someone like me, someone of my blood. Now I had that someone. He wasn't what I expected, but he was mine whether I liked it or not.

I only wondered how long I would have him as each breath struggled from his chest. When Hel decided to take him, he would no longer be mine, he would be Hers.

I sat down beside him and cleared my throat.

"I have another story you might like. No one dies in this one. Let me tell you the tale of Erik, the Whale Rider."

"Deliver us God, from the savage race of women who lays waste our realms."

Father Cristos

CHAPTER 16

✗

The island of Ignus rose up out of the water, a rocky beach that climbed up a grassy hill to a stone structure stretching high in the clouds. It was clearly pretending to be something else if we were all being honest with ourselves. It was an eyesore, an impractical tower that had been built in a sad attempt to get closer to the one god, who apparently watched everyone from some pious perch in the clouds.

The men and women of this church called the people of Helvar savages, monsters. They would not be pleased to see me on their shore. I worried they would douse me in the Ignusian Fire and cackle as the skin peeled from my bones.

I pulled one of the Perditian cloaks from our spoils and yanked it over my head. I buried my face under the mantle of fox fur, and tucked my steel hand into the sleeve in an attempt to hide myself.

"Carina," Nik called. "Drop the mainsail. Ready the anchor."

I moved to loosen the ropes for the sail. My back ached from sleeping in the chair next to Mateo's bed. The thing had to be made of stone and padded with needles. Between that, and the heat roiling off of Mateo's burning skin, I caught snatches of sleep here and there, during which I had nightmares of the rotting priestess. It had been a troublesome few days.

Mateo managed to survive, one night at a time. From here, that was all I could see for him--one more night. That was Mateo's life, broken down into breaths, days, hours. Whatever the Goddess chose to give him.

Nik jumped down from the wheel and ran for the anchor. I was still tangled in the sails, lost in my own thoughts. He released the anchor, letting the rope pull through his fingers to keep it from unreeling too fast. Our anchor caught on a rock, and we sidled up to the pier beside another cog ship much like this one with a white flag and blue lines on it, the mark for Ignus.

Before we could lower the gangplank, a line of white-robed figures streamed from the tower. One of them carried a flag bearing the image of their God on the front of it. He wore a sour expression and a gold crown. He didn't look so wonderful to me. Just a man with a frown.

I hid in the folds of my cloak as if the priests would know me by my face. I looked more like one of the Southern residents than the hands of Death from the North, but I was worried they would see something in my eyes—how much I despised being here.

The entourage stopped at the end of the docks, and the one in the lead cupped his hands around his mouth and called to us. "What brings you to Ignus?"

He was sweating from the short walk from the tower to the pier. Long stringy hair hung around his ears and a patchy beard covered his chin. It was as if he tried to make himself look like their one god. He was hardly someone to fear except for the small vial he wore around his neck. They all wore them. That had to be the Fire. My skin itched as if the poison already burned through my arms.

Nik took to the bow and called down to the priest. "We had a skirmish at sea. One of our crew was injured and has taken ill. We need help."

"This is one of the consul's ships of Fortis. Is it not?" the priest asked.

"Yes," Nik said. "His son is aboard."

"Well then. Let us see about this boy."

The priest waved two others up the gangplank, younger priests. I wondered if they would have been so apt to help if Flavian had not been with us. The Southern Emperor gave great deals of money to the island of Ignus. Flavian's father had probably delivered the coin himself, and in exchange, Ignus had given the Emperor their Ignusian Fire. The Emperor had used it in his conquering of the Eastern lands. These priests judged Helvar for worshipping Death while committing greater sins for the price of silver.

The two young priests climbed onto the deck. I leaned against the rails and hid under my hood, trying to disappear into the background like another crate or net. I refused to be burned with poison, not when I was this close to Fortis and my prize.

Nik showed them below decks, to Mateo. I scraped my metal fingers together impatiently and then stopped. One of them could have heard it. I clasped my fingers on my elbows and heard Flavian.

"A little to the left. No, right. Mind the hole in the deck."

He and Nik and the two priests carried Mateo up the stairs in a cocoon of sheets.

"Is it contagious?" the elder priest called.

"No," one of the younger priests called back. "It's an infection, a strong one. We may need to remove the rot."

I sucked air through my teeth. No. No, that was not what we had come for. We came for life or Death, yes or no, not more agony.

"No," I shouted against my own will. My voice had become a thing of its own.

"Who is she?" The priest said "she," as if it were an insult, and all he knew about me so far was that I was a woman.

He would find out exactly what kind of woman I was. *Carina the Unstoppable.* I charged down after Mateo and stood right in front of the man. "You will not take his leg," I said.

He laughed. "I thought you came to us for help. And now you're the doctor?"

My steel fingers twitched inside the cloak. One swat across his cheek would wipe the smile right off his face.

"What is your name, Little Mouse?" he asked.

"Carina." I bit back the Unstoppable, keeping my hand clenched inside my robes to stop myself from tearing out his tongue for calling me Little Mouse. Of all the priests and priestesses here, he wore the largest vial around his neck.

"Who are you to go cutting off young men's legs?" I asked.

"Father Augustus," he said. "And what would you have me do, let him die?"

Yes, I thought. Yes. I would rather see him die than watch him be hacked away bit by bit. But I couldn't bring myself to say it. "I would have you use your medicine to cure his fever before you go cutting him to pieces."

The priest frowned. He looked like a piece of leather left in the sun too long, hardened and wrinkled.

Something touched my shoulder. I spun around, tense, ready to draw my sword until I found Flavian next me. "Mateo is her brother, Father

Augustus. She is quite concerned for his well-being as I am sure you can imagine."

"Yes, I can understand…"

"Flavian Katrakis, at your service." Flavian folded into a flourished bow.

"Ah," the priest brightened. "Your father is the consul."

"Yes." Flavian winked at me, as if to say, do you see how simple things are, Carina, when you play nice? I supposed they were, as long as you had a wealthy, powerful father to call upon. "We would like the best care for my friend, Mateo. He is like a brother to me."

"Of course," the priest said. "See," he turned to me, "you have no need to worry, Little Mouse. Your brother is in good hands."

Little Mouse. Little Mouse. The words cut at my ears. Worse than Little Girl, he reduced me all the way to vermin, something that could have been quashed between the crooked toes peering from the ends of his sandals. We would see about that.

"I am not a little mouse!"

I pushed a tight, steel fist into the center of his stomach. He exhaled in a gasp and tumbled backward, and I joyfully watched as horror filled his wrinkled eyes. "I am Carina, the Unstoppable." I pulled my sword and pointed it to the end of his nose. He reached for the vial on his neck, and I slapped his knuckles with the flat side of my blade. The vial dropped from his hand, and I felt such a strong surge of satisfaction, it left a sweetness on my tongue.

"What is this?" he asked. "Why did you bring this abomination here? Go. Leave this isle and never return."

Beside me, Flavian sighed, and the hold on my sword faltered. What had I done? I had promised to help Mateo reach Ignus. I had promised to let Hel decide his fate, and now I may have clinched it. Had that been worth my pride? Another look at the horrible priest sprawled on the ground, and I couldn't decide.

"Carina has, ah, left her order," Flavian stumbled for excuses. He truly was a master negotiator, a clever player. "She has been our protection on this journey." He reached a hand out to help the priest from the ground and dusted the grass from the back of his robes. "Quite temperamental, of course," Flavian said. "We're continually working with her. Sadly, it's been a slow journey. Like training a wild dog. Please accept my apologies."

The priest cleared his throat. "Well, I suppose, seeing as how close your father is with the Emperor..."

"The best of friends," Flavian said. "In fact, we've been discussing funding more of your work here. I would love to talk to you about it...while your staff tends to Mateo, of course."

The priest clutched his vial in his fist. "I suppose we could do that. But we can't have her on the island. This is a holy place, and she'll taint it with her...her..."

Skill? I ached to say, and this time bit my tongue. I had made my point, Flavian had corrected it, and I would always have the memory of watching the priest roll to the ground like a cockroach on its backside.

"Exactly." Flavian put his arm around Augustus. "She will stay on the ship, and I promise, will be of no more trouble to us."

He gave me a look that suggested I would pay for this later, for him having to rub his nose in the back end of the Father's robes. He and the priests carried Mateo in his sheet cocoon up the hill and through a set of heavy wooden doors. When they closed behind them, I realized that anything could happen inside that tower, and I had been relinquished to the outside. Away from Mateo.

Nik stayed behind to secure the ship. Without looking, I could feel his gaze boring into my shoulders.

"I thought we decided—"

"I know," I said. Before we landed, we had all discussed how I would keep myself hidden.

"I'll grant you, he was rude and arrogant," Nik said.

"Not just rude." I spun around. "I did not train for nine years to be called Little Mouse."

Nik crossed his arms over his chest. "Why do you care what he says?"

Because I always have to fight, I thought. If Dagna missed a strike, someone clapped her on the shoulder, gave her another sword and told her, "You'll get it next time." If I missed the same strike, I was met with a dozen shaking heads. "This is why we don't let Southerners fight for the Daughters," they would whisper.

All of the other girls in training only had to focus on their sword play and archery, but I'd had two tasks to complete. I'd had to constantly prove to them that Merle had not made a mistake in keeping me. I was not my cowardly father. I fought to keep up with Dagna and her infallible tenacity, her long legs, and even longer, sword-reaching arms. Even after earning these claws, I had to work to show I deserved to keep them, and that foul, pinch-faced priest stole that all away with two words.

Little Mouse.

But I didn't say that to Nik.

"I don't want them to take Mateo's leg," I said instead and climbed the gangplank.

"Why not?" Nik followed me.

"You have to be joking." I stepped onto the warm deck and checked the ropes to make sure they were secure. We had different beliefs, yes, but I thought we could both agree that chopping off Mateo's leg was a bad idea.

"No, I'm not." Nik tugged on the rope I had just checked.

"Then you want Mateo to be short one leg?"

"No," he admitted. "But I want him to have a life. Mateo is not his legs. One leg. No legs. He can look at the stars and the water and the sky and navigate an entire ocean. He knows the history of Fortis back and front. He can recite Vasilios's work by memory. He can play his flute. None of that will change."

"Yes it will," I argued. "I will grant you, Mateo has tenacity in strides, but even tenacity can't make up for the loss of a leg." Nik hadn't seen the Disgraced, the one-handed women on Helvar struggling to balance ale pitchers. He hadn't seen the way the others looked at them. I would not wish that on Mateo.

"Would you rather he die?" Nik shook his head. "No, don't answer that. If Mateo were conscious, he would say the same thing. He would do what's best for his health."

"Are you sure? You don't even know what he wants. You've all fussed over him to the point that I think you actually enjoy holding him back."

"That's not true." He jabbed a finger at me, which told me I had uncovered a sea of truth.

"I would rather have him dead than tormented," I said.

"Of course you would. It always goes back to your goddess. You have been aching to cut Mateo open since we brought you onto this ship. I thought knowing who he was would change things. I hoped it would change things."

"It has," I argued. "I am trying to protect him. That man is going to tear Mateo up, and you are going to let him. You think because the leg is bad, it doesn't matter if you take it. It does."

Nik shook his head. "This has nothing to do with him. It has to do with you. You can't suffer the fact that Mateo is not a warrior. He can't fight like you do. He can't defeat a ship full of pirates, or challenge a man twice his size, and it doesn't matter. Not to him. Not to anyone else. He's happy being who he is, and if he were nothing more than the head on his shoulders, he would be a thousand times more valuable than you are."

His piercing gaze never wavered while he said it, but mine did. I couldn't look at him as the knot swelled in my throat. *Do not cry. Do not cry.* What did it matter what some orphan boy from Brezadine thought? He would be nothing if the glorious Nyssa hadn't dragged him from the gutter. But he was something. And I did care what he thought, and he thought I was nothing more than the sword in my hand. And Hel help me, I couldn't find the words to disagree.

"Stay with the ship," he muttered and stormed down the gangplank.

"Don't let them do it," I managed to choke out. "Please," I added, and noted a hitch in Nik's step before he stomped up the hill toward the tower.

I slumped onto the deck and clasped my knees to my chest. Was Nik right? Was I only trying to save Mateo's leg for myself? I'd been so proud of him when he'd defended himself against the Perditians. Was that the only Mateo I could accept? Would I rather have him dead than alive?

I didn't know. It shouldn't matter. I should sit back and let Hel decide, but I was afraid of what She would choose. I was afraid of what Nik and the priests would choose. I was afraid of what Mateo would choose.

This was why the wolf never spent time with the sheep.

CHAPTER 17

✗

No one returned to the ship for the remainder of the afternoon. I had no news of Mateo until just after dusk when a single figure emerged from the tower. It was Nik. I recognized his long gait, shoulders tight to his neck as if he were waiting for someone to jump out from the shrubs and attack him.

He always looked like that, which would make him harder to kill when the time came. He would be expecting it.

I busied myself re-knotting ropes to make it look as if I had not been waiting for him, festering about Mateo, pining over Nik's last words to me.

"If he were nothing more than the head on his shoulders, he would be a thousand times more valuable than you are."

Dagna used to tell me, "If you were pierced through with this arrow, no one here would weep for you."

If they both thought it was true, was it?

If I were in Mateo's place, I would wish for Death to take me. Because I did not know how to do anything else. I was the one defined by my skill and physical strength—not Mateo. He had strength in drawing, and course charting, astronomy, and music. He had even shown promise in sword play, and he had done it all with a greater disadvantage. Always persisting. If I were ever injured to the point of being incapable of fighting…I didn't know what I would have. Mediocre sewing skill?

Not enough.

Nik climbed up the deck. He stopped and tapped his foot on the new boards I'd hammered into the floor.

"You fixed the hole," he said in the Eastern language. It was what we both automatically fell into when we were alone.

"It was only a matter of time until Flavian tumbled into it," I said.

"Where did you get the wood?"

"Here and there." Mostly from the crate of Flavian's clothes. I had been bored, anxious all day. I'd needed to keep my hands busy, my mind occupied. "How is Mateo?" I asked.

Nik dropped his chin. "Not good. They bled the wound, re-treated it. But the fever isn't subsiding."

"Did they take his leg?" My heart stopped while I waited for an answer.

"No, but we've decided if the fever hasn't broken by morning...it's the only way, Carina."

I nodded. "He still has the night to pull through." I did believe in Mateo. I also believed Death would spare him once more. She was as benevolent as She was vengeful.

"He does," Nik agreed, not sounding as hopeful. "I wanted to apologize for shouting at you earlier." He leaned against the rails beside me. "What you said wasn't completely wrong. Flavian, Nyssa, and I...we've fallen into the habit of making things easier for Mateo. It's hard for us to watch him suffer. If anything, we're as guilty as you are of being selfish. We even tried to talk him out of coming on this trip, but he insisted. We all made a lot of promises that if he did come, we would bring him back. I'm trying to keep those promises."

"I understand."

I knew all too well the burden of promises. Standing here under the moonlight with Nik, I didn't feel the urge to kill him. But I owed the Goddess payment, and I owed Merle so much more.

"Carina." He put his hand on mine, calloused fingers on split knuckles. "I don't want to do it. Tomorrow morning, I am going to have to stand by my friend's bed and watch silently while they saw off his leg."

"Then don't let them do it. Let Death choose."

He shook his head. "I wish I could, but I saw your goddess make the wrong choices over and over again in Brezadine. Good people would suffer. Bad people would thrive. Mahmod and his bloodied hands always took more. It wasn't until I escaped that I saw something else. Mateo and Flavian, they are my family. Nyssa is dying. If Mateo goes...I can't be like that again. I can't be alone." His dark hair fell over his face. When he pushed it back, I saw tears blooming in his eyes.

"I don't want him to die, either," I said, even though it was a horrible thing to say. It was selfish to want to keep someone alive for yourself.

"It will be alright," Nik said and pulled me closer to him. I inhaled his familiar scent of sweat and seawater. He ran his fingers down my cheek and I stared into his dark, haunting eyes.

Then he kissed me, warm and soft. My skin tingled. My heart raced. His tongue brushed against mine I pulled him closer, kissed him harder, tasting the sea on his lips. This was bad, very bad. The wolf especially did not taste the sheep before slaughter, and I couldn't stop myself.

I felt like I had on the eve of my first raid, that adrenaline of the unknown. He was solid under my fingertips, like an island in the middle of a torrential sea.

I reached underneath his tunic and ran my hands across his stomach to explore more of this foreign isle. My hand slipped across his hip to his back and there I found the hills etched into his skin.

Scars. Rows and rows of scars. Whip marks. It reminded me of who we both were and where we stood.

"I can't do this." I pushed him away.

"Does it bother you that I've been beaten?" He wiped his mouth with the back of his hand, like he could erase that kiss.

"No, of course not." If anything, those scars made me admire him more. He fought like I had. He was unstoppable. And the Aldam could all burn in Niflheim for what they had done to him. "But I don't belong here with you. My life, my devotion is in Helvar."

He shook his head and sighed. "You know the Aldam used to tell me that too. 'You have nowhere to go without us. You will starve. You will die.' I believed it for a long time. I probably would have kept believing it if not for that last night."

"What happened?" I asked, cautiously.

He lowered his gaze. "Fahima. Javad forced himself on her. She screamed and clawed at him and he laughed, daring me to stop him. I grabbed a candle and thrust it into his side. His shirt caught fire. He released Fahima, and she ran. But I didn't have that option. Javad grabbed me by the collar and said, 'You stop me from having mine. I will stop you from having yours. I'm going to take what makes you a man.'" He closed his eyes and exhaled. "I left as soon as I could. I knew he would kill me next time."

I wrung my hands together. There was one thing men valued over everything else, and Javad took it from Nik. I wasn't certain that Hel could punish a soul like Javad's enough to pay for what he had done, and the rest of the Aldam were still there, torturing young boys like Nik.

I could do nothing about it. No one could. The Aldam ruled, and Hel's Daughters didn't hunt in Brezadine. It wasn't fair. It wasn't fair that Nik had been tortured, and Mateo was suffering, and I was helpless.

"Say something," Nik said in a cold, quiet voice.

"Why did you tell me all of this?"

"I thought you should know. I was ashamed for a long time, but now I'm not. These scars and marks, all of them, they've made me who I am, and I am at peace with that. But if I had stayed with the Aldam…I would never have peace."

"Helvar is not the same as the Aldam," I said.

"Are you sure?" He grabbed my wrist and ran his thumb along one of my scars.

I snatched my arm back. "I earned that. In battle."

"Most people don't put children in battle."

"That is why most people are weak." I rubbed my arm where he'd touched me.

"What about the girl who sold you to us?" he asked. "Did she care about you?"

"She was one person."

"Is she?"

I thought of everyone else, laughing at Dagna's insults to me, and of Merle's guarded smiles, only revealed when I properly cut or stabbed something. "Why are you trying to turn me against my people?" I snapped.

"Because I like you Carina. Despite your temper, and piss poor attitude, and your attempted murder of one of my best friends, when I see the real girl teaching her brother how to fight, tending his sick bedside and dancing with Flavian in a stupid dress, I like her."

"I don't have a piss poor attitude," I muttered, trying to untangle myself from this emotional web he made of flattery and ire.

"Not all the time," he agreed.

"I have to go home once this is done," I said. "I am a Hand of Death." I held up my metal hand as proof.

"If that's your choice." He tucked his hands into his pockets and headed for the stairs. "I'm going to get some sleep."

I followed him a short time later, once I was sure he would be asleep, and he wasn't. He watched me climb into the neighboring bunk above Mateo's. I pulled the sheet to my chin and stared at the wooden boards over my head.

This was awkward. More awkward than going to sleep in the longhouse after Von's stolen kiss. Because Nik didn't steal his. I gave it to him.

I rubbed my steel claws together and imagined driving them into Nik's throat to silence his life. The thought made my stomach churn. He had already been cut so many times. Was this a test from the Goddess? I was already sparing Mateo's life, could I ignore Nik as well?

The most profitable offering was Flavian. His life I could not forgo, but remembering the story of Baldur and Ulla, I liked to think the Goddess would forgive me for sparing Nik out of affection. I didn't love him. He just didn't annoy me as much as other people.

The breath from Nik's bunk turned soft and smooth. He finally succumbed to sleep. I could not, though. I kept reliving that kiss, and the foul priest carting Mateo away. I thought of him lying in that bed, sick and feverish with only hours to decide his fate.

I needed to see him for myself. I needed to see that taking his leg was the only option.

I slipped out my bunk and silently went to the deck. The ominous stone tower loomed in the darkness. Only a few flickering candles illuminated the stained glass windows. I'd tried to use the spyglass earlier to peer inside. The colored glass acted like a shield against prying eyes. I didn't know where they kept Mateo.

I used the spyglass to survey the grounds. As far as I could tell, only two priests stood in front of the main doors and both looked as if they were on the verge of falling asleep. I didn't see another door, but there was one window slightly ajar, five windows up on the right side of the tower.

It wasn't that high. I could do it. Sneak in, see Mateo, and leave before anyone caught me. Stealth was a strength of the Daughters.

I pulled on my cloak, a crossbow, and a curl of rope. Head low, I crept down the gangplank to the pier and waited there, watching the two priests. My pulse throbbed in my neck. One splash of their poison and I would be reduced to bone. Sneaking into a darkened village had been so much easier with a hundred Sisters at my back.

Keeping low, I hid myself behind a large rock jutting from the ground. From here to the tower, there was nothing but ankle high grass. I would be fully exposed. I closed my eyes and took a breath.

You are a Daughter of Hel. You will not hide from priests.

I flung my eyes open and made the run as low and fast as possible.

When I reached the stone wall of the tower, I pressed against it and waited for the shouts and screams that never came. I stayed another few minutes before moving again, then I pulled the crossbow from my back.

I tied the rope tight to one of the bolts and took a few steps into the open to get my aim. I rested the crossbow on my shoulder and squinted at the open window. My goal was to hit the wood frame surrounding the window. I pulled the trigger and held my breath. The crossbow made a snapping sound that echoed in the still night. The bolt soared with the rope trailing out behind it and stuck in a crack a few stones shy of the window.

The added weight of the rope ruined my shot. Everyone on Helvar would be laughing if they saw that. It was a novice mistake. I tugged on the rope to pull it free for another strike and found it was stuck, lodged deep into the crack. This might not be so terrible after all.

With both hands, I held the rope and let myself dangle there for a few breaths. The rope did not come loose. I braced myself against the wall and pulled myself upward, hand over hand. If I fell now, I would be alright. Then I passed that point of safety, to the place where I would surely break something if I fell, and I kept climbing.

I focused solely on the window ledge above. Even when I reached the bolt, I would have to climb a little further on the stones. I pushed myself up on a stone that protruded from the wall, and the bolt pulled free.

I jabbed my steel fingers into another stone crevice as the rope fell to the grass far below. I wedged one foot and one hand in the wall. I pressed my cheek to the cool stones and took a moment to compose myself.

It wasn't that far to the window. As soon as I could sink my claws into the soft wood of the frame, I would be safe.

With my other foot, I scrambled for another foothold and caught on the edge of a stone. I pushed and pulled with my steel hand, reaching up. My muscles burned. I needed another foothold and found it. The window frame was almost there, almost there. My sweat-soaked hand of flesh slipped, and I reached with everything I had to get my steel claws into the wood. They bit into it, and I hung there, drawing on reserves of strength.

I would not die in a heap outside of this church.

Swinging myself to the left, I got up enough momentum to grip the other end of the windowsill, and I hauled myself upward. I sat on the edge of the window, fighting to catch my breath. My arms ached from the climb, and…Hel's fire, one of my claws was bent.

Slowly, I nudged the window open wider. It led to a bedroom, small and simple with only a dresser, a picture of their frowning god on the wall, and single bed with a small figure curled in the blankets. I slipped inside and tiptoed past the bed to the door. The sleeping figure didn't stir.

I nudged open the door and peered into the hall. A torch burned on a sconce. The hallway went around the building in an arc like the tower, which would make it hard to see if someone approached or not. I also didn't know where they kept Mateo. Was he up or down from here? I should have asked Nik, but if I had asked him, he would have told me not to come.

I was on my own. I gripped the hilt of my sword and pushed the door open wide.

"Stop," a voice whispered behind me. I paused, slowly turning my head over my shoulder where I found a girl sitting upright in bed.

CHAPTER 18

✕

I didn't move. If the girl had the Ignusian Fire with her, it would be easy enough for her to spray it across my back and burn the flesh from my shoulders. My crossbow was unloaded. I would have to reach her with my sword and either hope she had clumsy aim or I stabbed her first. Before I could make a decision, she spoke again.

"You're here for the boy, aren't you?" she whispered.

I swallowed. "Yes."

"Do you mean to hurt him?"

"No. I just want to see him. He's my…my brother." That word had been harder to say than I thought it would. It stuck to my teeth like honey.

"Well you can't go out there like that. Sister Eugenia is working the clinic floor. She will douse you with poison if she catches you."

I turned to face the girl. I would leap from this window before allowing someone named "Sister Eugenia," to get the best of me.

"Wait here." The girl kicked back her blankets, and I bared my claws. She held up both hands. "I don't have anything," she said, lip quivering. She couldn't be more than thirteen, small and meek, barely over the crest of being a child. "I'm going to give you one of my robes. You can wear it to reach your brother. I'm just going to the wardrobe." She placed her foot on the floor, and I let her, keeping my claws raised.

"Why would you help me?" I asked.

"Our God teaches us forgiveness and to help those in need. You seem as if you are in need."

I raised an eyebrow. I wasn't sure she and the other priest worshipped the same god. Father Augustus hadn't been very forgiving or helpful, at least not until Flavian waved the promise of coins under his nose.

"How long have you been a priestess?" I asked.

"Three months," she said and reached for her wardrobe. I placed my other hand on my sword, in case this was all a ruse to get her stash of poison. When she wrenched open the door, five white robes appeared and nothing more.

"It will probably be a little small for you." She took one robe from the hanger. "But better than going on as you are." She held the robe out to me, and I snatched it from her fingers. I swallowed when I touched it. It was the same white cloth as the robe the priestess had worn, the one who haunted my nightmares. I pictured it stained with the blood from her crossbow bolt wound, and I was sure this priestess would not be so kind if she knew I had led Merle to kill another woman from her order.

I decided it would be best not to mention it.

I held up the robe, eyeing the reach of the sleeves. It would never fit over the cloak, or the crossbow. I unslung it from my back and tossed it onto her bed, followed by the cloak. When I pitched it across the room, something dropped out of the pocket and skittered across the floor.

The damned rune stone. It nearly hit the priestess's bare foot, and she bent down to pick it up.

"Rorik's stone." She held it in her palm like a fragile egg.

"A copy," I said quickly. "One of my shipmates is a carver. He made it for me as a gift."

"Oh." She handed it back to me. "Why would you want a copy?"

"I have my reasons." I took the stone, put it in my pocket, and tugged her small robes over my head. Everyone seemed to know about this stone.

When I got the robes around my waist, they cinched me in like sausage casings. I would have to crouch to cover my boots and cradle my arm over my chest to keep my claws hidden.

"Father Augustus has been looking for the real stone," the young priestess said.

"Why?" I asked. "Is there someone he'd like to raise from the dead?"

The dead priestess appeared in the corner in a flash. She was gone before I could shudder.

"Yes, and no," the young priestess said. "The stone doesn't exactly raise the dead, it only shrinks the gap."

"Shrinks the gap?" I tugged on the too short sleeves.

"Between this world and the afterlife. Niflheim you call it, I believe. The stone makes a window; it closes the distance. You can see the other side as long as someone is waiting to receive you…at least that is what the legends say. Rorik eventually went mad, able to see his sons but not recover them. As such, the stories are very scattered."

That made more sense. Death could not be reversed, even by Hel herself. It would also explain the nightmares. Perhaps it was the priestess peeking through at me. I know your trick now, old woman.

"How did your friend make the copy?" she asked. "It looked so real."

I changed the subject. "Where's Mateo?"

"Oh, he's two floors up," the priestess said. "Go right from this room and take the first door on your left. That will lead you to the stairwell."

"I appreciate your help, but I need some insurance." I snatched her arm and swung her around, claws jabbed into her back. She went stiff and still, trembling.

I caught a whisper of Flavian's voice in my head. *"Good God, Carina, the girl is trying to help you. Could you try not stabbing her?"* Somehow he could annoy me even when he wasn't here.

"I won't hurt you," I said to her. "But I don't want to get doused with poison in case this goes wrong. You take me to Mateo, and then you can go back to sleep. What is your name?"

"Sister Angele," she whispered.

"I am Carina…just Carina." I nudged Angele ahead of me and kept one claw in her back as I pulled the hood of her robe over my head as far as I could. "Open the door. Slowly."

She pulled on the door with a long creak. I peered over her shoulder in both directions. The hallway seemed to be clear.

One step at a time, we made our way down the hall. She opened a door, and it did indeed lead to an inner stairwell lit with flickering torches. We rounded them upward, one step at a time. Two floors up, Angele stopped at another door.

"This is it," she whispered.

"Open it."

She nodded and pulled open the door, going completely still. "Fourth door on the right," she whispered over her shoulder before striding into the hall. She slammed the door behind her.

"Sister Eugenia," she said loudly. Purposefully.

"What is wrong, child?" Another woman's voice called. I pressed myself against the stones.

"I can't sleep. I have a horrible stomachache. Would you make me that drink with the mint leaves? I would appreciate it."

"Of course. You should not have waited so long."

I heard footsteps retreating and another door slam closed. Sister Angele could have easily passed me to Eugenia. Instead, she let me go.

I would not waste the gift she had given me. I would not forget it, either.

I pushed open the door a second time, scanned the hall, and ducked out of the stairwell. Angele and the other women spoke softly behind the first door. I counted three more and nudged the fourth door open. A familiar wheeze called to me—Mateo. He still lived. I slunk into the room and sealed us inside.

Five beds pressed up against the wall. Mateo lay in the furthest one, and barely made a lump in the sheets. They clung to his body, soaked through with sweat. His complexion had turned from yellow to gray, and the room smelled like rot and alcohol. More like rot than alcohol. The fever was winning, beating him down as hard as Horrible Hild and her heavy, steel fist. But Mateo had defeated worse, and it took only one well-placed hit to topple even the largest foe.

I crossed the room and knelt beside him. I pressed my hand to his forehead and nearly burned my fingers. Carefully, I curled the sheet away from his chest, down his sweat-soaked middle to his leg. They had re-bandaged it. Likely seeped some of the infection and re-stitched it too. They did all they could with medicine, and it wasn't enough.

I closed my fingers into a tight fist.

If Nik hadn't caught me with the pillow and told me the truth, I could have saved him from this misery. The Goddess could save him too, take him away instead of leaving him to suffer. Why didn't She? Did She want him to live? Or was She trying to prove a point?

"Fight it," I whispered to him.

"Tahlia," Mateo muttered in his fever dream, and I wondered who she was. Who else had Mateo left behind in Fortis? Who else would miss him if he left?

***

"Tahlia."

I snapped my head upright. My mouth tasted as if I had swallowed a ball of wool. My tongue clung to the roof of my mouth. Red and blue light filtered in from the stained glass window over Mateo's bed. It shone on his cheeks, giving them the appearance of health. I had fallen asleep here, stretched beside Mateo in his sweaty sheets that turned cold. I needed to go before someone caught me. I slipped out of the bed, and Mateo's eyes fluttered open.

"Carina?" He sounded surprisingly lucid for someone at the edge of Niflheim. I touched my fingertips to his forehead. It was cool. Cooler than my hand. By the grace of the Goddess, She set him free. I had not angered Her after all.

"What are you doing here?" He tried to push himself upright and couldn't. He had fought the infection, but he wasn't well. The Goddess only left him with another chance.

"I wanted to make sure the priests were treating you well. We can talk later. I'll send Nik in as soon as I can. I have to go and don't tell anyone I was here." I made for the door and hoped this ill-fitting robe would serve me well enough to escape the tower. I peered into the hallway. A stern-faced priestess approached. She saw me and dropped the towels in her hands.

"She-devil!" She pointed an accusing finger.

I slammed the door and leaned against it. My plans for an easy escape disappeared with her shrieks.

"What is happening?" Mateo gasped.

"I'm not supposed to be here." I grabbed one of the empty beds and slid it in front of the door.

"Why not?"

"I might have punched a priest."

"Carina..." He sounded disappointed and not-surprised.

"He was insulting." I tore the sheets from another bed and tied them together.

Fists banged on the door. "She's in there," a voice cried, the same one that had shrieked at me moments ago.

I tied the end of the linens to the bottom of Mateo's bed and tugged on my makeshift rope. Hopefully Mateo's weight would be enough to hold me. I stood on the edge of his bed and unlatched the window. Something slammed into the door, enough to shift the bed blocking it.

"You can't jump," Mateo said.

"Well I can't stay here, and I can't go through that door. What would you have me do?"

I couldn't fight them, not with their Ignusian Fire. The bodies slammed into the door again, and this time the cot slid across the floor. Two priests dove into the room. I tangled my hand around the sheets and leapt through the window. I slid down to the end of my rope, which wasn't nearly long enough to reach the ground, but I could reach the window below.

"Don't touch me," I heard Mateo shout.

I kicked off the wall to give myself momentum. When I swung back to the tower, I closed my eyes and sank my claws into the sheets. My body crashed through the window, and I rolled to the floor in a heap of cloth and broken glass.

The floor was wet, and this time male voices shouted at me. I raised my head and made out the bottom of a golden tub.

"What is she doing here?" one man shouted and pointed at my steel hand. The others reached for towels and robes to cover themselves. It would seem I had crashed into the men's baths.

"I thought I told you to stay out of here." Father Augustus stood on the stones, dripping water from underneath the folds of his towel that did not quite cover all of his unmentionables. They were as over-tanned and wrinkled as the rest of him. I felt sick.

"I'm leaving now," I said and scrambled to my feet.

He reached for his jar of poison, hanging from the chair beside the tub. I hurried toward the door, crunching over blue and yellow glass. There was something familiar sitting in the shards—my stone. It must have fallen out of my pocket when I crashed through the window.

Let it go, I told myself as I was already reaching for it. But I could not, would not, let the insulting Father Augustus have it. I would rather die.

I closed my hand around the rock and something splashed on my knuckles, something like liquid fire. I snatched my hand back as the skin bubbled and blistered. The stone fell from my fingers.

Father Augustus clutched his open vial of poison in one hand and reached for the fallen stone with the other.

"What is this?"

"Nothing," I said. "A trinket."

Streams of blood rolled down my fingers. The pain crawled up my hand into the rest of my arm. Pain like I had never known, even though I had been hit with arrows and stabbed with knives.

Father Augustus held up the stone and smiled. "I think we both know

146

this is more than a trinket."

CHAPTER 19

✖

The dungeons in the priests' tower were surprisingly clean. Better accommodations than I had been given on the ship when Flavian, Nik and Mateo had kidnapped me. This at least contained a bucket to relieve myself and a straw stuffed mattress to lie on. The priests had been cleverer, though, and bound my hands behind my back, which made it infuriatingly difficult to use the bucket and eat the watery soup they brought me. My shoulders ached almost worse than my hand. The intense burning stopped, but the memory still prickled across my knuckles in waves of heat.

Perhaps the Goddess wasn't pleased with me after all.

A door opened in the hall. I stood up and scrambled to the back of my cell, below the barred window. I hoped for Nik with his knives, or Flavian and his flattery and bribes. Surely they would come for me. I was their prize. They needed me to bring back to their precious Nyssa. Yes, I would have to suffer the rest of this venture with Flavian gloating about how he rescued me, and I could suffer it as long as he took me far from this awful island and Father Augustus.

But the visitor was not Flavian. Or Nik. I recognized the steps, squirrelly and over-confident—Father Augustus. He peered through the bars of my cell, still grinning.

"How are the accommodations?" he asked while his fingers toyed with the vial at his neck in warning. I pressed myself deeper into the wall.

"Where is Flavian?" I asked.

"Leaving," he said.

"That's not true."

"Look for yourself. Through the window." He nodded to the bars where the late afternoon sun streamed through.

It had to be a trick, a way to get me to turn my back. I pressed my shoulder to the wall and stood on my toes, one eye through the window, one on him. From here, I could make out the docks, and Flavian's ship, moving away from the shore.

It felt as if another arrow pierced my shoulder. Flavian swore he would do anything for Nyssa and last night, Nik practically begged me to stay.

What a fool I had been. I believed Nik's kisses, Flavian's bold honesty, and again, I drank the poisoned wine.

I closed my fist. "What did you say to them?" I asked.

The priest twirled the vial in his hands. "I told the boys it would be one or the other: they could take their sick friend, or you. It did not take them long to decide."

Of course not. I was disposable. Dagna had pushed me off the island; Flavian and Nik left me here. I belonged nowhere. To no one.

"If he were nothing more than the head on his shoulders, he would be a thousand times more valuable than you are."

A knot rose in my throat. I shoved it down with a steel fist. This was not Mateo's doing. He was too sick to make decisions. His two mother hens made the choice for him and left me here to rot.

"You bastard," I snapped at the priest. "You despise my people for bringing peaceful Death when you use human lives as bargaining tools." I lunged at him, and he held up his vial as a shield. I skidded across the stones and stopped halfway across the floor.

He still had the advantage, but his hand shook. I frightened him. Even in these chains, behind these bars, he recognized a desperate animal with nothing left to lose. The most dangerous bears in the forest were those who were already snared.

"There are things that matter more than your pitiful life," he finally said.

"What about Flavian's father? Doesn't he fund this island?"

The priest shrugged. "Along with many others. Losing one donor won't destroy us, and I doubt I will lose him. What would the consul of Fortis care for a Daughter of Hel trapped in our dungeons? He might even reward me for disposing of you."

He was right. The Daughters' power came in numbers. We were only fearsome and respected and admired as a group. Without them, I was just a pathetic girl with a steel hand, currently bound behind my back.

"I want to know about this." He removed the stone from his pocket and held it out to me, the snake side facing the bars. It chafed me to see *my* rock in his filthy hand.

"What do you want to know?" I asked.

"Where did you get it?"

"My shipmate carved it for me. I'm sure he would have made you another if you hadn't chased him from the isle."

He closed his fist around the stone. "Liar. I have seen copies, from master craftsmen, and none of them have been this good. So tell me now." He shook his vial of poison. "Where did you get this stone?"

"Alright," I sighed, backing away from him. "There was a church." Another step. "With a dried up, disgusting priest." Step. "When I killed him, I peeled off his skin and found the stone tucked behind his brittle bones."

I managed a small grin before he uncorked the vial of poison and splashed it through the bars. "You disgusting creature!" he shouted.

I pressed against the far wall, and even there, a few droplets of the poison splashed onto my leggings, quickly chewing through the fabric like angry moths before it bit into skin

Panicking, I searched the cell for a way to cool the pain. On the way to my bed, I tripped over the bucket and splashed cold urine on my leg. I sighed as the Fire subsided. The river of urine stretched under the bars of my cell, and the priest stepped back, frowning.

"I would think carefully about your answers next time." He shook his vial. "I have vats of this in the tower, and I will burn away your skin from toe to chin to get my answers."

He shuffled down the hall, and I stayed stiff and still until the other door slammed closed. The stench of urine rose up from the floor. I hated being caught. I hated being caged.

I paced the inside of my cell. As soon as I got out of here and retrieved my sword, I would let Gut Spiller earn its name. The leader of the Ignusian church would be a fine prize for Hel, and his poison would be an even finer gift for Merle. This could be yet another opportunity, a test.

Except as far as I could see, there was no way out of this cage, and no one was coming to rescue me. My only escape had already sailed away.

I slumped onto the corner of the mattress and shifted my arms to keep blood flowing to my fingertips.

"It's painful isn't it?"

I snapped my head up. I knew the voice. It haunted my nightmares nearly every night, except this time, I was wide awake and staring at the dead priestess in the corner of the room. Her skin hung ashen and waxy from her cheeks, and her white robes were stained with soot. But Father Augustus had the stone now. I shouldn't be seeing her.

"I'm going mad," I said.

"Not yet." She smiled, and the black beetles crawled between her teeth and across her lips before sinking into her gums.

I tried not to look. "I don't have your stone."

"I know."

"Then why are you here?"

"Because I want you to get it back." She stopped a few feet away. Beetles and worms and centipedes crawled out from beneath her robes and circled her arms. "We don't have much time. You and I are both attached to the stone for now, but that connection will fade the longer it is out of your hand."

"Good," I muttered. Not being haunted sounded delightful.

"You're angry with me," she said.

"I don't like being haunted."

"I didn't enjoy being murdered. Forgive me if I used the stone to teach you a lesson."

"Have you been to Niflheim? Have you met Hel?" I asked. No one had ever seen the land of the dead and returned. I wanted to know what it was like. If the legends were true. If our Goddess was as infinitely beautiful and terrible as the *skalds* described.

"No. I haven't been anywhere yet," she said. "You called me with the stone."

"I did not."

"Yes, you did, with your guilt. With the stone in your hand, you thought of me, so here I am."

I did do that, unfortunately. "Then I send you away. I want a new ghost." One of my dead Sisters or kinsmen. Someone useful.

"You cannot do that. The stone only connects two, and it cannot be undone until the stone passes to another. I used to speak to someone of my order, Sister Birte. She warned me of this before you came. I was talking to her when you entered my church. She told me a girl would come, and the stone would go to her, and I would be her other. I obviously did not want to believe it, but here we are." Another beetle skittered from her mouth across her nose. "We do agree on something, young Daughter of Hel--no one should come back from the dead. Father Augustus cannot have the stone, and you must get it back from him."

"I'm not in the position to do that right now." I shifted my bound arms.

"You'll have to find a way. That poison you despise so much?" She lifted her robe and along her exposed leg, black beetles skittered up to her knee. "Father Augustus has grand plans for it. He wants to conquer the world, and believe me when I say the North, your island, will not be immune from it. He believes he can wash sin from the world with his Ignusian Fire, except he has a limited supply. When Father Titos, the man who created the poison, found out what Father Augustus planned to do with it, he killed himself and took the means for making the Fire with him. If Augustus has the stone, he will call Father Titos to him and have control of the Fire."

The burn on my fingers ignited once more. I did not want that. Neither would Merle.

"How much time do we have before the stone becomes his?"

"Days, maybe. The transfer will be instant if he kills you."

I nodded. "Then help me out of this cage. I'll take it from him and slit his throat."

"I cannot help you from the cage." She reached for the wall and her ghastly fingers went right through the stone. More bugs dropped to the floor. "You'll have to figure it out for yourself."

"That's it?" I gasped. "You tell me I have to get this stone back or awful Father Augustus will burn the world and you leave me with nothing? You can't send those roaches after the key?"

"I'm afraid not. I can only give you this." She held out a palm, and one of her roaches circled the center. "A lone roach away from the rest of its intrusion may seem like nothing." She clapped her hands together and crushed the cockroach in between. "But it's still nearly impossible to kill." She opened her hand, and the cockroach sat on her skin, stunned but alive.

I couldn't decide if it was better or worse to be compared to a cockroach versus a mouse.

"I need more than that."

"Then how about this? I underestimated you. I thought you would be cold and callous as the other killers. The concern you exhibited for your brother…it has shown me otherwise."

"I am so glad you approve, but that's not going to undo these chains."

"Don't be so dismal," the priestess said. "You'll see. Others have noticed. Have faith in your friends. Things are not always as they seem." The insects swarmed over her last words, covering her mouth and arms. They ran down her neck and legs until they became a cockroach cloak. When they scattered, trailing through the window, they took the priestess with them.

I tried not to vomit.

I thought of all the dead warriors of old I could have called with the stone instead. Gunhold Strongarms or Helga Hammersmith. She was a legendary smelter. She made the first of the steel hands. Surely she would know how to break a puny chain, but no. I had a worthless priestess, crawling with roaches.

I shifted my right shoulder forward and bent my arm. Pain lanced through me, neck to wrist. I pushed it down into my stomach and turned one of my steel fingers upward, sliding it back and forth over the metal link of one of the chains. I only hoped these chains were thinner than that cursed lock had been.

CHAPTER 20

✕

When I awoke, I couldn't feel either of my hands. I sat upright, and the chains clattered against my steel fingers. Thank the Goddess. My hands had not been burned away by Ignusian Fire in the night; they had only gone numb from the tightness of the chains.

Pale moonlight filtered across the floor, and the stench of stale urine burned my nostrils. Sleep crusted my eyes. I did my best to rub it out with my shoulder, and decided to get back to work on sawing through the chains. I didn't have much time.

Before I contorted my arm to get the right angle, I readied myself for the pain. It helped to think of a goal. As soon as I got myself free, I would find the priest. I would get my stone and then use my claws to carve out his heart and offer it to Hel on a platter. Then I would take his vials of poison and deliver them to Merle with whatever gifts I gained from Fortis. I would be welcomed back as Helvar royalty.

But those dreams shattered as soon as I heard the door open at the end of the hall. I flattened out on the bed and feigned sleep. The footsteps did not belong to the priest. There were two sets, and they were slow and cautious. Soft.

Two robed figures appeared on the other side of the cage door, one short, one tall, both hidden behind white hoods. I watched them through a fringe of lashes as the smaller one shoved a key into the lock. I pulled my knees closer to my chest.

One night Dagna tried to carve runes into my forehead, and I'd heard her before she could. I was, by habit, a light sleeper. I felt the rumble of her footsteps quiver through the bedframe. I heard her breath in the night air. As she poised her knife over my forehead, I tightened my calf and swung out hard, striking her in the kneecap. She walked with a limp for days afterward.

I would do much worse to these intruders. I flexed the muscles in my leg, thigh to ankle, and waited like an arrow about to strike.

"Carina?"

I released my leg. "Nik?" I sat upright. His dark eyes found me from under the white, priest robes. He came back for me...after leaving me to rot for a day, long enough that my arms went numb, my leg was burned, and I bathed in urine.

"Get me out of these chains," I snapped. He had wasted enough time already.

"Are you alright? Have you been hurt?" He grabbed one of his knives and shoved it into the lock, twisting it back and forth.

"Of course I've been hurt. He wasn't feeding me cakes and wine in here." The lock snapped free. I pulled my arms loose and rubbed the feeling back into them. "I watched you leave."

"We had to. Father Augustus had Mateo. He was going to keep him here instead of you if we didn't take him and go."

I understood. I was less than Mateo. I only mattered when it was easy and convenient.

The smaller figure threw back her hood—Angele. "We should go before someone finds us." She handed me a white robe.

"Why are you here?" I asked.

"It isn't right," she said. "Our God does not keep prisoners. He does not make bargains with people's lives. I'll show you the way out." She beckoned me to the door, and I watched her in awe.

She had reached some level of kindness and goodness and forgiveness I would never know. Father Augustus would likely never find it either. There were few who would.

"I can't leave," I said. "Not yet."

"We can't stay," Nik said.

"I need my stone and sword first." I looked him hard in the eye.

"We don't have time. The ship is on the other side of the isle. We need to reach it by morning if we want to leave here alive."

"Then go ahead," I said. "I'll catch up." I stretched my claws, and apart from the bent one, they were sharp and ready to gut Father Augustus.

"I'm not going without you," he said.

"And I'm not going without my things." I crossed my arms over my chest. "This is non-negotiable."

"It's the real stone, isn't it?" Angele said in her sweet, whisper voice.

I did not answer her. "Where is his room? He'll have it with him," I said instead.

"The top of the tower," she said. "But you cannot go there."

"I rarely go where I'm welcome."

I pulled the priestess robe over my head. This one fit better than the last. Before anyone else tried to argue with me, I made for the open cell door. I wondered if it would help convince Nik if I explained it all to him: the true nature of the stone, the dead priestess, Father Augustus's plans, but I did not owe him any explanations. I owed him nothing.

"If you insist on going," Angele said. "I will come with you."

"No, you've done enough. Go back to your room."

She touched my arm, eyes wide as a doe's. "I know why he wants the stone," she whispered. "And I believe you do too. I'll show you the way to his room, just promise me when you have it, you will take it far from this island."

"You have my word on the Goddess Hel," I said. "If you help me get the stone, you will never see it again." She would also never have to see Father Augustus alive again either, but I did not tell her that.

She waved her arm. "This way."

"I'm coming with you," Nik said.

"No." I pointed a claw at him, the bent one unfortunately. "I don't need your protection. Start for the ship. I will catch up."

"I know you're angry," he said. "But remember you left me too. I woke up on the ship, and you were gone. I didn't find out where you were until Flavian came rushing onto the ship to tell me you crashed through a window in the men's baths."

"That was an accident," I said. "And I left—"

"If I may," Angele interrupted. "We should hurry."

I snapped my claws at Nik. "Then come if you want. But try to keep out of my way."

We hurried past the other cells…why a church needed so many cages, only Father Augustus could answer that. Nik followed close behind, breathing down my neck. My shoulders rose around my ears. For some reason, at this moment, the memory of our kiss slunk into my thoughts. I mentally carved it out in the same way I would carve out Father Augustus's organs.

Nik grabbed a torch from inside the stairwell and held it in front of us. We circled up the stairs, pausing to listen for other voices or catch the shadow of flickering lights. The air in the stairwell hung thick and warm, clinging to my shoulders. To reach Augustus, we had to climb from the bottom of the obnoxious tower to the top, circling around and around. By the fifth or eight turn, I broke into a sweat. By the tenth, my breath turned heavy. I was shocked the priest did this every night. I imagined his brittle bones creaking and popping at every turn.

"This is it," Angele whispered and pointed to a door.

Ten more steps reached above us, probably leading to the roof. The door in front of us was carved with a design of two priests in long robes, arms outstretched, reaching for the same star. The carving was oiled and waxed to a deep, rich brown.

Nik held the torch over my shoulder. "Are you sure you want to do this?"

"Yes." I pushed open the door, driving a claw into one of the carved priest's eyes. Nik stretched the torch into the room. Faint firelight cast across the stones, finding Father Augustus under his sheets.

The burns on my hand and leg pulsed at the sight of him. Behind him, against the back wall sat a desk piled with parchment, a plush, green armchair with a high back, and a glass cabinet sealed with a lock and filled with varying jars and vials.

Propped against the side was Gut Spiller. I smiled, glad to see an old friend.

Nik grabbed my arm. "Careful," he mouthed.

I shook him free. "I can handle this." As if he had any right to tell me what to do.

Heel to toe, I made my way across the stones. The blanket rose and fell with Augustus's breath. The vial of his poison sat on a table near this pillow, less than an arm's reach away. I quickened my pace and snatched my sword.

Quickly, I scanned through the glass cabinet, looking for the stone. It wasn't here. I spun around to Father Augustus. He would keep the stone close, like the poison.

I made my way to him. Angele watched me wide-eyed from the door. Nik tensed, ready to leap into the room at any moment. I leaned over the sleeping priest. I clicked my claws. If I jabbed his neck, he would bleed out quickly enough. But first, I needed the rock. If he had hidden it somewhere, I would need to coax the location out of him before he bled to death.

I grabbed his vial of poison and shoved it in my pocket before I opened the drawer to the nightstand. He kept a book inside with another vial of poison resting on top. I took that one too. No sign of the stone. A flicker of movement caught my eye. A cockroach raced across the sheets and crawled up the priest's arm, stopping on his hand.

Ahh, so now the priestess could help me, and since I knew where he hid the stone, he had no reason to live.

I raised my sword and angled it to cut through his ribs. I moved to drop it and someone screamed...Angele. The priest rolled to the side faster than I thought he would. My sword struck the mattress. Feathers burst in a plume.

Father Augustus's wrinkled eyes went wide. He reached for his vial of poison that I had already taken. I swung my sword a second time and slashed through his fingers. They dropped to the ground like bloodied worms, and the stone fell between them.

"Devil!" he shouted, clutching his bleeding hand.

I grabbed the stone and aimed my sword for a second strike. "You have no poison. No chains."

"You will pay for this," he said.

"No, I think you will."

"Carina!" Nik shouted. "We have to go." He touched his torch to the curtains, and fire ripped through them.

"In a moment." I needed to gut the priest first. I turned back to Augustus just in time to watch him disappear through a secret door in the wall.

Hel's fire.

The room filled with smoke. The flames from the curtains spread to the sheets. The air singed my skin. I ran to the door, past Angele who watched me like a frightened little rabbit. This would probably be the last time she helped a stranger.

"Come on." Nik waved me down the stairs, a knife in each hand.

We circled down the tower, and on the third pass, we ran into another priest and priestess. I flashed my bloodied sword, and they backed against the wall, giving us ample room to pass. I clutched the stone in my steel fist

158

and tried to piece together how everything had gone wrong. Why had Hel let that man escape?

"This way." Nik tugged my sleeve, and we darted into the kitchens. He shouldered into a small, wooden door. It broke apart, and we were in a storage pantry, filled with sacks of flour and grain.

"This is perfect," I said. "You led us to a closet."

"Not a closet." He moved a bag of flour aside and revealed another door. When he broke this one open, we were in a long dark tunnel with no torch.

"Keep going straight." He reached his hand back for me. I ignored it and held onto my sword. He shrugged and jogged forward. I kept right behind him, close enough to see the folds of his tunic which became harder to find the further we moved from the pantry door.

This was worse than the cage on the ship, the one in the church. It had no openings, no windows.

"Where are we going?" I asked Nik.

"This should lead right to the stables," he said in heavy breaths.

"How do you know?"

"Flavian. He has a way of getting information."

Something brushed my cheek. I hurriedly wiped it away and moved closer to Nik's shoulders. "How much longer is it?"

"I don't know." He paused. "I don't like small spaces either."

"I'm fine," I said. It wasn't as much the space as the pure, impenetrable darkness. Without the moon or stars to guide me, I couldn't find my way.

A few more steps, and a small sliver of light appeared. The closer we moved to it, the more shape it took: a rectangular outline of a door. Nik and I crowded around it. The hinges were rusted shut. It took both of us to wedge it open, and even then, we only opened it wide enough to slip through the crack.

I crawled into knee high grass with a high moon hanging overhead covered in haze. The smoke came from the priest's tower, ignited in flames like a giant torch. This was why Augustus had lived, to see everything he made brought to ruin.

I threw off the priestess robes and dropped the stone in my pocket next to the vials of poison. Merle had always wanted some of it and could never reach it. When I gave it to her, she would smile, pat me on the shoulder and say, "You've done well, Carina."

Unfortunately, though, that approval never seemed to last. It would fade the next time I made a mistake, which was why I had to take Fortis. It was the only gesture grand enough to shield me.

"This way." Nik waved me toward the barn.

Inside the horses slept in their separate stalls. I rapped my steel knuckles on the door to wake them. Three stirred to life. Nik grabbed tack from the hooks and opened the stall door for a brown mare. I chose a brown and white dappled stallion. He looked strong and fast, possibly the most coveted horse on the isle—Augustus would be upset to find him missing in the morning.

I fastened my sword to the saddle and hoisted myself onto the stallion's back. I kicked my heels into his haunches, and he leapt through the barn doors. Outside, the fire in the tower continued to burn. As I watched the flames lick the stones, I hoped I would meet the priest again, for a second chance to take his life.

CHAPTER 21

✗

nik and I rode under the cover of darkness, following a narrow path up the rocky hill with only the moonlight to guide us once we left the blaze of the fire. Few trees sprouted from the grass, not like on Helvar. No tall pines to hide underneath or hearty oaks to stand behind. This island was made of rock, tall grass, and low, fat shrubs. We would have to keep moving to stay concealed.

Behind us, the smoke lingered as a gray haze on the black sky. I wondered if the priests were behind us with their vials of Ignusian Fire. They had a limited supply, but likely enough to burn me alive if they chose.

I kicked the horse in the haunches to push him forward faster.

"Can I ask a question?" Nik asked.

"Was that the question?" I retorted. Whenever someone requested permission to ask a question, the question was never good.

"Did you drag me up there for the stone? Or because you wanted your vengeance on Father Augustus?"

Both, I didn't say. "The stone is mine."

"That's it, then? Your only answer?"

"If you don't like my answer, why did you bother asking the question?"

He sighed and shook his head. "I'm trying to understand, Carina, but I can't if you won't explain."

"Fine, I wanted him dead."

"Because he hurt you?"

"I don't need a reason." Death didn't need a reason to take a life. Her reason could simply be because it was there.

"But you had a reason."

"Yes," I said. "He took my sword. He took my stone. He threatened my brother's safety and…" I stopped myself before I mentioned the dead priestess and Father Augustus's plans for lightning everyone on Fire.

"And what?"

"Nothing." I nudged the horse again, weaving ahead of Nik and his brown mare. I was tired of being interrogated.

We crossed another hill, and the path disappeared, swallowed by even taller grasses that brushed the tops of my shins. My horse plodded along undeterred. On Helvar, Merle kept a black stallion named Coalfire. He stood as tall as two women, a glossed ebony black. He could run the length of the beach in minutes. This horse wasn't as fast or grand as that, but he did have a tireless work ethic.

Patches, the Unstoppable Stallion.

Patches. Had I just named a horse, Patches? Not Ironhooves or Bonecrusher? What in Hel's name was wrong with me?

The grasses cleared ahead around the circle of a small pond. Patches, or Ironhooves, veered toward it. I yanked the reins to pull him back, and he jerked his head to the water. I tugged again, and he reared up on his hind legs, threatening to throw me off if I did not let him have a drink. Ironhooves the Stubborn.

"Fine." I gave in and let him turn to the pond.

Nik and his horse came up beside us. "We should keep moving," he said.

"Tell it to the horse." I slid off Ironhooves' back and rubbed my shoulders. They were still stiff from being chained behind my back for the better part of the day. The smell on my clothes had not improved with age, either. If anything, it turned worse, sour and spoiled.

I waded into the pond beside the horse, fully clothed, hoping I could wash away the memory of this entire venture, but even as I splashed my face with cool water, I could still see Flavian's ship, sailing away from me. I had that gut-sinking feeling of being stranded.

Nik slid off his horse and knelt by the pond. He scooped water into his palm and sipped it, his back to me. How easy it would be to slice him through the neck and remove him from my life. One swing of my sword. I could tell Flavian and Mateo the priests killed him. Burned him with their poison. They would still take me to Fortis, and I would lose nothing.

"You shouldn't have done that," he said in a low voice, jarring me back to the moment.

"The horse needed a drink, I said. "And I needed a bath." I crawled from the pond.

"I don't mean this. I mean before. You shouldn't have gone to see Mateo. If you had stayed on the ship like you were supposed to, none of this would have happened."

"I don't have to follow your orders." I should have killed him when I had the chance.

He combed his wet hands though his hair. "You're angry. I understand. But we had no choice. We never intended to leave you there. We moved the ship, and then I started walking across this damned island to get to you."

"It's fine." My clothes ran wet with pond water. I wrung out my tunic. "It's done."

"It's not done."

"It is done. You don't get to decide when things are done or not done, either."

"What do you want from me Carina?" He raised his arms. "I am sorry. We are all very sorry. Flavian, Mateo and I are all in hearty agreement that Father Augustus is a monster, and I hope his entire tower burns to the ground. But there were only three of us. Mateo was still injured. He was going to take your place, and we wouldn't let him do it. We had to save him from himself, and despite it making us sick to do it, Flavian and I both knew you would be strong enough to survive it."

"Because I had done it before? Because I had been caged, and starved and tormented?"

He closed his fist. "I am not going to apologize for that again."

I couldn't remember him ever apologizing for it. "Then don't. Don't apologize for anything. I don't care." I reached for Ironhooves' saddle, and Nik grabbed the reins.

"Carina, wait." He lowered his voice. "We hurt you, and I am truly sorry." He held my gaze. "Sometimes…no, no excuses. We made a mistake."

My shoulders eased. "As I said, it's fine."

"No, it's not. You're right. Flavian and I strategized. We thought about how to get Mat out, and you out, but we didn't consider the time in between. Mat was the only one who did. I was angry, and I shouldn't have punished you."

"You were angry?"

"I woke up and you were gone. I thought you'd left us. I thought I'd said or done something to put you off."

He thought I was ashamed of him, or disgusted by the kiss, and unfortunately, I was not.

"That wasn't why I left."

He raised his head. "You can't even apologize?"

Apologies did not come easily to me or any of the Daughters. Apologizing for an action meant regret, and the Daughters had nothing to regret. We did as we pleased. We fought, we killed, we ate large amounts of food, we drank wine, we spoke loudly, we punched people for disagreeing with us, and if by chance we overstepped some bound of decency, we put it all to rest over a horn of mead.

Unfortunately we had no mead at present.

I tried to make the words come past my lips. I'm sorry. That was it. I am sorry. But as I fought to dredge the words from my throat, I felt like I might vomit.

"It had nothing to do with you," I finally said. "But I would prefer if we never spoke of that night again. Let us pretend it never happened. Come on. Let's go. We need to get back to the ship." I pulled myself onto Iroonhooves' back, squelching in the saddle.

Nik hesitated before he climbed onto his horse. I exhaled when he kicked him in the haunches and rode ahead without another word. If only it were that easy to forget that night. If Nik leapt off his horse this moment and kissed me again, I was eighty percent sure I would return the gesture. It would be higher if I wasn't still stinging from being abandoned in the dungeons.

Nik was the worst possible choice for me. If I wanted to kiss boys, I should be kissing someone like Von. It would make everyone happy, apart from Dagna, who didn't deserve to be happy. But my thoughts didn't linger on Von. They went to Nik, his soft lips that tasted like salt and his thick, knife-throwing forearms wrapped around my waist.

No. I couldn't. I just had to push him out of my mind.

We rode through the night, up and down rocky hills until we finally crossed the last one. There the sun crested over the ocean, striking the edge of Flavian's ship. He stood on the prow waving both arms as if he were trying to flag down an army.

We led the horses down to the water where Nik uncovered the dinghy hidden in a cluster of bushes. I ran my hand over Ironhooves' nose as I stripped him of his saddle and bridle. "Go now," I said. "But not back to that awful priest. You can do better on your own." I swatted him on the backside to chase him away and tossed the saddle and bridle into the boat. They were both well-made, hand-stitched. They would be worth something to someone.

Alone in the dinghy, Nik pulled on the oars and I fought to look anywhere but in his direction. Even so, I caught flashes of his arm or knee, and I felt as if I were walking down that long dirt tunnel again, lost in the darkness with no idea of where I was headed.

I really liked Nik, and Mateo. But how would they feel when I slaughtered Flavian and absconded with his riches? Why did I care how they would feel? I had given myself to the Goddess Hel. Everything I was or would deign to be belonged to Her. No one else.

Only two more weeks. Then we would be at Fortis. If I could maintain my focus for two more weeks, then this would all be over.

The dinghy sidled up the Flavian's ship, and he leaned over the side, his black curls framing his high cheeks.

"For God's sake, Carina," he called. "You do know how to keep a man waiting."

"Pull us up," Nik said in a somber tone and threw Flavian the rope.

It took three times for Flavian to actually catch it, then he looped it around the pulley and dropped it back to us. Nik and I pulled on it in turns to raise the dinghy to the deck.

Flavian reached a hand out to me. I ignored it and drove my claws into the side of the ship. I swung myself over the railing and landed in a derisive, "thud." I reached back to the dinghy for the saddle and bridle and dropped them on the deck in a heap of leather.

"Why Carina, I haven't seen you this miserable since we first picked you up," Flavian said.

"Don't," Nik warned.

Of course Flavian ignored him. "That Father Augustus is going to be punished for this. He won't get another piece of my gold...my father's gold."

I waved him off. I already knew that threat was idle to Father Augustus. There were plenty of others with gold who supported him and his ideas.

Mateo sat across from us on the deck. Flavian had brought the chair up from his room, slumped Mateo into it, and buried him in blankets. Only a sallow face emerged with two sinking eyes.

"Carina," he said, breathless.

I made my way to him, and it was if I could feel our blood ties reaching out across the divide, pulling me closer. I knelt beside him and took his hand, and it was strange how natural it felt. How easy my fingers fit into his.

"I knew you would beat that fever," I said.

His thin lips quirked on one side. "This time," he said.

"I appreciate you offering to stay in the dungeons for me."

"They wouldn't let me." He nodded to Nik and Flavian.

"I know. They are far too overprotective."

"Are you alright?" he asked.

"Yes." I pulled my hand from his and tucked my burned arm behind my back. I stood up. "I hope you don't think this nearly dying makes you exempt from sword practice. I expect you to be back with the blade as soon as you feel ready."

"I thought you might say something like that." He lifted the blanket and there sat Flavian's jeweled rapier, propped up against the chair. Mateo had already learned so much more than Flavian. Never be without your blade.

He covered the sword. "I had a dream you were going to kill me," he whispered, "and I wanted you to kill me."

I said nothing.

"It wasn't a dream, was it?" he continued.

I still said nothing. I thought back to that moment where I held the pillow to his face. If Nik hadn't stopped me...I shook my head. I didn't want to think about it.

He sighed. "I was only four when I caught the plague and I spent most of that time in and out of doctors' rooms. But as soon as I was well enough, Mother became obsessed with the Daughters. We both did. We read books upon books. I drew maps of the island and chartered every possible route to reach it. We kept hoping we might find you, even though in all of the books we read, the Daughters never left survivors." He paused to let out a rattling cough. "But they did. They do. You're still alive."

"I am a punchline to a long standing joke," I said. "A joke played on my father...*our* father."

"I don't think you're a joke," he said. "I also don't think you're a monster."

I shifted to look him in the eye. He would be saying differently when I killed his closest friend.

"Death must be satisfied. That is your pledge isn't it? But what the books don't say is *who* decides how she is satisfied."

"The chieftain decides," I said. Merle plotted the raids to give towns time to rebuild, to feel safe before we struck them again.

"And what about now? How do you decide?"

He meant on my own, without Merle whispering in my ear, without Dagna leading the way. "I don't know," I lied. I had decided to kill whoever would offer me the most glory. Who could assure my place on Helvar.

"Carina, can you give us a hand with the sheets?" Nik called. Thank the Goddess. He gave me an excuse to leave.

I turned to the prow and found Flavian tangled in the ropes. Useless. I untangled him and hoisted the sail.

"I heard you went chasing after your rock again." Flavian said.

"It's mine, and I will keep it." I patted the lump of the stone in my side. I decided not to tell him it worked. The more people who knew about the stone, the more desirable it became.

"Nik also told me we hurt your feelings when we left."

My lip curled. The way he said it made me sound like a pouting child. They hadn't taken away one of my toys. They left me in a cell with a horrid priest armed with burning poison.

"You boys talk too much," I said and looked to Nik, wondering what else he had told Flavian. If he told him about the kiss, I would have to cut out Flavian's tongue or I would never hear the end of it.

"I will admit," Flavian stroked his chin, "we did not consider your feelings when we made the choice to leave you there. We should have listened to Mateo. Nik and I have a dreadful habit of making decisions for him, and I'm beginning to think Mat might actually be the smartest and most capable one of us."

"Might be?"

Flavian rolled his eyes. "Very well, he unquestionably is, and so I would like to offer you my own apology."

"I've heard enough apologies."

"I know," Flavian agreed, "which is why I am offering you my version of one." He straightened his spine, folded his hands behind his back, and squinted one eye. "You can hit me."

"Hit you?" My heart fluttered at the thought. How many nights had I gone to sleep aching for the chance to strike the arrogant grin off his face?

"Yes, I will release you from your promise not to harm us and allow you one hit." He held up a finger. "But, I am begging you not to break anything or leave permanent damage. My face is really my best asset, and I think we can both agree without it, I would be like you without your steel hand and that menacing sneer you've perfected."

I pulled my lips together. I was wearing the sneer now. "Alright, I accept your apology." I pulled my hand back and eyed his face, aiming for the best place to strike. My heart pattered. I felt like a child with a new sword.

Flavian pinched his eyes closed. "Not too hard. I am a delicate creature."

I curled my steel fingers into a metal fist. This would be for everything. For when they dragged me onto this ship and left me in that cage. For later, when Flavian dressed me in that gown and forced me to dance, for having to endure the priest's torment, for knowing that the mother who abandoned me was still alive.

I swung my arm and at the last second, opened my fingers. I struck Flavian across the cheek with a flat, steel palm. It hit with a menacing crack. His head snapped, his body spun, and he toppled to the deck in a heap of fine linen, velvet, and jeweled rings.

"Good God, Carina. I think you've shattered my perfect bone structure," he cried

He gently patted his jaw, already turning pink in the shape of five, distinct finger marks.

I held out my hand to help him up. He took my fingers, and I yanked him to his feet.

"Nothing is broken," I said.

"How can you be sure?" He leaned over the side of the ship as if he could catch a glimpse of his reflection in the moving waves.

"If it were, you wouldn't be talking," I said.

That would all change later, of course, when the swelling set in, and we would all have at least a day or so of silence from Flavian, until we had the ultimate silence. When I killed him.

"Ask no questions, both I intend to kill; long have I desired to cut short your days."

Edda of Saedmund the Wise

CHAPTER 22
✖

I knew the priestess was there long before I opened my eyes. She left an odor of stale bread and mold in the air. It was distinct to her presence, decrepit and sour.

"Are you still haunting me?" I asked.

I rolled onto my back and looked first to Nik, asleep in the bunk below and across from me. Flavian was with Mateo in the captain's quarters. Flavian stayed to keep watch on Mateo, and I was sure because his skin was too delicate for the hard, crew bunks.

"If he wakes up." I nodded to Nik. "Will he see you?"

"Only you can see me," the priestess said. "We are matched that way. If you gave the stone to him, he would call his own spirit."

"Where would you go?"

"To Him." She raised her chin to her god's realm.

"You mean to Her." I lowered mine to Niflheim.

"I suppose I will have that answer when I pass."

She clasped her hands together, white and waxy in the moonlight. She looked different tonight. More like a doll instead of a rotting corpse, with pale skin pulled tight on her face. Too tight in some places. Her eyes bulged from the sockets far enough to see the red lines around them.

"Is that what you want?" I asked. "For me to release the stone so you can pass?"

"Yes and no. Yes, I want my rest, but the stone cannot be hidden, it can't be destroyed. It wants to be found, and it will be found. It was my burden to look after it in life. It seems I have been given the same burden in death. If you keep it, I can continue to watch over it."

"I'm not going to keep it. I am going to give it to my chieftain."

Her eyes bulged wider, nearly popping from her skull. "I would advise against that."

"It's our rule." I spun the stone in my fingers. "All earthly rewards go to the chieftain for distribution."

"Who do you think she will call upon?" The priestess asked.

"I don't know," I said, which was not entirely true. I had an idea. She might call upon Ragnhild the Red, one of our former chieftains, named because she performed well above her required offerings to Hel and sought to expand Helvar to other islands. She felt it was our right to claim the land with the death of their inhabitants. Before she could enact it, though, she was struck through the eye with a crossbow dart. Merle always admired her ideas, though.

If we are entitled to the gold in the coffers, why not the land beneath their feet?

And if that was Merle's desire, to follow in Ragnhild's footsteps, I would follow her.

"I would think well on that before you make your choice," the priestess said.

"The stone is mine. I will do with it what I choose."

Below me, Nik groaned. "Carina? Who are you talking to?"

"No one." As I said it, the priestess drifted into shadow.

I stuffed the stone in my pocket and climbed down from my bunk. I needed some air and to escape Nik's unwavering gaze.

On the deck, cool wind rolled off the water and grazed my cheeks. Despite us moving south into warmer waters, this deep in the ocean, the water stayed cold. I tucked my fingers into my pocket and ran my thumb across the stone's sleek surface.

"Carina?"

I snapped my arm back. Of course he followed me. "I needed some air," I said.

"I heard you talking in the bunkroom. To no one. Is something wrong?"

"You boys need to mind your own affairs."

He joined me by the rails. "My ship. My affairs." The wind caught a piece of his hair and curled it around his cheeks.

"It's Flavian's ship," I said.

"I'm the captain. I say where we go, but it's fine if you don't want to talk about it."

"The stone works," I said, to make him stop talking. "Except it doesn't raise an undead army, or open the doors to Niflheim, it just makes a window, a very small window, large enough for me to see the priestess, the one I should have killed and didn't. The stone was hers, and I called her here by festering about my mistake. Now she's haunting me."

Nik went very still apart from that one piece of hair dancing on the wind. "I think you should go back to bed," he finally said. "You might have come down with a fever."

"I don't have a fever. You asked me for the truth. Here it is."

He crossed his arms over his chest. "Alright, then call the ghost. Let me see her."

"It doesn't work that way. Only I can see her."

The muscle in his jaw flexed. He thought I had lost my wits.

"Believe it or don't," I said. "It's not as if I enjoy being haunted. But if I don't keep the stone, someone else have it, and they will call a different spirit. Father Augustus wanted it to call upon the man who made his Ignusian Fire so he could burn the world. Think about what would happen if your Mahmod had it. Who would he call?"

"He's not *my* Mahmod." He tightened his hold on his ribs. "He could call Javad back. He could find out who killed him."

"I won't let that happen," I said. I would never let that man return. "I'll bring it back to Helvar. We will protect it." As I said the words, the rock weighed on my pocket, as if it had grown ten times its original size.

"I'm glad you told me," Nik said. "It would be best not to tell Flavian. Or Mat for that matter. Mat will tell Flavian, and Flavian will tell his father who will feel obligated to bring it to the Emperor. We don't want him getting the stone either."

"You're not loyal to the Emperor?" I asked.

He played with the top of one of his knives. "When the Emperor conquered the Eastern lands, he killed the caliph and any local rule. He gave rise to the Aldam. He is no friend of mine. If he could use that to get access to the Ignusian Fire…"

"It will not leave my side," I said.

This rock proved to be more troublesome and valuable than I ever could have imagined.

When we returned to our bunks, I fell asleep with the stone clutched in my steel fingers. The priestess gave me a pass this night. No nightmares, and with my mind free to wander on its own, it found Nik, standing on the deck of the ship with his hair loose and blowing around him. I tried to catch strands of it and push it behind his ears, and they wrapped around my arms and wrists, pulling me closer to him.

I didn't fight it as much as I should have.

In the morning, the three of us hoisted Mateo from bed and perched him on the deck, covered in blankets. The warm air of the Southern waters seemed to do him well. His skin brightened. His spine straightened. Step by step he moved further from Hel's grasp...for now. You could never escape the Goddess completely. At some point, Mateo would become Hers. We all would. All we could steal from Her was snatches of time.

Nik locked eyes with me from the other side of the ship's wheel. I nodded to him in a sign of our shared confidence about the stone as Flavian strode toward me, twisting the rings on his fingers. He balled his fists on his hips and breathed deeply. "Already the air smells like home, doesn't it?" He spoke in thick words, but unfortunately, his jaw didn't swell enough to silence him.

"Not my home," I muttered.

"My sister is going to insist on meeting you," he continued. "She'll probably want to drag you to a party or two, to shock the locals. Helene loves to create a stir."

"No parties. No dresses. No dances," I said. He would be dead before that could happen, but I doubted I could avoid meeting the mother. That was the purpose of their journey, and it would earn me five hundred pieces of Flavian's gold. But after that, I would spend my time planning my route, the remainder of my take, and how I would escape. If all went well, I would be out of Fortis within days and on my way to Helvar with a new ship stuffed with treasures.

"You are no fun, Carina," Flavian said.

"Stop bothering her," Mateo replied on my behalf and saved me the breath.

"I'm not bothering her." Flavian rocked back on his heels. "I'm simply making conversation."

Mateo and I both turned to Flavian at the same time, with the same exasperated glare.

Flavian raised his hands in surrender. "It might be a good thing we're separating you two soon. That was positively eerie." He stepped away from the rails and dipped into the flask from inside his tunic.

"I know he can be annoying," Mateo said. "But his heart is in the right place."

It wouldn't be for long. Not when I carved it out of his ribs.

"I'm worried. I had a dream last night," he said. "Mother died and came to apologize to me for not being stronger, for not waiting. I think we might be too late."

"It was just a dream." I was not that lucky. There was no possible way that the Goddess would show me favor by taking the horrible Nyssa before I arrived. It would be a kindness too great. One I hadn't earned yet.

"You don't know how sick she was before we left, and we've been gone longer than we planned."

I couldn't keep trying to convince him she lived in part because I didn't want her to live. I changed the subject. "Who is Tahlia? You spoke about her in your sleep."

He swallowed, and his complexion turned a shade paler. "Well, I don't know if she's a friend of mine or not. She's my sister."

My heart stopped. "There's another sister?" I could not suffer another unknown sibling.

"No, she's you. That was your name before."

Tahlia. I rolled it on my tongue. It was a weak name. A plain name. One I carried for three years until Merle took me and renamed me Carina, which meant "dear one." Another joke because I wasn't dear to anyone. My father discarded me like waste, and yet I preferred the mocking name to "Tahlia."

"Don't ever say that name again," I whispered.

"I won't," he stammered, and I walked away from him, moving automatically toward Nik. When the emotional waters turned too deep for me, I gravitated toward him, a rock I could safely land upon.

"How is the ship handling?" I asked him as I looked up to the mainsail, puffed out with strong wind, pushing us ever faster to Fortis Venitis and Nyssa.

"Did you really come to talk about the ship?"

"No…I suppose there is no way I can avoid meeting this mother, is there?" I agreed to their venture to worm my way into the spoils of Fortis. They thought I agreed for a pocket full of Flavian's coins and a ride home. But I wasn't sure I could stand there and let this sick woman look at me like she owned me, like I was her Tahlia. I also wasn't sure I could scream in her dying face, knowing the reason she left me behind was for Mateo.

"You can't give a dying woman her wish?"

"No."

"You don't want Flavian's coin?"

"Oh I do want that," I said. "Do you think he'll give it to me regardless?"

"Carina." He steadied the wheel with his knee so I could have his full attention. "No one is going to hold you at knifepoint and force you to see her. But I think you should. I never met my mother, and my father died when I was five. I barely remember him. Don't you want something of her? This could be your last chance."

"I buried her a long time ago. I don't need to dredge her up from the grave."

"Then do it for me, and not that you owe me any favors. I'm asking because it's important to me to pay her back for all she's done, and this is the only way I can. Please." He pierced me with those charcoal eyes and my resolve wilted.

"Fine. For a minute. No longer."

"That's long enough."

If I had to sit there and listen to her apologies or whimpering, I might snap and take her life before Hel could snatch it.

"Land Ahoy!" Flavian shouted.

"It's Land Ho," Nik corrected him.

"Well whatever it is. It's there."

I followed the line of his jeweled finger to the prow where a shadow of gray rose from the water. Nik turned the ship slightly portside, and it stood in front of us, a monument lifting toward the sky--the white cliffs of Fortis Venitis.

I clicked my claws together, reminded of our raid on Frisia. I would be launching myself on unsuspecting victims…in a far different manner. Instead of charging across their island with my Sisters beside me, I would slip through it alone under the shield of three of their sons. I could do this, I told myself, and focused on sailing into Helvar with a new ship, piles of gold, and weapons all marked with the Southern Emperor's crest. The *skalds* would sing themselves hoarse telling my glory, and this time, it would be true.

On the starboard side of the ship, another small island drifted on the water--Orsalia. Even though the Southern Isles consisted of six separate islands, and I hadn't been here since the age of three, I knew that one had been my home, the island the Daughters raided, where Merle killed my father and claimed me as her prize. It had the right landscape, small with a smooth beach and right under the Emperor's nose.

If the South hadn't been suffering under the plague, Merle might never have slipped by the three war ships docked conveniently within sight. It was as if everything came together to enable the raid, and it was falling into place again, for me.

Nik steered the ship toward Fortis port. White buildings with blue domes dotted the cliff, standing up in rows. From the port, only a single one-horse road curved up the side, nothing large enough for an army or a horde of steel-armed women, which was why Fortis remained protected.

"Pull the sheets," Nik shouted.

I jumped down the stairs and grabbed the rope for the mainsail.

Flavian stood beside me, waving his red handkerchief. "Your long lost son has returned!" he shouted.

Nik dropped the anchor. The ship slowed, and Flavian nearly toppled over the side. He caught himself on the rails, but he did lose his handkerchief.

Mateo used both hands to free himself from his blanket. He leaned heavily on his cane, hunched over it like a sagging sack of grain. He wore a nervous grin. He wouldn't be at ease until he saw Nyssa alive. I wouldn't be at ease until I sailed away from here in the other direction.

Except I wanted Mateo to get his wish. One day with his Nyssa and then she could do me a great favor and die. It would make killing Flavian and leaving here much easier if they were all prostrate with grief.

Nik slid the gangplank over the side. Flavian strutted down it, holding out his arms as if he were the Emperor himself, returning home. Nik held Mateo's elbow while he hobbled down. I kept in front of him, in case he should topple forward.

"Paulo!" Flavian waved to a man on the docks. He was short and squat, dressed in a cream-colored vest and a floppy, green hat. It looked like bird nesting on his head. The Southern fashions were more ornate. Less utilitarian.

"Master Flavian?" The man squinted one eye. "You're home!" He held out his arms and frowned. "What happened to your face?"

Flavian gently touched his mottled cheek. "Oh some nasty business with pirates. Go fetch us a horse and cart. We need to get home immediately. How is Nyssa? Is she well?"

The man's face dropped, and I clenched my teeth. I knew the look of bad news.

"We tried to reach you, sir. No one knew where to find you."

"What happened," Flavian said, his smile falling too.

The man removed his hat and ran his fingers around the brim, spinning the cap around and around. "Well, Miss Nyssa took a turn for the worse…and…the doctor did everything he could. Miss Helene sat by her side until the end."

"The end?" Mateo gasped.

"I'm so sorry, sir. She passed two days ago this morning."

Whatever strength Mateo used to get off the ship, disappeared. He slumped into Nik's arms and landed in a pile of shaking whimpers. A knot formed in my throat. This was what I wanted, for her to be gone, to never have to look at her, and it didn't feel as vindicating as I thought it would.

Two days.

If not for Father Augustus, or the stop at Isla Mortem, Mateo might have made it in time to say farewell. I couldn't question the Goddess's choice. If She took Nyssa, then it was her time, but it was poor timing for Mateo. He never could seem to grasp any shred of good fortune.

"I knew we were too late. I knew it." Mateo's sobs burst from his chest. I worried they would tear him apart.

"It's alright, Mateo," I said. "It will be alright. She's with the Goddess now."

Mateo raised his head long enough to throw me an icy glare. "I don't want to hear about your horrible goddess. This is not alright!"

I took a step back with undeniable proof that I was terrible at consoling.

CHAPTER 23

✳

"**W**here is she?" Flavian asked the man Paulo, barely audible over Mateo's wheezing sobs.

"In the cemetery at the church. We buried her yesterday. We would have waited, but we had no word of when you'd be back. It was a beautiful service. Mister Sergio's daughter, Lia, sang in a voice like a siren."

"That's lovely to hear." Flavian twisted the ring on his middle finger, no trace of his jovial grin on his swollen jaw. "Please, go get us a horse and cart. We would like to see her."

Nik tried to pick Mateo up. He shoved him away and kept weeping. I kept my distance, an outsider to this whole affair. I didn't share in their grief. On Helvar, we understood that death was not an end, simply a parting.

Mateo didn't want to hear that, though.

Paulo returned with a small wagon drawn by a single white mare. Mateo allowed Flavian and Nik to pick him up and place him in the back. With the three of them wedged in the cart, I climbed onto the bench and sat next to Paulo. He stared, slack-jawed at my steel hand, not as impressive with the bent claw.

"You're....you're..."

"Yes." I stretched out my fingers. They were getting stiff again. I had been rationing my goat fat to last the journey.

"Just go, Paulo," Flavian said. "Carina is fine. She was Nyssa's daughter."

"Oh, I see it now. You have her face."

"It's my own face," I said and pointed forward, as instruction to start moving or I would show him my claws more clearly. Even dead, I could not escape this woman. She would haunt me in her own way, from the other side of the mirror.

Paulo snapped the reins, and the small, thin cart bounced up the small, thin road that wound up the mountainside. The air smelled of warm spices and sweet honey, different spices from those in Brezadine and not entirely foreign. We twined around the white cliffs and I began taking inventory of what the city had to offer: fine shops and cafés. A music shop stocked with violins and lutes. A dress shop with glittering, tiered gowns. A glassware shop with imported plates, ornately painted in gold leaf.

Because of Fortis's built-in cliff protection, they were able to grow and prosper without worry of attack. Hel had been absent from this island for far too long. It was time they knew that Death reigned supreme, and for every life I sent to Her, She would leave me their worldly possessions in return. More than Dagna had ever claimed on any raid.

I salivated over the wealth like a dog with a bone while Mateo whimpered behind me.

We turned around a bend and encountered another cart headed in the opposite direction. Our wheels scraped in the pass. The security of having such thin roads carried a price. The amount of time it would take to bring a load of cargo from the harbor could be more than a day. It could also be a problem for me. The Daughters attacked shoreline towns to enter and exit quickly. I could easily get trapped on this road with no way out, something I would have to consider.

The higher we climbed, the further we moved from the sea. Down below, our ship looked like a toy, and we were wending higher still, toward a smooth, white building with a blue top, and four columns. Here the wagon stopped, and Flavian and Nik helped Mateo from the back.

A fountain stood out front with a small stone figure in the center. It was one of the old goddesses. The Southerners used to worship many gods and goddesses until the Emperor brought with him a new religion with only one god. This simpler religion spread quickly north, perhaps because of the simplicity of it. Those of us in Helvar were the only ones who did not follow.

But here was this small statue, the one reminder that things were different once.

"Wait for us, Paulo," Flavian said.

"Yes, sir."

Flavian and Nik partially-carried, partially-dragged Mateo past the fountain and underneath the columns to a small courtyard, lined with tightly packed marble stones in a field of grass. I stayed behind, at the edge of the cemetery. I did not want to inadvertently grin or laugh at Nyssa's grave and send Mateo into a new fit of sobbing.

The three of them circled around a white stone over a patch of dirt that had yet to grow its covering of grass. Mateo knelt beside it and buried his face in his hands. The weeping returned in full force. Flavian rested his hand on the stone and bent over it as if in prayer, and Nik stood to the side, arms crossed, head shaking as if he could not believe the perfect woman had the audacity to die.

I couldn't read what the stone said. I could only assume it was something like, "Perfect mother, teacher and friend. The entire world will suffer for her absence."

Ridiculous. If I told her tale, it would be a very different story. The one of a sad woman who married a weakling fool. Who chose one child over another. Who let her lost child drift for thirteen years, grow comfortable in a new life, only to tear her away from that life and make everything so confusing.

I was supposed to be a Hand of Death, and here, I was, already forced to spare Nik and Mateo, and with Flavian's soft crying, I felt sorry for him too. She ruined me! Again and again she ruined me!

I sank my fingers in the dirt and pulled up a ball of mud. "I hate you!" I launched the dirt at her gravestone. It crumbled across the crisp, white stone, leaving behind a brown stain. A mark on her perfection and not *nearly* enough.

I grabbed another handful.

"I despise you more than that awful Father Augustus." Another spray of dirt. "It's your fault that Mateo was injured." Another clod. "It's your fault I am a flawed Sister." A larger clump of dirt. "You had a thousand chances to come for me and never did. You are the worst mother I could possibly imagine, and I hate you for dying before I could say this all to your face. You selfish, horrible, harpy."

I grabbed a loose rock from the ground and flung it as hard as I could at the grave marker. It struck the corner, and a piece of the flawless white stone snapped free. All three boys stared at me as if a second head had emerged from my shoulders.

I gently touched my cheek and found tears. Now this monster mother had pushed me to weep, for Death.

"AHHHHH!" I shrieked at her grave one last time, loud enough she would hear me all the way in Niflheim.

I stomped back to the church and leaned over the fountain. I splashed cool water on my face to erase the tears. My chest ached. I hated her, a thousand times I hated her. If she had held on for the last two days, I would have choked the life from her, hang all promises and vows.

With my claws, I raked my hair from my face and caught my breath. Behind me I heard the slow shuffle of Mateo. He reached the fountain and leaned hard against it, dropping sweat into the cool water.

"I'm sorry," he said. "I didn't know you cared so much."

"Excuse me? You mistook that for caring? The only thing I care about is getting away from this place."

He dipped his finger in the water. "Achelois," he said and pointed to the stone figure above the trickling water. "She who washes away pain." He scooped up a mouthful of water and held it to his lips.

"Then she is terrible at her job. You were right to abandon your old gods."

He wiped his chin. "I'm sorry we didn't come for you sooner."

"It's fine," I said.

"You know, I grew up with a ghost too. Mother kept a bed for you, always. A second empty bed in my room. I went to sleep every night staring at the folded sheets and woke up with it there, always empty, always waiting. Each year, on your birthday, she'd leave a gift on it. Then she would spend the night sobbing. She blamed herself, you know. That was why she didn't come for you. Gone, she could convince herself you were still alive. She was afraid if she went searching she'd find…well, you know what she thought she'd find."

"How horrible that must have been for her," I said.

"It was a mistake."

"Are you saying the perfect Nyssa wasn't so perfect?"

"No, she wasn't. No one is." He shook his head. "I blame myself. She was afraid to leave me to look for you. If I had been stronger, healthier—"

I stopped him there. "Don't be foolish," I said. "It's not your fault. I was fine where I was. No one needed to come for me."

"I'm glad we did, though. I'm glad we found you even if we were too late." He offered me a weak smile.

I sighed. "I am too." They led me right to Fortis, and I didn't mind knowing Mateo. Nik.

"I can tell you what she would have done if you had said those things to her in person," he said. "If you want to know."

"I'm sure she would have cried, and then made me feel terrible for making her cry."

"Yes, and then she would have agreed with you."

Of course she would have. Perfect Nyssa couldn't have given me the satisfaction of keeping my hate.

"Has everyone calmed down?" Flavian gingerly poked his head around one of the white columns.

"Yes." I smoothed my hair from my damp cheeks.

"Good." He clapped his hands together. "Then let's go home. I need a bath before I visit with my mother and father and try to explain where I've been for the past four months."

We all piled into the wagon and turned further up the hill, and as we did, the grandeur of Fortis shone brighter, in massive private homes with golden shutters and mosaic tiling. Our wagon stopped at one of the grandest of them all —the home of the consul.

The shabby wagon clacked on white stone, around a spewing fountain, under a tiled awning. Servants appeared from nowhere, dressed in white and blue robes. One of them appeared at my side, hand outstretched.

"Can I help you down, miss?"

"Of course." I stretched out my steel hand and smiled as he curled away in horror. The boy helped Flavian with Mateo instead. A wise decision.

Nik remained in the wagon. "Paulo, can you take me back down to port?"

"Of course." Paulo looked to Flavian for approval. "Do you need anything else from me, sir?"

"No, no." Flavian waved his fingers. "You can take Nik home and go back to whatever you were doing before we arrived."

"Thank you, sir." He ducked his head and slapped the reins. The white mare circled around the cobblestones back to the main road with Nik tucked inside. My rock on this journey.

"Where is he going?" I asked.

"Home," Flavian said. "Nik rents a room down by the harbor. I'm sure we'll see him later, after we get things settled."

I didn't know if that were true. As soon as I had my plan of attack, I needed to leave. That might be the last I ever see of Nik, and I didn't have a chance to say goodbye. And what did it matter? Once I left here on Flavian's ship, I would never see him again anyway. He would never *want* to see me again.

"Don't look so miserable, Carina," Flavian said. "I'm starting to wonder if you and Nik were carrying out some secret romance on the ship." He winked, clearly thinking he had made a joke.

My face blanched. "Don't be crass."

Flavian sent another boy to fetch our things from the ship. One wave of his gilded fingers, and ten people leapt to serve him. I would have to be cautious of them too. So many eyes on Flavian would add another level to my escape.

Flavian leaned closer to the boy who had tried to help me from the wagon. "Where are the consul and his wife at present?" he whispered in his ear.

"Visiting Master Gregor, sir."

"Good. Good." Flavian sagged with relief. "I'm going to return to my rooms and take a bath. Please send word as soon as you see them return. I would like a few moments to prepare myself. And fetch Maris. Tell her to see Miss Carina here to our finest room, the one next to Helene's that overlooks the terrace. She is to have everything and anything she needs, do you understand?"

"Yes, sir." He cocked his head to the side and squinted one eye. "What happened to your face?"

"I..."

"I slapped him upside the head," I said. The boy looked shocked. Not surprised. I was sure I was not the first to slap Flavian. Or to want to.

"Yes." Flavian ran his tongue over his teeth. "Remember to warn me as soon as you see the consul returning." He marched up the stone steps into the grand house. Before the boy raced off to fetch Maris, he looked to Mateo.

"We're all very sorry about Miss Nyssa," he said. "If we had known..."

"Yes, I know. Thank you," Mateo said and waved away the offer of help to get inside the house. He leaned on his cane and made his way up the marble stairs on his own, step by painful step.

The foyer of the house shone in the sunlight. White marble lined the floors, and huge columns supported the ceiling. Various statues and art decorated the main room, along with satin curtains and a rug woven in the shape of a herd of horses.

So much to take, but I would have to be careful in that too and only take what I could carry. My gaze went to two more jeweled rapiers hung crossed over the fireplace. As useless as they were as weapons, they boasted rubies and emeralds and the Emperor's hawk insignia. Those I could take.

"You like the swords?" Mateo asked. He noticed I was staring.

"I always have an eye for a sharp blade," I said. "You grew up here?"

"As part of the staff," Mateo said.

"Did you have to jump when Flavian called and satisfy his every wish?"

"No, but I did have to complete all of his arithmetic lessons."

A young girl skittered down the stairs in a rush. The skirts of her beige robes flew behind her in a flurry. She reached the tiles and skidded to a quick stop in front of us. Her eyes went wide and she ducked her head.

"Oh Mateo," she said. "I am so sorry about Miss Nyssa."

I sighed. I would never hear the end of this woman.

"I am too," he said, his voice cracking. "Maris, this is Carina, my sister."

"A pleasure to meet you." She bent in her knees in a quick curtsey. "I'll show you to your room."

"If you need me," Mateo said. "My rooms are down here." He pointed to a hallway that ran underneath the stairs.

"I don't need a minder," I said and followed Maris up the stairs.

The house smelled like soap and spices. On the second floor, a servant dusted an ornate vase, painted with the image of a tiger. It was lovely. And large. I could never carry it. I needed to keep watch for small things. Valuable things. Rare things.

"You'll be in here," Maris said and swung open a door. Two more serving women were inside, hastily scrubbing the floor. They probably washed the floor constantly to keep the shine as glossy as it was.

The back doors opened onto a small terrace that overlooked the city. I liked that this room held two exits. I couldn't get boxed in. I tugged on the gossamer curtains flowing in the breeze and peered over the balcony to the winding road below. From here, I could barely make out the harbor. It would be a long trip. I wondered if I could plan a route going down on the rooftops.

"Miss Carina?" Maris said. I turned around "Do you need help with your bath?" she asked.

"No."

"Then I'll bring you some fresh clothes and something to eat." She eyed my salt-crusted, blood-stained tunic and continued to hover.

"I don't need anything else," I said.

She wrung her hands together. "May I ask…," she shook her head and tried again. "Mateo doesn't seem well. Did something happen to him on the journey?"

"We were attacked by pirates," I said.

"Oh my." She covered her mouth with her hand. "That must have been terrible."

"Well, it wasn't pleasant," I said, wondering what else she wanted to know.

"I've hardly been able to sleep, worrying about him for months, and then Nyssa passed…this must all be awful for him."

She sounded overly concerned for just an acquaintance. "Are you and he…" I couldn't force myself to say the word, "together." As soon as I thought it, I began picking her apart. She was too short for Mateo, too fidgety.

"Oh no." Her cheeks turned a bold shade of crimson. "I'm just a maid, and he…well, he's the best mapmaker in Fortis. The consul depends on Mateo greatly for the shipping routes. I could never…he could never."

I held up my steel hand to silence her. "I don't really care."

"Of course not. How silly of me." She picked up the skirts to her robe. "We'll leave you to your bathing."

She waved the two other maids from the room and closed the door behind her. I needed some silence, some time to think.

I found the bathroom in an adjoining room with a copper tub already filled with warm water and topped with flower petals. I stripped out of my clothes and sank deeply into it, washing away the last remnants of my journey here.

Once I cleaned up, I could make my way through the city, find the best route to the harbor and look for a couple of men who would help me sail to Orsalia for some of Flavian's coin. I couldn't have Nik bring me back. He wouldn't, not after I made my offerings to Hel.

In Orsalia, I could pick up an entirely new crew, men who knew nothing about me, and sacrifice them once we reached the shores of Helvar. There would be no living remnants of my journey here. Just the bounty I claimed.

I scrubbed all the grime from my skin, and stepped out of the tub. I dried my hair and piled my claws with some lavender oil. They moved freely and smelled pleasant. I only needed to straighten out the bent one, and they would be perfect.

In the bedroom, I found a neat set of folded clothes next to a tray of food, stuffed grape leaves and a bowl of olives. I stabbed one of the olives with a claw and shoved it into my mouth. My few things had also been brought from the ship, my cloak from Merle and my silver cuff. I slid the cuff onto my arm and left the cloak on the bed.

Death does not show mercy, the runes read.

I wouldn't. Not this time. I would leave enough blood behind in Fortis to prove my devotion.

"Flavian!" A deep voice shouted, loud enough to cause me to drop my next olive. "Where in God's name have you been?"

That had to be the consul.

"Ah, Father." Flavian's honey smooth voice answered in response.

"Don't you dare speak!"

"Goodness," a shrill woman said. "What happened to your face?"

I recovered my olive and bit into it, trying not to smile.

"Nothing, Mother. I tripped," Flavian said.

"This is the end," the consul shouted. "I have given you far too much freedom. It's time you take responsibility for your actions and show some respect for your position."

"I have great—"

"Do not speak!" The consul said. "I've spoken to Emperor Basil. He is granting me an enormous favor by allowing you to court his niece, Ileana."

"Ileana?" Flavian said. "She wouldn't be my first choice."

"She is now," the consul snapped. "You will remain in this house until I say otherwise. No cavorting in town. No sneaking out of this house. The staff has been notified. When Ileana's caravan arrives, you will be the picture of a suitor, or you will find yourself out of this house, do you understand?"

The voices went silent for a breath, and I waited for Flavian's clever retort, his liquid voice to spin some tale of woe or innocence.

Instead I heard, a meek, "Yes, sir."

This wasn't the Flavian I knew. Granted, it was one I preferred, compliant and accommodating, but…I was disappointed. I wanted him to fight.

CHAPTER 24

✗

I dressed in the new clothes. Not quite the same as my Helvar made wool and linen tunics. I had been given tight, black leggings and a white tunic with a low neckline. It came down my chest and laced together, trying to give me the appearance of having a bosom and also revealing the five scars on my collarbone.

I ran my thumb across them. They had been my gift the morning after Von's stolen kiss. I woke up with Dagna perched over my bed. My claws were new. I moved to stop her and my burned hand went stiff.

"Never touch him again."

She jabbed me in the chest, and left me with these marks. A warning. A reminder. Not seven weeks after that, the Daughters went on a trade run to Brezadine, where Flavian, Nik and Mateo found her. She must have been so delighted to pass me off to them. Looking back, I remembered how much her mood brightened on the return trip.

She must have spent the last weeks reveling in her glory of finally ridding the island of me, and I couldn't wait to see her shock and disappointment when I returned.

I picked up my plate of food and decided to eat on the terrace, to get a better view of the city. When I stepped outside, I realized this terrace wasn't private. A woman sat in one of the plush lounge chairs, dressed in a thin, blue gown with her dark hair piled in braids on top of her head.

"Oh Good God," she said, her mouth falling open. She sounded exactly like Flavian, with a higher pitch. This had to be his sister.

"Helene." She stood up and held out her hand. "And you must be

Carina. I cannot believe that we have a Daughter of Hel, here, on our terrace."

I ignored her outstretched hand long enough that she let it drop to her side.

"You must tell me everything. What is it like to live in the cold North? How many people have you killed? What does it feel like to take a life?" She thrust her hand forward as if she were jabbing a sword into someone's heart, and by the one gesture, I knew she would do far better with a sword than Flavian.

"It's cold," I said. "I lost count of the number after a Perditian ship attacked us, and it feels…" I paused, searching for a word I couldn't find because there wasn't one. Of the few I had killed, no death was the same. The first man on Frisia had felt freeing, necessary. The others I killed to make up for the lost priestess. The pirates had been to protect myself and my shipmates. Their captain was a sorry loss. "I don't know," I finally said.

She closed her eyes and inhaled a deep breath. "My father will not let me touch a sword. I think he believes I would use it too capriciously, which I probably would. All of the uptight, wealthy daughters would find their hair removed, or their favorite dresses slashed to bits. I cannot stand being in a room where someone looks better than I do."

Yes, she was definitely Flavian's sister: vain, beautiful, verbose, and despite all of that, interesting.

"Do you have everything you need? Has the staff treated you well?"

"Yes." Although a tunic with more chest coverage would have been nice.

"Oh good. We were so very sorry to lose Nyssa. I sat with her to the last breath. She was like a second mother to Flavian and me." She dabbed her eye with the tips of her fingers. "I am going to cry away my face if I keep going on like this."

She had been a second mother to everyone. And no mother to me.

"There you are!"

Flavian strode through the double doors, freshly washed, hair curled, dressed in a white, blousy tunic and blue vest embroidered in silver thread along with tight-fitting gray leggings. He wore his usual smile, no sign of the argument with his father. It made me wonder how many other things he hid under his mask of rouge and narcissism, and why did I care? He would belong to Hel soon enough. He would be Her problem.

"I see you two have met." He plucked a grape leaf from my plate without permission and poured himself a glass of wine from a nearby carafe.

"Flavian, what happened to your face?" Helene pressed a delicate hand to her cheek.

It looked as if Flavian tried to cover the injury with powder or cream or something, only succeeding in turning the purple bruise an unsightly brown.

"It is dangerous business being at sea." He sipped the wine.

"Father and Mother were furious," Helene said.

"Yes." Flavian drank more wine. "I gathered that as he screamed at me. I am to start courting the Emperor's niece, Ileana, immediately."

"I know. I am sorry."

He waved his fingers. "Why be sorry? Ileana is a lovely girl with mass amounts of wealth. I am sure we will be quite happy." He drank the last of his wine and refilled his glass. I almost wanted to tell him he wouldn't have to marry anyone. He would be free soon. Relieved of the troubles of living once I jabbed him in the stomach.

"What did Father say about Carina?" Helene asked.

"Oh." Flavian twisted the ring on his finger. "You can stay, Carina, as long as you like. Here." He unhooked a sack from his belt and handed to me. "Your coins as promised. When you're ready to go home, I will arrange it."

I tossed the sack in my fingers. It felt like the promised five hundred. Flavian remained true to his word.

"Don't look so surprised. Did you think I wasn't good for the coin?"

"No." I tied the sack to my belt, although if he had stiffed me on the coin, I would feel better about killing him later.

"When will you sail back?" Helene asked. "There is a tea party on Sunday next—"

"No parties," I said.

"Carina is not the 'partying' type. She prefers shouting and stabbing," Flavian said to Helene.

"Oh I do hope she runs into Father while she's here."

Flavian grinned. "Yes, it would be fun to see our Father scared out of his wits. You see, Carina, you two have much in common. You both like to bully people, only he prefers to deal in silver and threats. I think, though, your sword would win that battle. He's a coward at the core. Like me."

Helene stole Flavian's wine and drank deeply. "God, Flavian." She handed it back to him. "I keep waiting for Nyssa to come through those doors, to tell me to sit-up straight and hand me a book of poetry."

Flavian smiled. "Yes, she would certainly have something to say about us speaking ill of Father and drinking before supper." He held up his chalice. "To Nyssa, for tirelessly trying to enrich our lives and make us better people."

"To Nyssa." Helene raised an imaginary glass as her eyes flooded with tears.

I had to go. I couldn't stand any more tears over the wondrous Nyssa.

"I'm going to explore the city," I said and handed Flavian my plate of grape leaves.

"Sadly, I can't accompany you," he said. "I'm bound to the house." He slumped into one of the plush chairs and set the plate on a nearby table.

"I can't either," Helene said. "Not without an escort."

"It's fine," I said. "I can manage on my own."

As I headed down the stairs, my sword and coins clanked against my belt, drawing the attention of every servant as I passed. They whispered in one another's ears, talking about me no doubt. Being the strange element in this house would make it more difficult to do what I needed to do.

In the foyer, I glanced down the dim hallway where Mateo said his rooms were. I decided to take a walk that way to see if there was anything of value in this wing. The hall opened into a catacomb of rooms. I peeked inside to find mostly servant's quarters, small and simple with only a few things of personalization—clothing, art, unfinished sewing projects. Neither Merle nor I had any interest in these.

At the end of the hall, I heard the shuffling of papers. That had to be Mateo's room. I hesitated before I continued onward. I didn't really want to see Mateo, but I did want to see his rooms. I was curious about where he'd come from.

In the center of the stone floor he sat, caged in by piles of books. Above him hung an oil painting of whom I guessed was the wondrous Nyssa, though one of the eyes was drooping off the side, and her hands were strangely small, like a doll's.

"Is that her?" I pointed to the painting.

Mateo jerked upright and clutched his chest. "I didn't hear you come in," he said. His eyes were rimmed in red. He'd been crying again.

"I can go." I stepped back.

"No. No. You belong here as much as I do, and yes, that painting is of Mother. Helene made it for her as a gift. It was one of her earlier works. Not her best."

"Ah." I nodded. That explained the tiny hands, except I almost liked this version of Nyssa, showing some imperfection. She might have been kind and charitable, loving and musical, but she had a face that looked as if it had spent too much time near the fire. Hands that couldn't hold a fork.

"I was just going through some of her things." He nodded to another door. The attached room held a small bed bathed in sunlight and a mosaic design on the wall in red, gold and yellow.

"They're your things too," he continued. "If you want to have anything."

"I don't…" I started and bit my tongue. No, I did not want to keep any reminders of her, but she might have something of value. Hel gave the riches of the dead to the living, and in a way, Nyssa's life belonged to me, in the same way that if Merle died, she would leave some tokens to me: a cloak or a set of knives.

I wandered into the bedroom. It smelled like sickness and lemon oil that had sadly tried to bury the sickness. It smelled like weakness.

Against the bed sat a simple wooden chair. Helene must have sat there to witness Nyssa's dying breaths. In the other corner, there was a tufted footstool with a lute resting on top. I went to the bookshelf and ran my claws over the spines. Unknown words ran the length of them, except the runes for 'Hel.' I could recognize those in most languages.

I snatched the book and flipped through the pages, stopping on an ink drawing of a Daughter of Hel, foot on the prow of her boat and a severed head hanging from her steel fingers. She was no one I knew, just a woman with a sneer and a steel hand, made to look like every Daughter of Hel—a monster.

I turned the book to Mateo. "We're not like this." I showed him the drawing.

"Then what are you like?" he asked.

"Well, we don't go dragging around body parts," I said. "You might not like Death, but She is necessary part of life."

"Yes, I know. I've faced it enough times and nearly escaped to realize that, but as I said before, I think we're all capable of dying on our own. We don't need help."

"It's not help," I said and slammed the book. "It's sacrifice."

"Whose sacrifice?"

I shoved the book onto the shelf, bending the cover in half. "Everyone's," I snapped and turned to the vanity beside the shelf. I was not that ugly thing in the book. They made a monster out of Death to justify their fear of it. But that was not me.

I opened the drawer of the vanity and found a silver-handled brush twined with dark hairs, a few gray ones. I plucked one of the dark ones out with my claws and held it next to the end of my braid. It matched perfectly. The exact shade of brown hair. No one on Helvar had this particular hue.

I dropped the brush into my pocket. It was the only thing I could see of value. The silver in it would fetch a few coins at market.

"What are you going to do with that?" Mateo crawled to his feet and stood on a shaky legs.

"You said I could take something."

"Yes, but why that?"

"It's silver," I said.

A line dug into his forehead. "I didn't mean for you to sell it."

"I will do with it as I please. She had no problem sacrificing me."

He hobbled toward me. "I know you are angry with her, and you are justified in that, but don't punish me for it. Anything you take from this room, you vow to keep. Otherwise, leave it behind."

"I am not going to make any vows," I said. Even after she was gone, Mateo fought for her useless things. "What are you going to do? Build a shrine for her?"

In a surprising move, he lunged for the brush, trying to take it from my pocket. I easily blocked him with one arm. He struck my elbow and fell back onto the ground. He made an "oomph," sound and didn't rise again. He simply sat there, wheezing, glaring.

"Keep it then." I threw the brush at him and stepped over him to leave.

I had to make my offering to Hel and go. I couldn't stay here, not under Nyssa's shadow. She left no room for anyone else to breathe.

CHAPTER 25

✗

On foot, the riches of Fortis shone even brighter. I found some empty grain sacks outside the kitchen of Flavian's home. I could use those to carry my take down the harbor. I walked up and down the main road four times, deciding my best route. The higher up on the clifftop, the more value the shops and homes held. Closer to the water, the scenery changed to shipping warehouses, fish markets, and dingy pubs.

I decided my best course of action would be to kill Flavian, take his jewels, a few of his fine cloaks, grab the swords in the main room and leave. Then I could kill the jeweler and his wife, clean out their wares, raid the smithy's stash of weaponry, and from there leap down in the alley behind the haberdashery, and carve a path through the shops to the water. I would only have to follow the main route for the last turn.

If I killed quick and clean and didn't get hung up anywhere, I could be from Flavian's to the water in under an hour. My final task would be finding a crew who would be willing to help me sail Flavian's ship across the water to Orsalia. I would kill that crew and pick up new men on the other side to hide my trail.

I made my way back down the cliffs to the waterside. I'd spent the entire afternoon plotting my course. The sun dropped into the water, and the lanterns came aglow with flickering flame. Good. The seedier residents would be easier to find in that dark. That was when they came crawling out of their holes.

At port, I walked past Flavian's ship. The barnacles had been scraped from the hull, the wood freshly polished and the hole in the deck repaired with fresh boards. The consul's staff had been busy this afternoon. If I could find a crew tonight, I could finish my raid and abscond before daylight. Again, the Goddess showed me favor.

I followed the scent of stale beer and filth on the wind to a tavern at the end of the pier, the Rusted Anchor. It looked like a place where I could tempt a few sailors to help me steal the consul's ship and sail it across the bay.

As I entered the tavern, several heads turned. Of those heads, most looked once and turned back to their drink. Only a few lingered longer. I rubbed my claws together, and their gazes drifted away.

One man sat alone at the bar, hunched over his drink, hiding under a stained cloak. He appeared to have something to hide or run from and might be looking for a way out of Fortis. I sat down beside him and dropped the sack of Flavian's coins on the bar.

"I'm in need of a good sailor or two," I said.

He raised his head and his hood fell back to reveal a familiar sheen of black hair and a curved nose.

Nik picked up the bag of coins and shook them. "Were you planning on leaving us?" He tossed the bag back to me.

"Yes," I said. "That was the plan." What did he think? I would experience some drastic change of heart upon meeting Mateo, abandon my Sisters and live here in Fortis for the rest of my days? "I can't stay here under Nyssa's shadow. I did as you asked. I came back. I saw what was left of her, now I can go."

"I will bring you to Helvar." He ran his finger over the top of his glass.

No, he wouldn't, not when I came running down the hill splattered in blood. "You should stay here. I'll find a crew. They can bring me back on Flavian's ship and return it after I'm returned to Helvar."

Nik sipped his beer. "If that's how you want it, I know some men who would be up to the journey. I'll introduce you to them later. Here. Have a drink." He raised his arm to signal the bartender. She was pretty with dark hair that fell in curls down her back, and she wore a blouse similar to mine. However, she wore hers much better.

She winked at Nik when she delivered my beer and I wanted to stab a claw in the back of her hand.

I took a hearty gulp of the ale. I needed to settle my nerves or dull my senses or something.

"I'm sorry we didn't get you back here in time," he said.

I set the mug down and wiped my mouth. "Don't be. I'm delighted she's gone."

He winced when I said that.

"I mean, I wish you had the opportunity to say your goodbyes, but the purpose of bringing me here wasn't for my well-being. It was for her."

"If you say so." He sipped his beer.

What did he mean by that? "You know I was perfectly happy on Helvar before you showed up."

"You keep saying that."

"It's none of your concern. I'll go where I want, with whomever I want."

"Just make sure you say goodbye to Mateo before you go. Don't leave him with another missed connection."

I pressed my lips together.

Nik swung around on his stool. "You can't do that, Carina. You can't just leave him."

"I can do whatever I want," I muttered.

"Yes, you can," he said. "But that doesn't mean you should. He missed Nyssa by two days. Don't make him miss you too."

I gulped more beer. "He doesn't care. He doesn't want me."

"That's not true."

"He just attacked me over a hairbrush. He told me to take Nyssa's things and when I tried, he went into a rage."

"Mateo went into a rage?" he snorted.

"It wasn't a *terrible* rage."

Nik shook his head and finished his beer before waving the bartender for another round. "He's your brother. You fight. Flavian, Mat and I have been at each other's throats a hundred times. We always shake hands in the end."

That didn't sound right. Dagna and I never shook hands after a fight. Whoever won would gloat over it, and the loser would spend her time imagining a more devious assault. Hence, my drugging and capture. That had been my punishment for kissing her brother, for earning my claws.

"I'll see what I can do," I said and continued to sip my beer.

Once the glass was empty, Nik ordered two more. He introduced me to the two men who would be sailing with me. They seemed strong and unmemorable. They would be easy enough to kill when the time came, and they promised to be at the ship before daybreak. We could leave right before the sun rose.

Nik ordered another round of beers. He could have kept up with Thorvald the Drunkard if he were here. I, on the other hand, was having difficulty standing straight, and had too much pride to refuse the next round.

The evening crowd filled the tavern, and a group of musicians settled in the corner, playing quick and loud. Nik took my hand, and I followed him to the center of the dancers. This wasn't a slow, close dance like the one with Flavian. This was more like Helvar music. We stomped on the floor and shouted along. The dust shook from the roof and landed on my shoulders.

I spun around, and in my haze, saw a familiar figure in the corner—the priestess. She pointed a finger toward the door like an admonishing parent. I made a face at her and tugged on Nik's arm.

"I need some air."

She was right, though. I needed to sober up and get back to Flavian's.

Nik and I tumbled outside, covered in sweat and smelling like ale.

"Is everything alright?"

"I'm fine." I swallowed. "Too much beer."

"You need something to eat. We both do. Come on." He waved me toward the rickety wooden stairs on the outside of the building. Eating sounded like a fine idea. I needed a full stomach before completing my raid, and I had hours before dawn.

He unlocked the door upstairs and led me into a small apartment. His apartment, I realized, when he lit the lantern and illuminated a small work table and a shelf of carved soapstone figures.

"You live above the tavern," I said.

"When I'm ashore."

The music blared through the floorboards. Nik lit a fire under the stove and pulled two fresh fish from a small box. He tossed them in the pan with some lard, and they popped and sizzled.

I made my way to his shelf of soapstone carvings. His work table wore a fine layer of white dust and various knives scattered across the surface. On the shelves above, rows of small carvings lined up like warriors. A fish leaping from the water, a whale with its tail raised, a horse reared up on both legs. Each one was beautiful in its own way.

"There are so many," I said.

"You can have one if you want." He turned the fish in the pan, and the air filled with the scent of thyme and onions.

I picked up the fish carving and rolled it in my fingers. Each scale had been meticulously carved into the side. I set that one down and picked up another, a bust of a woman holding a lute.

Her face was oddly similar to the painting Helene made of Nyssa, apart from the eyes being straight and the hands being the right size. It was the most detailed figurine on his shelf, down to the sparkle in her eyes and the individual strands of hair. Of course he would carve his perfect Nyssa to perfection.

"I don't have time for trinkets." I put the stone Nyssa back in her place.

Nik removed the fish from the pan and divided it onto two separate plates with a crust of bread. He ate standing up. I sat at his work table and dipped the bread into the grease oozing from the fish. He really could cook anything anywhere.

While I ate, I kept looking at the sculpted Nyssa. Her eyes seemed to follow me everywhere.

"I made that for her, for her birthday," Nik said.

"Did she give it back?"

"No. I never gave it to her. It didn't seem right."

I stabbed a piece of fish with my claw. "Is that what you all did? Composed songs for her? Painted portraits of her? Sculpted little figures of her to properly worship her? Who will you all use for a muse now? She selfishly took all the music and art with her when she died."

Nik set down his plate. "She's gone, Carina. You don't need to be jealous of her anymore."

I set down my plate as well. "I am not jealous of her."

Except I was. I was jealous because she had abandoned me and taken care of everyone else instead. Because the entire world seemed to lament her loss, while Dagna gave me away. These weeks I had been missing, had anyone asked about me? Did anyone care?

"I just don't understand why everyone adores her."

"She wasn't perfect, Carina." He moved closer to me. "We loved her because she wasn't. She was a sad woman. She would spend days in bed at a time, depressed. She felt like a failure. She looked after us because we were a distraction, Carina. She would focus on Mateo's health, or my education, or Flavian and Helene's manners to keep herself busy."

His knee brushed mine as he leaned over the table. I tried to shift away and couldn't. This space wasn't big enough for both of us. He grabbed a small box from his desk and lifted the lid. Inside was another carving. He dropped it into my palm.

"It's our imperfections that make us perfect."

I looked at the little stone figure. A girl with a braid wrapped around her shoulder, whipping in the wind. She wore a fierce expression, lips slightly parted, sword raised. He had even carved in the lines of muscle on her arm and the points of her steel claws.

"It's me," I said.

"Almost," he said. "I can't seem to get the eyes right."

"Why?" I asked. "Why would you carve me?"

"I don't know." He shrugged. "When I close my eyes, you're the face I see in the darkness."

He ran his fingers along my cheek, and I didn't push him away. Perhaps it was the ale or because this would be the last time I would ever see him, but I moved closer, tilting my chin up until my lips met his. I set the figurine down and swept my hands through his long hair. A small voice inside my head told me to stop, this was a terrible idea. Tomorrow I would be escaping on Flavian's ship, leaving behind a trail of blood, which was why I had to do this now. Tomorrow he would hate me.

He wrapped his arm around my waist and kissed me deeper, his tongue brushing mine. I pulled him toward the single cot in the back, running my hands along the underside of his tunic. He flinched when my steel claw grazed his stomach. I held it back and let my other hand circle around his back, to the whip marks I'd felt before.

There were so many.

He lifted my tunic and found one of the scars on my stomach. His finger played across it.

"Knife wound," I breathed against his skin.

He unlaced the ties on the tunic with one hand and yanked it over my head. His lips traced the scar as we fell back onto his mattress. I reached for the ties of his leggings, and he roughly grabbed my hand.

"I can't," he said, breathless.

"If you ever set foot on Helvar," I said. "You would know that plenty can be accomplished without a penis."

He released my hand and I pulled him down on top of me.

CHAPTER 26

✗

I woke up hours later, pinned under Nik's arm. He slept next to me with his dark hair splayed on the pillow and a thin smile on his lips. My body tingled with the same excitement as it had on the evening of my first raid, except this time I didn't make any mistakes.

I pushed Nik's arm aside and rolled to face him. I ran my finger down one of the lines on his back and thought about what he had said to me, about once asking a Daughter to kill the Aldam for him. I wondered who it had been. I wondered if it had been the great Merciless Merle.

It wasn't right. We shouldn't stay our blades in Brezadine for the sake of trade. The Goddess wouldn't do that. I meant to bring it up to Merle when I returned and ask why we cowed under the power of the Aldam when we were the Hands of Death.

I pressed my lips to his warm shoulder before I sat up and dug my tunic and sword out from under his bed. Before I left, I stopped at Nik's table. I picked up the small figurine of myself and dropped it into my pocket. He said I could have one, and I had the feeling if I didn't take this one, in the morning he would crush it the moment he heard about Flavian.

I paused at the door. I wanted Nik to wake up, to ask me why I was leaving, to beg me to stay. I might have if he asked. But he didn't. I left to fulfill my promise to the Goddess, that was my one and only objective. But I hated that tomorrow Nik would despise me. He would regret ever letting me into his room.

No more music burst from the tavern. When I stepped outside, the moon dangled in the sky like a jewel. A man slept underneath the stairs. He smelled strongly of wine and vomit. I crept around him and kept to the shadows, making my way up the hill.

The city was dark, quiet. I only heard the gulls on the cliff and the slap of the water against rock. I reached the consul's home, grabbed one of the empty sacks and slipped in through the darkened kitchen. I passed by the swords in the entryway. It would have been easier to take them first, but they weren't mine until I gave Hel Her due.

I crept down the hall to Flavian's rooms. *You will return to Helvar a legend. The first to conquer Fortis Venitis. You will never have to prove yourself again.*

I drew my sword and leaned against his door. No noise came from inside. Slowly, I nudged it open, and the opulence of it stunned me. He and someone else slept under the covers of a four-poster bed, shimmering in gold. A mosaic covered the far wall, a portrait of Flavian made in small, colored tiles. On his gilded dresser, ruby and sapphire rings scattered across the surface, along with two daggers, one silver and one gold, each one crusted in gemstones.

I salivated. I hadn't even rifled through the drawers yet, which would no doubt hold more things of value. I knew Flavian well-enough to understand he didn't keep anything that wasn't ornate and ostentatious. I imagined Merle's face when I unfurled the sack before her and left her with a pile of offerings in exchange for the soul of the Southern consul's son.

You have served us well, Carina. I knew you would.

Cautiously, I moved toward the bed, sword raised. This was not the way of the Daughters, to sneak up on someone asleep, but this was my only way to escape Fortis alive. Flavian's lover slept on the side of the bed closest to the door. I recognized him from the sculpture Flavian kept on the ship. This was the infamous Arturo. His thick, black lashes flattened on his cheek. His muscled arm dangled over the side of the bed.

I moved to the other side, to Flavian. His black curls were tussled on the pillow, and he slept with a smile across his face. He must have been having a good dream. Not a bad place to die, in the middle of a dream.

I swung my sword back. If I took a broad stroke with a heavy swing, I could take both their heads at once. It would be bloody, no doubt, but quick. They'd never wake. Yes, that was what I would do.

My grip tightened on Gut Spiller. My muscles clenched. I focused on the pulse of the vein in Flavian's neck. I heard Merle's voice in my head, shouting at me.

"Strike fast and quick. No hesitation."

"Death is not for us to choose. It is for us to deliver."

"Don't disappoint me again, or I will make sure you're the one we send to Hel."

I also thought of dancing with Flavian on the deck of the ship, and his father, cowing him into courting someone he didn't love. But I couldn't spare him. I couldn't go back to Helvar empty-handed.

I also couldn't kill him. Despite his many, many failings, I liked him.

My sword lowered as Arturo rolled to the side. His eyes fluttered open. He caught me, sword dropping.

"Flavian," he shouted.

"Again? Already?" Flavian jerked when he saw me leaning over his bed, but not for the reason he should have. "Carina, is everything alright? Is it Mateo?"

He didn't suspect, even for a second, that I had come here to kill him. However, Arturo did.

Someone in the room laughed. I turned to the dresser where the priestess stood, her blackened mouth wide with laughter.

"I knew you could not do it."

"Quiet," I hissed.

"Carina, what is it?" Flavian threw back the blanket.

"I need to go."

I ran from the room, down the hall, to the kitchens. I left everything behind. I had not earned it. The coins, the stone, the vials of Ionian poison, and the ship would be enough for Merle. But I had forsaken the Goddess Her souls, and She would punish me for it in the end.

When I skidded out the back door, I stopped short. The priestess blocked my way with her graying, blood-stained robes.

"I don't have time for this," I said. "You can laugh at me later."

"I'm not here to laugh." She raised her hand, and a cockroach skittered over her fingers. "I'm here to warn you. Father Augustus sent his men for you. They'll be arriving in port before daybreak. They're going to claim you stole the stone from him."

"That's ridiculous. I didn't steal it. He did."

"Who do you think the consul, the Emperor, will believe? A well-respected priest or you, a murderer from the North?"

I thought of Mateo's book, the one with the sharp-toothed Daughter holding a severed head. That was how they saw me here. They would have me hanging by my neck before the end of the afternoon, and Father Augustus would have his stone.

Ironic I would be pinned for a crime I did not commit.

"I'm going. Immediately."

"Good."

I ran past her following the escape route I had planned. With this new information, I would not have a second chance to remedy my mistake. I would not have time to find a new soul to claim. Perhaps I could stage a small raid on Orsalia before I headed north, but that would not be the same as making my mark on Fortis. Fame and glory had been within my reach and I had forsaken it for pity.

I took the last leap onto the docks and found the shadow of a dark ship looming closer to port. Hel's Fire. The priests were already here. I had no time, and I needed a crew. I ran to one place I knew--the tavern, and I raced up the steps two at a time. I banged my steel fist on the door, and it swung open on its own. Nik hovered over his work table with a piece of soapstone and a knife in hand.

"You have a bad habit of sneaking out in the night," he said.

"I need your help. I have to go."

He set the knife down. "What happened?" He searched my claws and sword, looking for signs of blood. Perhaps he knew why I had left. Perhaps he knew what I intended to do, and he let me go anyway.

"Father Augustus's men are coming for the stone. They'll be here within the hour."

He stood up and reached for his tunic. "I'll fetch Zach and Sergio. They'll help us across."

"We don't have time. We will be sailing past them as it is. Just help me get to Orsalia. I can pick up a new crew there. We should be able to manage the ship that far."

"Alright," he said. "Alright." He snatched his tunic from the bed and pulled it over his shoulders then drew on his belt, lined with knives.

"Keep to the shadows. Get to the ship and raise the anchor. I'll unlash it from the dock."

We ventured outside, and under the moonlight, the Ignusian ship loomed ever closer. It might have been easier to escape on a smaller, less noticeable ship, but I needed a large ship to reach Helvar, and I needed a prize.

Nik and I crept up the dock while the Ignusan ship made port. We reached Flavian's ship and Nik held a finger to his lips. I nodded and grabbed one of the tow ropes. Feet against the ship, I pulled myself hand over hand, step by step. I heard the ropes of the other ship hit the deck along with loud voices. Nik bent down and began untying knots.

A cockroach crawled from the top of the ship and ran in circles on the back of my hand. I froze. A member of the Fortis guard rode by on a brown mare, carrying a white banner with the Emperor's crest—the image of a hawk with a snake in its beak.

"Who let this ship dock?" he shouted. "The pier is closed until sunrise."

Sunrise quickly approached. The first tips of the sun rose over the water. I kept pressed to the side of the ship, clinging to the rope as more of the Emperor's guard clattered by. Nik curled into the shadows, almost invisible.

"They're from Ignus," another man shouted.

"We're looking for a girl, a Daughter of Hel," one of the priests said. "She maimed our head of church and burned the tower. She's also stolen something."

I looked to Nik. The tower was his doing. Not mine.

"There are no Daughters on these shores," a guard man said.

"Yes, there is," another said. "Master Flavian has one staying with him."

"How dare your suggest the consul has a murderer in his home?"

The cockroach remained on my hand, a warning to stay put, but if I stayed here, we would be found. I shook the roach from my hand and climbed higher.

"Hey," a voice called. "Who's there?"

Curses. A circle of lantern light moved toward Nik's hiding place. I left all caution behind and slammed my claws into the ship to pull myself higher.

"Stop right there!" A crossbow dart struck the side of the ship, nearly cutting through my cheek. I lost my hold on the rope and skidded down the side of the ship. I hit cold water and sank fast. My steel hand and sword and Flavian's five hundred coins tugged on me. I jabbed my claws into the pier struts and yanked myself to the surface. When I broke through, I sucked in air.

Heavy footsteps raced overhead. A whistle blew.

"Let me go," Nik shouted. Through the cracks in the pier, I saw him struggling against two men. They pinned him by the arms.

The cold water stiffened my muscles. I climbed slowly up the struts, hanging from the barnacles. I threw myself to the top. More men in chainmail gathered on the dock, swords raised. Behind them, the pious priests smirked, victorious in their lies.

"There she is." One of them jabbed a finger to me.

I rolled to the side and loosened my sword from my belt. One man lunged at me while I remained prostrate. I kicked my boot between his legs. He gasped and tumbled off the pier. I leapt to my feet and shook the seawater from my sword.

I swung wide and low, catching one of Nik's captors in the back of the knees. Blood sprayed across the deck, and he toppled like a pile of stones. The other man released Nik and came for me. Nik, finally freed, threw one of his knives and hit the man between the shoulder blades. He dropped at my feet.

"Go swiftly to Niflheim," I said and kicked him into the water.

Tonight, Hel would have Her due. Her payment in souls. Not in the way I had intended, but Fortis would still bleed. I punched another guard in the neck with my steel fist. His face turned blue, and he clutched at his chest, wheezing for breath. I cut him across the stomach and his offering stained the pier.

"Go swiftly to Niflheim."

With the back of my hand, I wiped sweat and blood from my brow. We'd defeated the first round of soldiers, but more approached, racing down the thin road. The priests, undefended, scattered.

"Get to the ship," Nik shouted.

"Right." I moved for the ship and one brave priest lunged for me.

He caught me by the arm. "Give us the stone. It belongs to us. You stole it from our church!"

A horde of cockroaches poured through the slats in the pier and climbed up the priest's legs, to his chest. He shrieked and released me, trying to brush them off.

So now the priestess could be helpful.

Thirty soldiers rounded the docks, hooves smashing into the wood. I made for the ship. A series of arrows struck the pier. Nik sawed through the ropes holding the ship. I held my sword in front of me and backed to the ship. Another round of arrows, and one struck me in the thigh. I yelped and faltered as the men nocked new arrows on their bows.

This was the Goddess seeking Her due.

"Don't disappoint me again, or I will make sure you're the one we send to Hel."

I would die here on this dock, defending the stone and Nik, and I did not regret that decision in the smallest bit. I would die satisfied.

I clutched my sword while blood streamed down my leg.

"Carina, come on," Nik shouted.

"No, you go. I'll hold them off. Take the stone." I removed it from my pocket and threw it to him. He caught it in one hand and hesitated.

"You can't let Augustus have it," I said. I reached into my pocket for one of the vials of Ionian poison. It would be my last weapon.

I took a breath and readied myself to be struck through with a hundred arrows. It would not be a quick or painless death. I would suffer and bleed, and it was no less than I deserved. However, if the Goddess saw fit to punish me, I would accept it. As the first of the arrows flew, striking the ground beside me, three more riders appeared.

They leapt over a rooftop and clattered in front of the guard. Flavian, Helena and...Hel's fire, was that Mateo? He held the horse's reins in one hand, the jeweled rapier in the other, and that miserable scowl I had hated so much was now aimed at the Emperor's guard.

"Stop this, immediately," Flavian shouted. He raised his hand and the men lowered their bows. I exhaled.

"Master Flavian," the lead man said. "This woman is a criminal."

"What has she done?" Flavian said before he noticed the blood at my feet. He shook his head, disappointed. I supposed I should have just let them kill Nik and me. "Regardless, you had no orders to attack. We don't take orders from Ignus."

"No, we take them from the consul, who takes them from the Emperor. We don't take them from you. Men!" He waved his sword overhead and the guard picked up their bows.

Helene tugged on her horse and moved to block their path. "Oh my. All this excitement...I'm going to faint." She pressed her palm to her forehead and tipped her head back. As she slid from the saddle, three men rushed to catch her. One managed to grab her before she hit the wood.

Clearly Flavian's dramatics were inherited.

As Helene drew everyone's attention, Mateo rode his horse around the fringes to stand by my side.

"You should have come to say goodbye," he said

"I didn't have the time."

"Well you do now." He pulled something from inside his tunic—the brush. "Take it."

"Even if I sell it?"

"You won't sell it."

I shoved the brush into my belt. I probably wouldn't sell it.

"Go. We'll keep them back," he said.

Nik stood at the top of the ship and threw a rope down to me. I wrapped it around my claws, and he pulled me up the side. A few arrows struck the wood, and Helene shrieked again. "Someone, fetch the doctor!"

This would unquestionably go down as the most haphazard rescue in history.

"I'll find you again," Mateo shouted after me.

"Not if I find you first."

Nik grabbed my arms and hauled me onto the ship. "Take the wheel," he said, glancing at my blood-stained leg. I made my way there as he drew the sheets. Almost immediately, they plumed with a strong wind, launching us north.

As the sun crested the water, the tips of the waves turned a shade of rust, a sign that I had earned Her forgiveness. I had claimed Her souls on Fortis, and I would return with their offerings for my people. Not all of the gifts had been earned through death, though. Some I had earned through sparing life, and perhaps that was what the Goddess wanted me to learn-- Death spares life as easily as She takes it.

"There is only sorrow in loving someone who loves another. Better to let him go and share in his joy, than be the reason for his weeping."

From the story of Baldur

CHAPTER 27
✖

Nik and I couldn't stop in Orsalia to pick up more crew. The Fortis guard set out for us less than an hour after we left, and I had an injured leg. I would be useless on foot. Thankfully, Mateo's maps were on the ship, and in a further stroke of good luck, a thick fog rolled in later in the afternoon to hide our escape. We took to Mateo's routes and disappeared, another lone ship drifting at sea.

Nik and I adopted a routine in order to sail a four-sailor ship with only two. It was fine when the wind was strong and the water smooth. When it wasn't, it required sleepless nights and aching legs from running up and down the deck repeatedly.

Despite the effort, I enjoyed being at sea with Nik and no one else. We worked well together. We could sail the ship in near silence, as we both knew exactly what to do. It was our own dance, beautifully coordinated, no heavy dresses required.

We kept on a course due north, to Helvar. I had the Goddess's blessings and enough gifts to secure my place, but I traveled with one unintended gift – Nik. I did not know what to do about him. I didn't know if Merle would welcome him or insist we sacrifice him. I could not let that happen. I needed to make a decision soon.

"The ship is secure for the night." Nik came into the captain's room. We shared it--despite it still smelling strongly of Flavian's perfume. I set

Nyssa's brush on the vanity after I swept it through my hair one last time. Until I needed to sell it, it worked well as a hairbrush.

"I'll wake up in a few hours and check it," I said and stretched out my right leg. The arrow wound was healing, but because I kept racing across the ship on it, it was taking its time.

Nik sat on the edge of the bed. "I'm still stunned how much easier it is to sail this ship with a good sailor."

"I have more skills than sailing." I crossed the room and sat on his lap, laced my fingers behind his neck, and kissed him.

Since we left Fortis, he seemed…sad. He was more burdened by the end of our journey than I was. He couldn't go forward. He couldn't go back. In choosing my side, he became a criminal. If he ever returned to Fortis, he would be hanged.

He never said he regretted helping me. He didn't have to.

When we both collapsed into bed, sweaty and breathless, he took my hand and pressed my knuckles to his mouth. My spine stiffened. It was these gestures, these tender gestures I couldn't take. Something about it was too intimate. Too permanent.

"I can't go to Helvar," he said.

I drew my hand back. He was going to force me to talk about this now. "I can't go many places. Not with these steel fingers." I waved my metal hand as a reminder. Any town or village the Daughters raided would hold me accountable. The Daughters' strength and reputation came in numbers. Alone, I would be torn to pieces. "I also have the stone," I said. Father Augustus would not let it go, not until he or I were dead, preferably him. But I couldn't face him while he hid behind his Fire.

"I've thought about that," he said. "We can stay on the ship. We can move cargo. We can fish. We can keep to the sea."

The, we, in his suggestions felt like claws down my back. I didn't plan to abandon him. I also didn't plan on committing my life to him.

"I can't do that." I moved to leave the bed. He grabbed my wrist.

"Don't walk away," he said. "It was just an idea."

I twisted my arm loose. "I'm supposed to go home." I grabbed my tunic from the floor and pulled it over my head.

"I can't go home," he said.

I flinched. "I didn't ask you to—"

"You didn't have to." His voice rose. "I did it because I love you."

I flinched at those words too.

"You're impossible, Carina. You want to be a Daughter of Hel. Go ahead." He stood up and stretched his arms wide, baring his chest. "Kill me." He pounded his fist on his chest. "Indiscriminate Death wouldn't hesitate, would She? Kill me right now. Please, I'm begging you because it will be better than being in this in-between."

I stared at his chest, the separation of his ribs. I knew exactly where to slip a knife or a sharp pointed claw to pierce his chest. I could jab through his kidneys from the front or behind. I could pierce his lungs and wait for them to fill with blood, and he would eventually suffocate. I could kill him in a thousand different ways, and the thought made me sick.

"I'm leaving." I picked up my leggings and turned from the room. I slammed the door behind me.

I went to the bunkroom instead, crawling onto the hard mattress I'd slept on before. Even Death loved someone once—Baldur. And She'd let him go. Perhaps that was what I needed to do, let Nik go. The thought twisted like a knife in my side. I couldn't devote myself to Nik. I couldn't let him go. What could I do?

I fell asleep, alone, and woke to a sound of footsteps on the deck above. I rubbed my eyes and rolled out of bed. I'd told Nik I would check the ship. I'd slept too long, and he'd done it for me. I wasn't ready to face him. I also didn't want him to complain in the morning about how I'd shirked my duties.

I crawled to the deck, half-asleep. One of the mast ropes hung loose. The sail flapped in the wind. I snatched the loose rope and tied it tight. No sign of Nik. The rope must have been the sound I heard. We were still on a track north, evident by the leading star, dead ahead. If we kept to this course, in weeks we would hit Helvar.

"You are beautiful," a voice whispered, a woman's voice. I braced myself for a vision of the priestess and found her by the rails in a billowing white dress. It clung to her legs like smoke.

"Well, well, well," I said. "I thought maybe you'd decided to stop haunting me." I hadn't seen her since Fortis and her little cockroach trick.

"I'm sorry. This is the only way." The priestess turned from the rails, and dark hair striped with silver trailed behind her on the cool, night wind.

This was not the priestess. She was too young, too lovely, as perfect as the sculpture Nik had made of her.

"Nyssa," I whispered. "Where's the priestess?"

"She gave me a pass to see you."

"I thought the stone could only work with two, one ghost, one person."

Nyssa's ghostly lips spread into a smile. "The priestess said rules can always be broken, and not to worry, this is only a one time pass. She'll return to you soon."

"Wonderful," I muttered. I hated that priestess. She couldn't leave well enough alone. She couldn't leave Nyssa dead and buried.

I took the stone from my pocket and marched to the rails. "If I drop this into the sea, will you sink with it?"

"I don't know." She stepped toward me, and I stretched my arm further over the water. I didn't care if Father Augusts got his stone. I only wanted Nyssa to go away.

"Oh Carina, you are as beautiful as I imagined. And strong. Brave."

"You're as annoying as I imagined."

"I know." She bowed her head and the wind pulled at her gossamer, white gown. "I know you're angry with me, and you have a right to be. I was afraid. I was afraid you would be gone, and so I never went to look. It was easier to live with the lie than the truth."

"You almost killed Nik, Flavian, and Mat to find me."

"I had no choice."

"Yes, you did. You could have left me on Helvar. You could have left them on Fortis."

"I couldn't," she said, "but yes, I take full responsibility. After I lost you, I was terrified I would lose Mateo too. So I kept him close, too close. I never let him stray far from the house, learn to use a sword, or play games with the other boys. I always wanted him within arm's reach.

"Then I became ill, and I worried, if I died, there would be no one to look after him. I asked Nik to go find you, so Mat would have someone after I was gone."

"I'm not his caretaker."

"But you are," Nyssa said. "You did what I could never do. You let him go. You let him shine."

"He didn't need my help to shine. He just needed to stop being suffocated. Now go. You've said your peace. I'd rather the priestess and her roaches than your lies."

Nyssa's ghost paled to gray. "Before I go," she whispered, "will you tell Mateo that I left him a message in our book? And tell Nik his sculpture of me was beautiful. He's too critical of his own work. Don't let Flavian give into his father, and remind Helene, ladies never drink before dinner."

I rolled my eyes. "That will be difficult to do. I'm not welcome on Fortis anymore."

"You will find a way."

Now I was her messenger. "Anything else?"

"Yes." She reached a wispy hand to me. "Don't let Nik go. I made the mistake of leaving someone behind once, someone I loved very much, and I have never been able to forget it. Please, don't make the same mistake, Carina. You both deserve so much more."

My throat tightened. I pulled the stone back from the water and returned it to my pocket. "I'm not going to let him go."

"Good," she said and let her wisp fingers graze my cheek. "My beautiful, steel-handed daughter. I'm sorry for all the pain I've caused you. Don't let my mistakes poison you against love."

She pulled her hand back and the mast creaked. I turned over my shoulder to check it, and she was gone. I touched my fingertips to my cheek. It was cold where she touched me.

I felt raw, as if I had been scrubbed and boiled, and I was tired. Instinctively, I crawled back to the main cabin where Nik slept. I'd forgotten we were in the midst of an argument and when I saw him sleeping there, face down on the sheets, I crawled in beside him and curled into his warm side anyway.

He draped his arm around me.

"I don't care," he muttered. "We can go to Helvar if you want."

"No," I said. "We'll stay on the ship, like you said. We can run cargo, or something." There were plenty of odd jobs to be done at sea for those who were good with sails and swords.

He pulled me closer to his chest, and I listened to his breath while I stared at the ceiling. Everything was fixed. We had a plan, a destination, and I still felt as if something were missing. Nik rolled onto his side and showed his back to me, and the eighty-eighty whip marks lining his smooth skin. We had been together long enough I'd had time to count them.

I curled my steel fist. As long as I bore my claws, I was a Hand of Death, a messenger of the Goddess, and Her hands had been too long absent from the shores of Brezadine. The Aldam needed to learn that there was no greater power than Death.

I slipped away from Nik and out of the bed.

"Are you sneaking away again?" he asked.

"Just for a minute," I said. "We should stop for supplies. I'm going to shift the sails."

East, toward Brezadine.

Death must be satisfied.

ACKNOWLEDGEMENTS

First and foremost, I have to thank my husband, Barry Menard, who has read more draft young adult novels than he ever could have imagined when he said, "I do." I am also grateful for my die-hard writing partners, Arleen York and Marie Ventura. And Dani Baum for her amazing cover design. If you need an artist for hire, snatch her up quick because she is going to be wildly successful. And I can't forget Jill Pierce, my biggest fan and long-time friend. Whenever I worried my work wasn't good enough, she would text me with, OMG this is so good! I probably would have given up years ago if she wasn't there with an ego boost right when I needed it.

Carina is a character very near and dear to my heart. She was featured in the third novel I wrote with a slightly different name. I decided to shelve that book for various reasons, but I could never forget my love for the girl with the steel hand.

Six-years-later, enter Carina, out-of-place teenaged Viking warrior. I wrote this for myself as a reader, who is tired of safe characters who don't challenge ideas and world views. Carina is not out to save the world or win the crown. What she wants is acceptance, to not feel like an outsider.

Please don't take anything I wrote in here as actual fact about Vikings. There are some truths in here, but I drew from historic data spanning over three-hundred years and embellished *a lot* with my own imagination. If you are looking for real data about Vikings, I encourage you to read *The Sea Wolves: A History of the Vikings* by Lars Brownworth. I read it as part of my research and found it to be a thorough and entertaining exploration of Viking culture.

Thank you for reading, and if you have a moment to share your thoughts, I love reviews. Especially those with gifs.

ABOUT THE AUTHOR

RACHEL MENARD earned her degree in marketing from ASU, during which time her work was featured in the university paper and her own, self-published punk zine, *Chelsea*. She was also a college radio DJ. Her short work has appeared in *The Final Summons* anthology and on *Cast of Wonders*. For more of her writings and ramblings, visit www.rachelmenard.com.

Made in the USA
Middletown, DE
27 July 2019